CARROLL & GRAF

The Diary
of a Country Priest

GEORGES BERNANOS

The Diary
of a Country Priest

TRANSLATED FROM THE FRENCH BY
PAMELA MORRIS

Carroll & Graf Publishers, Inc.
New York

I

MINE IS A PARISH like all the rest. They're all alike. Those
of to-day I mean. I was saying so only yesterday to
M. le Curé de Norenfontes—that good and evil are
probably evenly distributed, but on such a low plain,
very low indeed! Or if you like they lie one over the
other; like oil and water they never mix. M. le Curé only
laughed at me. He is a good priest, deeply kind and
human, who at diocesan headquarters is even considered
a bit of a freethinker, on the dangerous side. His outbursts fill his colleagues with glee, and he stresses them
with a look meant to be fiery, but which gives me such a
deep sensation of stale discouragement that it almost
brings tears into my eyes.

My parish is bored stiff; no other word for it. Like so
many others! We can see them being eaten up by boredom, and we can't do anything about it. Some day perhaps we shall catch it ourselves—become aware of the
cancerous growth within us. You can keep going a long
time with that in you.

This thought struck me yesterday on my rounds. It
was drizzling. The kind of thin, steady rain which gets
sucked in with every breath, which seeps down through
the lungs into your belly. Suddenly I looked out over
the village, from the road to Saint Vaast along the hill-

side—miserable little houses huddled together under the desolate, ugly November sky. On all sides damp came steaming up and it seemed to sprawl there in the soaking grass like a wretched worn-out horse or cow. What an insignificant thing a village is. And this particular village was my parish! My parish, yes, but what could I do? I stood there glumly watching it sink into the dusk, disappear. . . . In a few minutes I should lose sight of it. I had never been so horribly aware both of my people's loneliness and mine. I thought of the cattle which I could hear coughing somewhere in the mist, and of the little lad on his way back from school clutching his satchel, who would soon be leading them over sodden fields to a warm sweet-smelling byre. . . . And my parish, my village seemed to be waiting too—without much hope after so many nights in the mud—for a master to follow towards some undreamed-of, improbable shelter.

Oh, of course I know all this is fantastic. Such notions can scarcely be taken seriously. A day-dream! Villages do not scramble to their feet like cattle at the call of a little boy. And yet, last night, I believe a saint might have roused it. . . .

Well, as I was saying, the world is eaten up by boredom. To perceive this needs a little preliminary thought: you can't see it all at once. It is like dust. You go about and never notice, you breathe it in, you eat and drink it. It is sifted so fine, it doesn't even grit on your teeth. But stand still for an instant and there it is, coating your face and hands. To shake off this drizzle of ashes you must be for ever on the go. And so people are always 'on the go.' Perhaps the answer would be that the world has long been familiar with boredom, that such is the true condition of man. No doubt the seed was scattered all over life, and here and there found fertile soil to take root; but I wonder if man has ever before experienced this contagion, this leprosy of boredom: an aborted despair, a shameful form of despair in some way like the fermentation of a Christianity in decay.

Naturally I keep these thoughts to myself. But I am not ashamed of them. I even believe that they'd be easy enough to communicate, too easy perhaps for my peace of mind—that is to say, for the peace of my conscience.

Our superiors are no longer official optimists. Those who still profess the rule of hope, teach optimism only by force of habit, without believing in what they say. You need only raise the mildest objection and you find them wreathed in knowing deprecating smiles; they beg you to spare them. Old priests are not taken in. For in spite of appearances, provided you use the same official terms—terms which are in any case hard and fast—the themes which inspire official eloquence are no longer the same, and our elders would never be able to recognize them. For instance, time was when according to secular tradition a bishop's sermon had always to end with a prudent hint—full of conviction indeed, yet prudent—of coming persecution and the blood of the martyrs. Nowadays these prophecies are becoming far more rare, probably because their realization seems less uncertain. Alas, there is an expression current in every diocese, one of those awful 'front line slogans' which seemed humorous to our elders, I cannot think how or why—but which people of my age find so ugly and depressing. (Surprising it is, too, what a number of sordid ideas have been conveyed with dismal accuracy by trench jargon. Or was that the way they really talked in the trenches?)

Well, they will keep on saying: 'Why worry?' But what else are we here for, in heaven's name? I am quite aware that to 'worry' is the business of our superiors. But then, who gives them their material? We do! So all this crying up of monastic obedience and simplicity somehow or other doesn't strike home to me.

We can all of us manage to peel potatoes and feed pigs, provided we are given the orders to do so. But it is less easy to edify a whole parish with acts of obedience, than a mere community of monks. More especially since the *parish* would always be unaware of them, and the *parish* would never understand.

Since his retirement the Bishop of Bailloeil is constantly visiting the Carthusian Fathers of Verchocq. 'What I saw at Verchocq' was the title of one lecture which the Dean almost insisted on our attending. We heard many interesting things, enthralling even as far as the telling went, since this dear old man has never lost the guileless little mannerisms of his professorial days and is as scrupulously careful of his diction as of his hands. One might suppose he both hoped and dreaded the improbable presence among his students of the late M. Anatole France, with whom he was engaged in apologizing for God Almighty, Whose style leaves so much to be desired. All this with many a subtle look and knowing smile and delicate gestures, crooking his little finger. Apparently this ecclesiastical levity was very fashionable about the year 1900, so we did our best to give these 'telling sallies' (which told us nothing) a fairly good reception. By nature I am probably coarse-grained, for I confess that I have always been repelled by the 'lettered' priest. After all, to cultivate clever people is merely a way of dining out, and a priest has no right to

[4]

go out to dinner in a world full of starving people. To sum up, the dear old man kept regaling us with many anecdotes; he illustrated his lecture with little stories; he stressed his points. I think I managed to understand. And yet, alas, I was not as moved as I ought to have been. It is true that monks are past masters of the inner life. Yet most of those famous 'pointed anecdotes' are like local wines which should be supped on the spot. They won't stand transport.

And perhaps— Have I any right to say so? Perhaps a handful of monks living always together, day and night, can create unconsciously their own very favourable atmosphere. . . . I know something of monasteries myself. I've seen monks bowed to the ground, humbly accept without a murmur, the unjust rebuke of a superior, bent on breaking their pride. But within those walls, untroubled by all outside echoes, silence attains the rarest quality, a truly miraculous perfection, and ears grown exquisitely sensitive are conscious of the slightest rustle of sound. The very stillness of a chapter-house is as good as any burst of noisy applause.

(Whereas a bishop's reprimand—)

I have been looking over these first few pages of my diary without any satisfaction, and yet I considered very carefully before making up my mind to write it. But that is not much comfort to me now. For those who have the habit of prayer, thought is too often a mere alibi, a sly way of deciding to do what one wants to do. Reason will always obscure what we wish to keep in the shadows. A worldling can think out the pros and cons and sum up his chances. No doubt. But what are *our* chances worth? We who have admitted once and for all into each moment of our puny lives the terrifying presence of God? Unless a priest happens to lose his faith—and then what has he left, for he cannot lose his faith without denying himself? He will never learn to 'look after number one' with the alert common sense—nay, with the candour and innocence of the children of this world. What is the use of working out chances? There are no chances against God.

Aunt Philomène has answered my letter. She encloses two hundred-franc notes, just enough for my most pressing needs. Dreadful, the way money slips through my fingers, like sand.

Of course I must confess to being a prize fool. For instance the Heuchin grocer, M. Pamyre, who is a very good fellow (two of his sons are priests) has always been friendly and hospitable. Besides, he is the accredited purveyor to all my colleagues. He never failed to invite me to his back room for a glass of elderberry wine and biscuits, and we would sit and chat. Times are hard for him; he still has a daughter to provide for, and two other boys both studying for the priesthood, who cost him a pretty penny. Well, one day as he was taking down my order, he smiled and said:

'Let me send you round three bottles of the elderberry as well. It'll buck you up.'

Like a fool I thought he wouldn't charge for them! A little pauper who at twelve goes straight from his wretched home into the seminary will never get to know the value of money. I would even go so far as to say that it is hard for us to be strictly honest in money matters. Better run no risk of meddling, were it ever so innocently, with what most laymen regard not as a means, but an end in itself. The Curé de Verchin, who is not always very tactful, must needs joke about this little misunderstanding in the presence of M. Pamyre. M. Pamyre was really upset.

'Of course,' he protested, 'I'm always delighted to see M. le Curé whenever he cares to look us up. It's a pleasure, I'm sure, to be able to offer him a drink. God be praised, things aren't so bad that a bottle or so makes all that difference! But business is business, I can't go giving my stuff away.' And it seems that Mme Pamyre chimed in: 'We tradespeople have our social duty to consider, same as others!'

This morning I decided not to prolong my experiment beyond the coming twelve months. On the 25th of November I'll stuff these pages in the fire and try to forget them. This resolution, which I made after mass, did not set my mind at rest for long.

It isn't exactly a question of scruple; I don't think I am doing wrong in jotting down, day by day, without hiding anything, the very simple trivial secrets of a very ordinary kind of life. What I am about to record would not reveal much to the only friend with whom I still manage to speak openly, and besides I know I could never bring myself to put on paper the things which almost every morning I confide to God without any shame. No, it is hardly a scruple, but rather a sort of unreasoning fear, a kind of instinctive warning. When I first sat down before this child's copy-book I tried to concentrate, to withdraw into myself as though I were examining my conscience before confession. And yet my real conscience was not revealed by that inner light—usually so dispassionate and penetrating, passing over details, showing up the whole. It seemed to skim the surface of another consciousness, previously unknown to me, a cloudy mirror in which I feared that a face might suddenly appear. Whose face? Mine, perhaps. A forgotten, rediscovered face. . . .

When writing of oneself one should show no mercy. Yet why at the first attempt to discover one's own truth does all inner strength seem to melt away in floods of self-pity and tenderness and rising tears. . . .

I went to see the Curé de Torcy yesterday. He's a good priest, very efficient, but I usually find him somewhat uninspiring, for he comes of well-to-do peasant stock, knows the value of money, and always manages to impress me with his worldly experience. There's some talk in the diocese of his being promoted Dean of Heuchin. . . . His manner with me is rather deceptive, for he hates taking people into his confidence, and knows how to discourage them with a huge jolly laugh—he's a lot slyer than you'd think. God, I wish I had his health and courage and sanity! But I think he makes allowances for what he is pleased to call my 'thin skin,' because he knows I'm in no way proud of it. Anything but! And it's a long while now since I gave up trying to identify with true pity—the strong gentle pity of the saints—my childish shrinking from other people's pain.

'Well, my lad, you're not looking any too grand.'

I was still upset by a scene old Dumouchel had made in the sacristy a few hours earlier. I only wish I *could* give away, together with my time and my trouble, the cotton tapestries, moth-eaten draperies and tallow candles, for which his grace's 'purveyor' rooks me, and that collapse with a frying-pan sizzle almost as soon as they are lit. But prices are prices. What can I do?

'You should've kicked the fellow out,' he said. And when I protested—'Of course you ought to have kicked him out. I know him all right, your Dumouchel! The old chap's got plenty tucked away. . . . Why, his late wife was twice as well off as he is—why couldn't he have buried her decently? Ah, you young priests. . . .'

He flushed scarlet and looked me up and down.

'I'm wondering what you've got in your veins these days, you young priests! When I was your age we had *men* in the church—don't frown, it makes me want to clout you—men I say—make what you like of the word—heads of a parish, masters, my boy, *rulers*. They could hold a whole country together, that sort could—with a mere lift of the chin. Oh, I know what you're going to say: they fed well, drank good wine and didn't object to a game of cards. Well, what of it? When you tackle your job properly, you get through it quickly and efficiently, there's plenty of time over, and it's all the better for everybody. Nowadays the seminaries turn out little choirboys, little ragamuffins who think they're working harder than anybody because they never get anything done. They go snivelling around instead of giving orders. They read stacks of books, but never have the nouse to understand what it meant when we say the Church is the Bride of Christ. What's a wife, lad—a real woman as a man'd hope to get if he's fool enough not to follow the advice of Saint Paul? Don't answer—you'd only talk rubbish. I'll tell you: it's a sturdy wench who's not afraid of work, but who knows the way of things, that everything has to be done over and over again, until

[9]

the end. . . . For all the efforts of Holy Church this poor world won't turn into a shining altar for Corpus Christi day. Once—that was in my last parish—I had a marvellou.; vestry woman, a nun of Bruges, secularized in 1908, one of the best. After the first week's rubbing and scrubbing, the house of God began to shine like a convent parlour. Honestly I couldn't recognize it. It was reaping-time, of course, not so much as a cat came near, and yet the confounded little woman *would* make me take my boots off —and I loathe slippers. I believe she bought me a pair out of her own money. Every morning to be sure, she found a fresh layer of dust over the benches, a mushroom or two sprung up over night on the choir tapestry—and cobwebs! Child, there were cobwebs enough for a bride's trousseau.

'I thought: keep it up, my girl, and wait till Sunday. And Sunday came. Oh, just an ordinary Sunday, no festival about it, only the usual crowd. But, oh, the next day she was at it till the small hours, scouring and polishing by candle-light. A few weeks later it was All Saints, a great feast when two Redemptionist fathers came down to preach, two fine fellows. . . . The poor soul was spending most of her nights on all fours, between her pail and floor-cloth, mopping and slopping till there was moss growing up the pillars, and grass sprouting between the flagstones. Ah, but she wouldn't listen to reason! If I'd let her have her way I'd have turned everyone out so the Lord might keep His feet dry. I ask you! "You'll be the ruin of me with all your medicine," I said. For she kept coughing, poor old thing. She took to her bed in the end with rheumatic fever, her heart gave way and—plouf!—there was my little sister before Saint Peter. In one sense she's a true martyr, no shirking it. The mistake she made wasn't to fight dirt, sure enough, but to try and do away with it altogether. As if that were possible! A parish is *bound* to be dirty. A whole Christian society's a lot dirtier. You wait for the Judgement Day and see what the angels'll be sweeping out of even the most saintly monasteries. Some filth! Which all goes to prove, boy, that the Church must needs be a sound housewife—sound and sensible. My nun wasn't a real housewife; a real housewife knows her home isn't a shrine. Those are just poets' dreams.'

I was ready for him at this point. While he was re-filling his pipe, I awkwardly attempted to point out that perhaps after all his instance didn't quite fit the facts, and this nun who had scrubbed herself to death had nothing in common with 'little choirboys,' little ragamuffins 'who go snivelling around instead of giving orders.'

'Not at all,' he answered rather harshly. 'They've both got the same bee in their bonnets; the only difference is that my little nun had more guts than the ragamuffins. As soon as *they* come up against it, they start whining that after all the priesthood isn't quite what they imagined, and they chuck it all up. What they want is jam on it. Well, a man can't live on jam, and neither can a Christian society. Our Heavenly Father said mankind was the salt of the earth, son, not the honey. And our poor world's rather like old man Job, stretched out in all his filth, covered with ulcers and sores. Salt stings on an open wound, but saves you from gangrene. Next to your idea of wiping out the Devil comes that other soft notion of being "loved." Loved for your own sweet selves, of course! A true priest is never loved, get that into your head. And if you must know: the Church

[11]

doesn't care a rap whether you're loved or not, my lad. Try first to be respected and obeyed. What the Church needs is discipline. You've got to set things straight all the day long. You've got to restore order, knowing that disorder will get the upper hand the very next day, because such *is* the order of things, unluckily: night is bound to turn the day's work upside down—night belongs to the Devil.'

'Night,' I observed (I knew I was going to annoy him). 'Surely there are monks to look after that?'

'Yes,' he replied coldly. 'They sing a bit.'

I tried to make him think I was shocked.

'Mind you,' he went on, 'I've got nothing against your contemplatives. Each man to his job. They provide us with bunches of flowers besides the music.'

'Flowers?'

'Certainly. When you've done the housework, washed up, peeled the spuds and laid the table, it's quite the thing to shove a few fresh flowers in a bowl of water. Of course that's just a way of putting it, and only idiots could be horrified at what I'm saying—because after all there *is* a difference. . . . The mystic lily isn't the lily of the fields. And anyway, if a man prefers a good tuck in of steak to a bunch of periwinkles, it's because he's a mere animal himself, a paunch. What I mean is, your contemplatives know how to do their job all right, and their flowers are well worth having. Unfortunately even in monasteries there's always the tendency to shirk—just as there is everywhere else—and only too often they're palming off artificial flowers on us.'

Throughout all this I could feel how closely he was watching me—sideways, without appearing to. At such times his eyes seem really very gentle and—how shall I put it?—somehow fearful, full of deep anxiety. We each have our separate burden. But I find it harder to keep my mouth shut. And when I do, my silence, alas, is due to constraint rather than courage, that particular constraint which doctors are also said to experience after their fashion and according to their own ways and cares. But he keeps his trials to himself at all costs, hidden under a crust of plain-dealing, more inscrutable even than those Carthusians who used to flit past me, pale as wax, in the cloisters of Z——.

Suddenly his fingers closed round my hand, fingers all swollen with diabetes; yet they gripped instantly, without fumbling, a hard masterful grasp.

'You'll tell me I don't know the first thing about mysticism. Don't be a fool, of course that's what you think! Well, old son, when I was a lad studying Theology, I remember a certain professor of canon law who'd got it into his head that he was a poet. He'd work you out some amazing stuff with the right metres and rhymes and feet and all—poor chap! He could have put his canon law into verse with ease. The only thing he lacked was inspiration, genius—*ingenium*—whatever you like to call it. Well, so do I. I'm no genius. Yet just suppose the Holy Ghost *did* give me the tip one fine day, you bet I'd throw away my brushes and cleaning rags and join up with the archangels' band, though I might be a bit out of tune at the start. But surely I may be allowed to snigger at folk who keep bursting into song before God has raised His conductor's baton.'

He sat thinking for a moment and his face, which was turned to the light, looked suddenly as if it were deep in shadow. Even his features had grown rigid, as though he were on the alert, expecting—either from me or from his conscience—some sort of protest or denial of all he had said. . . .

But he was serene again almost at once.

'Fact is, sonny, I've always had notions of my own concerning young David's harp. A gifted lad, to be sure, but not all his strumming kept him clear of mortal sin. Of course I know our poor dear old-fashioned scribblers, with their tuppeny *Lives of the Saints*, take it for granted that a fellow can find safety in transports of ecstasy, that he curls himself up all snug and safe as though he were in Abraham's bosom? Safe? . . . Oh, I grant you there are times when it's as simple as pie to attain such heights. God sweeps you up. The real snag is to stick there, and know how to get down again—when you can't hold on any longer. Brr! . . . Now come along and see my oratory, but mind and wipe your feet because of the carpet.'

I know very little about furniture, but his bedroom seemed luxurious to me: a massive mahogany bedstead, a wardrobe with three heavily carved doors, armchairs upholstered in plush, and a big bronze statue of Joan of Arc on the mantelpiece. But M. le Curé de Torcy was certainly not out to show off all this. He took me straight into the next room—a bare little room with nothing in it but a table and a *prie-dieu*. On the wall a rather hideous oleograph, like those one sees in hospital wards, of a very rosy chubby Holy Child lying between the ox and the ass.

'See that picture,' he said. 'My godmother gave it to me. I could well afford something a bit better, more artistic, you know, but I'd sooner have that. It's ugly and it's rather stupid, and that sets me at rest. You know, lad, my folk are all Flemish: big eaters, big drinkers—and a rich land. . . . You poor blighters from these parts, in your clay-fouled hovels—you can't imagine the richness of Flanders, of our black soil! It's no good asking us for pretty speeches to send shivers down the spines of pious ladies, but we've got our own mystics, my boy, quite a few of 'em. And ours don't go into declines! Life doesn't scare us. We've good red blood in our veins, rich and healthy, the sort you can feel pounding against your temples when you're lit up with gin or itching for a fight—ours is a Flemish rage, enough to fell an ox. That's it, thick red blood, with a blue dash of Spanish fire in it, just enough to set it alight. Well, well, you've troubles enough of your own and I've had mine—and I shouldn't think they'd be the same. No doubt you'll go to bed on thorns sometimes, but I've had to writhe and kick there, and more than once, believe me, lad. If I were to tell you —but I'd better tell you some other time, because you're not looking any too grand and I don't want to see you pass out. Well now, to go back to my Holy Child. Would you believe it, the Curé de Poperingue, in my part of the world, agreed with the Vicar-general, who was one to get his own way, that the proper place to send me was Saint-Sulpice! In their opinion Saint-Sulpice was a kind of military school for young priests, like Saint-Cyr, or the École de Guerre. And besides, my respected father—' (incidentally I thought this was a joke at first, but apparently M. le Curé de Torcy never refers to his father in any other way: does that date back to the eighteenth century?) 'my respected father had been feathering his own nest for some time, and so felt he should do the right thing by the diocese. But heavens above! Shall I ever forget my first sight of that foul old barracks of a place, with its stink of greasy soup! And those poor lads were all skin and bone: the front view of 'em was more like a side face. Anyway, I soon palled up with three or four, and we kicked up a fine shindy whenever we could, and ragged the staff like a lot of young idiots. We were always on the spot for work and grub—but regular devils the rest of the time. One night when everybody had gone to bed, we climbed up on to the roof and began mewing like so many tom-cats, enough to wake up the whole neighbourhood. Poor old novice-master! He stood at the foot of his bed making signs of the cross, thinking all the cats in the district had collected on the roof of this holy seminary to tell each other dirty stories—it was a ridiculous thing to do, of course. . . . At the end of the term these reverend gentlemen sent me home with a nice sort of character: quite capable, well-meaning, heart in the right place, and so on, and so on. The gist of it being that keeping cows was all I was fit for. I whose one idea was to be a priest! Either that or death! I was cut to the quick, so deeply that God allowed me to be tempted—yes, tempted to finish my own life. My respected father was a just man. He took me round in his pony-trap to see the bishop, with a little note from a great-aunt of mine, Mother Superior at the Visitation Convent of Namur. His Lordship was an equally just man. He received me at once in his private room. I knelt before him and told him how sorely I had been tempted; the very next week he packed me off to his own seminary, rather a mouldy old place, but sound enough. Anyhow, I can say I looked death in the face all right, and what a death! Ever since then I resolved to put all that sort of thing on one side and get down to brass tacks. No fooling about on or off duty, as the soldiers say. My Holy Child is too much of a baby to be very taken up with music or books. And I should think He'd probably start to bellow at folk who'd stand around casting their eyes up to heaven instead of bringing fresh straw for his ox, or giving the ass a rub-down.'

He ushered me out of the room by the shoulders, and the friendly tap of one large hand nearly sent me sprawling. Then we had a glass of gin together. And suddenly he looked me straight in the eyes, with complete assurance, commanding. He seemed to have become a different person, a man who would take orders from no one, an aristocrat.

'Monks are monks,' he said. 'I'm not a monk. I'm not a Father Superior. I'm in charge of a flock—a real flock. I can't go cutting seraphic capers with my flock—cattle, that's all they are—nice sort of fool I'd look if I did! Just cattle, neither good nor bad, oxen, donkeys, beasts of burden. . . . And I've he-goats too. What am I to do about my goats? No killing or selling 'em. A mitred abbot can pass on the job to Brother Janitor. Should there be any difficulty he can get rid of his goats in no time. I can't. We've got to make room for everything and everybody—goats included. Whether it be a goat or a lambkin, the Master expects each beast to be returned in healthy condition. Don't go trying to stop a goat stinking like a goat—a waste of time and a source of despair, I can tell you. My old pals think I'm an optimist, a Hopeful Sammy; young fellows like you take me for an ogre, think I'm too hard on my folk, too tough and soldierly with 'em. And you both grouse because I haven't my own little pet plan for making people good, like the rest of you, or maybe because I've forgotten it in one of my pockets. The old are always grunting about tradition and the young keep on squealing about evolution. Well, I think a man's a man and hasn't altered much since the days of the heathens. Anyhow it's not a question of what he's worth, but of who's to command him. Ah, if the men of the Church could only have had their way! Mind you, it's not that I'm taken in by the usual fairy-tale Middle Ages: people in the thirteenth century didn't pretend to be plaster-saints, and though the monks may have had more brains, they did themselves far better than to-day, and there's no denying it. But we were founding an empire, my boy, an empire that would have made the Caesars' effort look like so much mud—and peace, real peace, the Peace of Rome. A Christian people doesn't mean a lot of little goody-goodies. The Church has plenty of stamina, and isn't afraid of sin. On the contrary, she can look it in the face calmly and even take it upon herself, assume it at times, as Our Lord did. When a good workman's been at it hard the whole week, surely he's due for a booze on Saturday night. Look: I'll define you a Christian people by the opposite. The opposite of a Christian people is a people grown sad and old. You'll be saying that isn't a very theological definition. I agree. But it 'ud make some of those gentlemen think, that yawn all through mass on Sunday. Of course they yawn! You don't expect the Church to teach them joy in one wretched half-hour a week, do you? And even if they knew all the articles of the Council of Trent by heart, I doubt it would cheer 'em up very much.

'Why does our earliest childhood always seem so soft and full of light? A kid's got plenty of troubles, like everybody else, and he's really so very helpless, quite unarmed against pain and illness. Childhood and old age should be the two greatest trials of mankind. But that very sense of powerlessness is the mainspring of a child's joy. He just leaves it all to his mother, you see. Present, past, future—his whole life is caught up in one look, and that look is a smile. Well, lad, if only they'd let us have *our* way, the Church might have given men that supreme comfort. Of course they'd each have had their own worries to grapple with, just the same. Hunger, thirst, poverty, jealousy—we'd never be able to pocket the devil once and for all, you may be sure. But man would have known he was the son of God; and therein lies your miracle. He'd have lived, he'd have died with that idea in his noddle—and not just a notion picked up in books either—oh, no! Because we'd have made that idea the basis of everything: habits and customs, relaxation and pleasure, down to the very simplest needs. That wouldn't have stopped the labourer ploughing, or the scientist swotting at his logarithms, or even the engineer making his playthings for grown-up people. What we would have got rid of, what we would have torn from the very heart of Adam, is that sense of his own loneliness. The heathens, with their shoals of gods and goddesses, weren't so daft after all: at least they did manage to give the poor old world some illusion of rather clumsy co-operation with the Unseen. But you couldn't get away with that kind of thing nowadays. A people without the Church will always be a nation of bastards, foundlings. Of course they can still cherish the hope of getting the devil to acknowledge them. And what a hope! Let 'em wait for their little black Christmas! Let 'em hang up their stockings! The devil's tired of filling 'em with stacks of mechanical toys that are out of date as soon as they're invented. These days he just leaves a tiny pinch of morphia or "snow" behind him—or any filthy powder that won't cost him too much. Poor blokes! They've worn everything threadbare—even sin. You can't have a "good time" just because you want to. The shabbiest tuppeny doll will rejoice a baby's heart for half the year, but your mature gentleman'll go yawning his head off at a five-hundred franc gadget. And why? Because he has lost the soul of childhood. Well, God has entrusted the Church to keep that soul alive, to safeguard our candour and freshness. Paganism was no enemy of nature, but Christianity alone can exalt it, can raise it to man's own height, to the peak of his dreams. If I could get hold of one of those learned gents who say I obscure the truth, I'd tell him! I'd say: I can't help wearing an outfit like an undertaker's man. After all, the Pope rigs himself up in white and the cardinals in red, so what's the odds? But I'd have the right to go around adorned like the Queen of Sheba because I'm bringing you joy. I'll give it you for nothing, you have only to ask. Joy is in the gift of the Church, whatever joy is possible for this sad world to share. Whatever you did against the Church, has been done against joy. I'm not stopping you from calculating the procession of the equinoxes or splitting the atom. But what would it profit you even to create life itself, when you have lost all sense of what life really is? Might as well blow your brains out among your test-tubes. Manufacture "life" as much as you like, I say! It's the vision you give us of death that poisons the thoughts of poor devils, bit by bit, that gradually clouds and dulls their last happiness. You'll be able to keep it up so long as your industries and capital permit you to turn the world into a fair-ground of mechanical roundabouts, twirling madly in a perpetual din of brass and crackling fireworks. But just you wait. Wait for the first quarter-of-an-hour's silence. Then the Word will be heard of men—not the voice they rejected, which spoke so quietly: "I am the Way, the Resurrection and the Life"—but the voice from the depths: "I am the door for ever locked, the road which leads nowhere, the lie, the everlasting dark." '

He said these last few words so gloomily that I must have grown paler—or rather yellower, which has been my way, alas, of turning pale during the last few months —for he poured me out a second glass of gin and we changed the subject. His gaiety did not appear false or strained, because I think his very nature, his soul, is gay. But the look in his eyes somehow seemed at cross-purposes with the rest of him for a while. As I bent towards him taking my leave, he made a tiny cross on my brow with his thumb and slipped a hundred-franc note into my pocket:

'I bet you're without a bean, the first days are the hardest, pay me back when you can. Out you get, now, and mind you don't say a word about us two when you're with fools.'

'Bring fresh straw for the ox, give the ass a rub-down.' These words came back into my mind this morning as I sat peeling potatoes for my soup. The town-clerk came in unexpectedly behind my back, and I jumped off my chair without having had a chance to get rid of the peelings. I felt idiotic. Still, he was bringing me good news: the municipal council has agreed to have my well dug, which will save me the franc a week I pay the choirboy who fetches my water every day. All the same I ought to have had a word with him about that new cabaret of his; the latest idea is to arrange a dance for Thursdays and Sundays—he calls the Thursday one a 'family hop,' and even gets little girls from the factory to go: the boys think it rather a joke to make them drunk.

Somehow I hadn't the pluck. He has a way of looking at me and smiling, on the whole quite a pleasant sort of smile, encouraging me to go on talking as though it were a foregone conclusion that nothing I could ever say would be of any consequence. In any case it would be better to go and see him at his house. His wife is seriously ill and has been in bed for weeks, so that gives me a pretext. She is not a bad sort of woman, I hear, and came to church fairly regularly at one time.

'Bring fresh straw for the ox, give the ass a rub-down.' No doubt. But the simplest tasks are by no means the easiest. Beasts have few needs and these never vary, whereas human beings—! I know rustics are supposed to be simple. Yet I who grew up in a peasant family would judge them to be horribly complex. During my first curacy at Bethune I was overwhelmed by the way young workmen at our club would insist on taking me into their confidence, as soon as they'd broken the ice; they were for ever trying to discover what they really were, you could feel them overflowing with sheer self-appreciation. But a peasant seldom loves himself, and his callous indifference to those who love him does not arise from any doubts of their sincerity, but rather because he despises them for it. He may not make any effort to improve, but neither does he try to delude himself as to the defects and vices which he endures, stolidly, his whole life long, having made up his mind that he is incorrigible; he merely seeks to keep in check these useless and expensive parasites, and feed them as cheaply as he can. And since such monsters tend to thrive and grow

in the ever-secretive quiet of peasant lives, an elderly
man finds it very hard to endure himself, and all sympathy exasperates; he suspects it of somehow being in
league with the enemy in his soul that bit by bit is eating up his strength, his work and his property. What is
one to say to these poor devils? Sometimes you may find
a dying man whose avarice has simply been a harsh self-
punishment for the wastefulness of his dissolute ways, a
penance self-inflicted and endured for years with relentless determination. And down to the very threshold of
death, some agonized word torn from their lips will tes-
tify to the last of that hatred of self for which there may
be no forgiveness.

I fear the decision I made a fortnight ago to do without a charwoman has been somewhat misconstrued. And
matters are still further complicated by the fact that M.
Pégriot, my late char's husband, has just got a job as
gamekeeper at the Château. He took his oath at Saint
Vaast yesterday. And I thought it was so clever to buy
from him a small cask of wine! All I've done is to waste
Aunt Philomène's two hundred francs, since M. Pégriot
no longer travels for his Bordeaux firm, to whom he has
nevertheless passed on the order. No doubt his successor
will derive all benefit from my little extravagance. How
foolish!

Yes, indeed, how foolish! I hoped that this diary might
help me to concentrate my thoughts, which *will* go
wandering on the few occasions when I have some
chance to think a little. I had thought it might become
a kind of communion between God and myself, an ex-
tension of prayer, a way of easing the difficulties of ver-

bal expression which always seems insurmountable to me, due no doubt to the twinges of pain in my inside. Instead I have been made to realize what a huge inordinate part of my life is taken up with the hundred and one little daily worries which at times I used to think I had shaken off for good. Of course Our Lord takes His share of all our troubles, even the paltriest, and scorns nothing. But why record in black and white matters which should be dismissed as fast as they happen? The worst of it is I find in these outpourings such solace that this alone should suffice to put me on my guard. As I sit here scribbling in the lamplight, pages no one will ever read, I get the feeling of an invisible presence which surely could not be God—rather a friend made in my image, although distinct from me, a separate entity. Last night I became intensely aware of this presence and suddenly caught myself turning my head towards some imaginary listener, with a longing to cry that shamed me.

At all events I had better continue the experiment to the end—I mean at least for several weeks. I will even force myself to write exactly what comes into my mind, without picking and choosing (sometimes I still search for words, correct myself), then I'll stuff it all away in a drawer and re-read it later with a clear mind.

2

THIS MORNING, after mass, I had a long talk with Mlle Louise. I don't often see her during any of the mid-week services, for her position as governess at the Château makes it necessary for us both to be very discreet. Mme la Comtesse has a high opinion of her. It appears that she intended to take the veil as a Poor Clare, but devoted herself instead to an invalid mother who only died last year. The two little boys worship her. Unluckily the eldest daughter, Mlle Chantal, is most unfriendly and even seems to delight in snubbing her, treating her like a servant. Mere childish petulance perhaps, yet her patience must be cruelly tried, since I hear from Mme la Comtesse that mademoiselle is very well-connected and was given a splendid education.

As far as I could gather the Château approves of my doing without a servant. Yet they feel I ought to go to the expense of a 'daily' once or twice a week, if only for the look of the thing. It is evidently a question of principle. I'm living in a most comfortable presbytery, the best house in the neighbourhood next to the Château, so I can hardly go doing my own washing! It might look as though I were doing so for effect.

And maybe I have no business to single myself out from among my colleagues who are doubtless no better off than I am, but who know how to make the little they have go further. I honestly don't think I care about being rich or poor, but I should be grateful if our superiors would decide the matter once and for all. This setting of well-to-do felicity which we are expected to live up to, is so out of keeping with out penury. Real poverty need mean no loss of dignity. Why must we keep up these appearances? Why should we be made shuffling and needy?

I had been looking forward to some consolation in teaching the children the penny catechism, and in preparing them for private Holy Communion, as recommended by that saintly Pope, Pius X. And even now, whenever I hear their chattering voices in the churchyard, and the tapping of all those little iron-shod sabots, my heart seems to swell with tenderness. *Sinite parvulos.* . . . I used to dream of telling them, in the childish speech which comes back to my mind so easily, all those things that I must keep to myself and couldn't possibly say in the pulpit where I have been so warned against imprudence. Oh, I shouldn't have said too much. . . . But I felt so proud to be called on to speak with them differently, to get away from vulgar factions and civic rights, and those dreadful object-lessons, which are indeed *object lessons* and nothing more. And besides, I was free at last from that strange, almost morbid nervousness which I suppose every young priest experiences when certain phrases or similes come to his lips: a fear of mockery, of equivocations, withering up all our inspiration, so that we naturally stick to austere theological doctrine expressed in words so trite and hackneyed as to be certain of shocking nobody, and so colourless that at least they have the advantage of making the listener too bored to attempt any satirical comment. Too often one would suppose, to hear us talk, that we Catholics preached a Spiritualists' Deity, some vague kind of Supreme Being in no way resembling the Risen Lord we have learnt to know as a marvellous and living friend, who suffers our pain, takes joy in our happiness, will share our last hour and receive us into His arms, upon His heart.

And so I thought I would tell the children. But at once I felt antagonism among the boys, and I couldn't go on. After all, they aren't to blame if weekly visits to the pictures now supplement a precocious realization of sex, inevitably acquired from animals.

By the time their lips could first have shaped it, the word 'love' had already become a thing to ridicule, a dirty thing to be hunted with shouts of laughter, and stoned, much as they treat toads. But I felt there was more hope in the girls; especially in Seraphita Dumouchel. She is the best pupil in my catechism, very gay and neat, with rather a bold yet innocent stare. I had got into the way of singling her out among her less attentive little friends; I would often question her and seem to be talking rather more for her special benefit. A few days ago in the sacristy, as I was giving her the weekly prize—a pretty picture to go in her prayer-book—without thinking I put both hands on her shoulders and said:

'Aren't you longing to welcome Our Lord Jesus? Doesn't it seem a long time to wait till your first Communion?'

'No,' she answered, 'why should it? It'll come soon enough.'

I was nonplussed, but not greatly shocked, for I know the malice there is in children. So I went on:

'But you understand me, though. You listen so well.'
Her small face hardened and she stared.

'It's 'cause you've got such lovely eyes.'

Naturally I didn't move a muscle, and we came out of the sacristy together. All the other children were outside whispering and they suddenly stopped and shouted with laughter. They'd obviously planned the joke together.

Since then I have tried not to alter my manner, for I don't want to seem as though I were entering into their game. But the poor child—probably egged on by the others—pursues me now with surreptitious oglings, grimacing, apeing a grown-up woman in a way that is very hard to bear. She has a trick of deliberately lifting up her skirt to fasten the shoelace which serves as her garter. Children are children—but, oh, why should these little girls be so full of enmity? What have I done?

Monks suffer for souls, *our* pain is on behalf of souls. This thought came to me yesterday evening and remained all night long beside my bed, a guardian angel.

Just three months to-day since my appointment to this parish of Ambricourt. Already three months. . . . This morning I prayed hard for my parish, my poor parish, my first and perhaps my last, since I ask no better than to die here. My parish! The words can't even be spoken without a kind of soaring love. . . . But as yet the idea behind them is so confused. I know that my parish is a reality, that we belong to each other for all eternity; it is not a mere administrative fiction, but a living cell of the everlasting Church. But if only the good God would open my eyes and unseal my ears, so that I might behold the face of my parish and hear its voice. Probably that is asking far too much. The face of my parish! The look in the eyes. . . . They must be gentle, suffering patient eyes. I feel they must be rather like mine when I cease struggling and let myself be borne along in the great invisible flux that sweeps us all, helter-skelter, the living and the dead, into the deep waters of Eternity. And those would be the eyes of all Christianity, of all parishes—perhaps of the poor human race itself. Our Lord saw them from the Cross. 'Forgive them for they know not what they do.'

(It occurred to me that I might make use of this passage, touching it up a bit, for my Sunday sermon. But the *eyes of my parish* provoked a general smile and I stopped short in the middle of a sentence with a most definite feeling of play-acting. And yet God knows I was sincere enough. But thoughts which have stirred our hearts too deeply are always in some way troubled and confused. I know the Dean of Torcy would have scolded me. After mass M. le Comte remarked in his funny rather nasal voice, 'You certainly were moved to eloquence.' I wished the earth could have opened and swallowed me.)

Mlle Louise has conveyed to me an invitation to lunch at the Château next Saturday. I was rather embarrassed by the presence of Mlle Chantal, but nevertheless would have declined it if Mlle Louise had not discreetly signed to me to accept.

My charwoman comes in again on Tuesday. Mme la Comtesse has most kindly offered to pay her one day's wages a week. I was so ashamed at the state of my underwear that I rushed to Saint Vaast this morning to buy three shirts, some pants and handkerchiefs; the hundred francs from M. le Curé de Torcy were barely enough to meet this heavy outlay. And now I shall have to provide a midday meal—a woman who has been hard at work all the morning needs proper food. Fortunately my Bordeaux will come in handy. I bottled it yesterday. It looks a bit cloudy, but the bouquet seems right.

One day goes by, and then the next. . . . How empty they seem! I just get to the end of my day's work, but I always put off till to-morrow the carrying out of the little plan I had in mind. Obviously I lack method. And I spend so much time out on the road. My nearest boundary is a distance of three good kilometres—the other, five. My bicycle is not much help since I can't possibly ride uphill, especially on an empty stomach, without the most horrible pains. . . . Yet this parish looks so small on the map! When I think how it takes a teacher well into the second term to get to know a class of thirty or forty children of the same age and type, brought up and educated alike—and even then he won't always understand each one separately. . . . I feel that my life, all the sap of my life, will flow to waste in sand.

Mlle Louise comes to mass every morning now. But she is there and gone again so quickly that sometimes I'm not aware of her presence. The church would be empty but for her.

Met Seraphita yesterday with M. Dumouchel. That child's face seems to alter day by day: her quick-changing mobile expression has now become fixed with a hardness far beyond her years. Whilst I was talking to her she kept watching me with such embarrassing attention that I couldn't help blushing. Perhaps I ought to warn her parents. . . . Only of what?

On a scrap of paper which I found this morning,

doubtless intentionally left in one of the catechisms, I discovered a clumsy scrawl, the 'drawing' of a tiny woman inscribed: 'M. le Curé's bit of stuff.' Since I hand out the books at random every time, it would be no use trying to detect the humorist.

Of course I keep saying to myself that these annoyances are part and parcel of daily routine, even in the best-conducted schools; but I am only partly reassured. A teacher can always consult the headmaster, whereas I—

'Suffer on behalf of others.' I whispered this comforting thought to myself all night, but my angel did not return.

Mme Pégriot came in yesterday. She seemed so dissatisfied with the wages arranged by Mme la Comtesse that I felt obliged to offer her an extra five francs of my own. It appears that the wine was bottled much too early, without the necessary precautions, and so I've spoilt it all. I found a bottle in the kitchen later which she'd scarcely tasted.

Obviously this woman is dour by nature, she'll be very hard to get on with. But I must be fair: I give so clumsily, with a kind of ridiculous embarrassment that must make people feel very uncomfortable. And so I rarely get the impression of any pleased response, no doubt because I hope for too much. They think I'm begrudging them.

On Tuesday we held our monthly conference at the home of the Curé d'Hébuterne. M. l'Abbé Thomas, who took his degree in history, lectured us on 'The Origins and Causes of the Reformation.' The state of the church in the sixteenth century really makes one shudder. Whilst the lecturer was broaching his subject, which was of course bound to be rather monotonous, I sat observing the faces of his audience in which I could discover nothing beyond the merest formal show of interest, as though we were listening to some chapter from the history of the Pharaohs. Such apparent indifference would have enraged me at one time. But now I believe it to be a sign of deep faith and possibly also of profoundly unconscious pride. Not one of those men would ever suppose that the church could be in danger, no matter for what reason. My own faith is no less than theirs, but probably of another order. Their serene security appals me.

(I rather wish I hadn't used the word 'pride' and yet I cannot cross it out, for there seems no other to express a state of mind so human and tangible. After all the church is not an ideal to be striven for: she exists and they're within her.)

After the conference I rather timidly brought up the question of my 'plan.' Even so I cut it down by half. They soon managed to make me realize that to achieve but a part of what I had hoped would require a forty-eight hour day and a personal influence which I am far from possessing, and may never possess. Luckily they soon ceased to notice me, and the Curé de Lumbres, a specialist in these matters, dealt in a masterly fashion with the problem of village savings-banks and co-operative farming.

I walked home rather sadly through the rain. The few glasses of wine I had taken had brought on an acute pain in my stomach. I certainly seem to have lost weight enormously since the autumn, and people have ceased inquiring after my health, so I should think I must look worse each time they see me. Supposing I were not able to carry on! Somehow I can never quite believe that God will really employ me—to the utmost: make complete use of me as He does of the others. Every day I become more aware of my own ignorance in the most elementary details of everyday life, which everybody seems to know without having learnt them, by a sort of instinct. Yet I don't suppose I'm really more of a fool than most people, and if I stick to easily remembered rules of thumb, I can look as though I really understood what was going on. But all those words which seem to have such precise meaning for some folk, are pretty nigh indistinguishable to me, so that I often use them haphazard, like a bad card-player to whom one lead seems as good as another. Whilst they were discussing the savings-banks I felt like a child strayed into a room full of gabbling grown-ups.

Possibly my colleagues knew no more than I did, in spite of all the pamphlets with which they inundate us. Yet they plunge into such discussions with an ease that amazes me. They are nearly all poor and bravely resigned to it, yet money matters seem to have a strange fascination for them. Their faces at once become solemn, with an air of assurance that disheartens me and keeps me tongue-tied, filled with something approaching respect.

I fear I shall never be practical, and I don't improve with experience. To a casual observer I look much as every other village priest, I am just a peasant like all the rest. But I come of very poor forebears, jobbers, unskilled labourers, farm-girls—we've always lacked a sense of property, or must have lost it in the course of centuries. In this my father was like my grandfather, and he was like *his* father who died of hunger during the terrible winter of 1854. A franc would burn a hole in their pockets and out they'd rush to get drunk with a neighbour. The other boys in the seminary knew instinctively: though mother was always careful to wear her Sunday-best petticoat and prettiest bonnet on visiting days, she could not change that humble furtive look, that wan smile of the poor creatures whose lot it is to bring up other peoples' children. At least if it were only my sense of property that is lacking! But I fear I am no more able to give orders than I am to possess. That is more serious.

Still, mediocre and poorly gifted scholars sometimes make their way to the front, though they will never be exactly brilliant. I have no ambition to change my nature, I merely intend to conquer my dislikes. Since my life is first and foremost a cure of souls, I have no right to remain ignorant of cares—on the whole quite legitimate—which loom so large in the lives of my parishioners. The head of the school here, although he's a Parisian by birth, often gives lectures on crops and pastures. I mean to swot up those subjects.

And I really ought to be able to start a sports club, like most of my colleagues. Our boys are very keen on football and boxing and speed-records. Must they be denied the pleasure of talking such matters over with me, merely because these quite legitimate amusements don't appeal to me? I wasn't strong enough for military service, and it would be absurd to take any active part in their games. But I can keep up with their interests, were it merely by reading the sporting news in the *Echo de Paris*, which M. le Comte lends me fairly regularly.

Last night after writing this, I knelt at the foot of my bed and prayed that Our Lord might bless my resolutions. Suddenly I was overwhelmed by a sense of destruction, a feeling that all the dreams, hopes and ambitions of my youth had been broken down. I got into bed shivering with fever, and never slept till dawn.

Mlle Louise knelt all through mass this morning with her face buried in her hands. At the last gospel I could see she had been crying. It is hard to be alone, and harder still to share your solitude with indifferent or ungrateful people.

Ever since I had the unfortunate idea of recommending to M. le Comte's bailiff an old seminary friend of mine who is a salesman for a large chemical firm, the headmaster cuts me. Apparently *he* represented *another* large firm.

I am due to lunch at the Château next Saturday. Since the primary, perhaps the only use of this diary, will be to encourage a habit of complete frankness towards myself, I must admit I am not disappointed, I am even rather pleased. . . . And I am not ashamed of this feeling. At the seminary they were always rather down on local squires, and there is no doubt that a young priest must always be careful to keep his independence with such people. But in this matter, too, I remain the son of very poor folk who never knew the strange jealousy and bitterness of the land-owning peasant towards the ungrateful soil itself, for eating up his strength, and towards the idler who merely draws revenue from that same soil. It's a long time since *we* were in touch with the gentry! For centuries we ourselves have been the property of those same land-owning peasants, and there are no masters more harsh and difficult to please.

[35]

Received a very strange letter from l'Abbé Dupréty. He was my best friend at the seminary, then he took his degree somewhere else, and the last I heard of him he was doing assistant duty in a small parish of the Amiens diocese, as the vicar was ill and required some help. I can remember him very vividly—tenderly almost. In those days he used to be held up as a model of piety, although I secretly considered him far too highly strung and sensitive. During our third year he used to sit next to me in chapel, and I often heard him sobbing with his face buried in his small hands, invariably inkstained and so white.

His letter comes from Lille (where I seem to remember one of his uncles, a retired police-officer, had a grocer's shop). To my surprise he in no way mentions the priesthood, which apparently he has left owing to illness. He was said to be tubercular. His father and mother both died of consumption.

Now that I have no maid living in, the postman slips all my correspondence under the door. I found the letter just as I was going to bed. It is a very unpleasant time for me and I put it off as long as I can. Stomach-aches are usually quite bearable, but there is nothing more wearing in the long run. The pain grows on the imagination bit by bit, the mind itself becomes tortured, and it requires great determination not to get up and walk about. I don't often give way to this temptation, because it's so cold.

So I opened the letter with a foreboding of bad news —worse still, of a whole succession of unpleasant tidings. . . . Certainly not a good start. But I don't like the tone of this letter anyhow. There is a forced gaiety about it which I find almost unseemly in the likely eventuality of my poor friend having had to give up his work, at all events for the time being. 'You're the only one who can understand me,' he says. Why? I remember he was far more gifted than I, and was sometimes a little scornful with me. Which made me the more attached, naturally.

Since he wants me to go and see him as quickly as possible, I shall soon know what it's all about.

I am very preoccupied about my coming visit to the Château. The success of some important schemes very dear to me may depend on this first contact, for the money and influence of M. le Comte would certainly allow me to achieve them. As usual my inexperience and foolishness, combined with a kind of absurd bad luck, always seems to complicate the simplest matters. I find that my best cassock, which I had been keeping for special occasions, is now too big for me. Moreover, Mme Pégriot, at my request, has been getting the stains out, but she has done it very badly and the petrol has left horrible rings, like the iridescent spots that float over the surface of too greasy soup. I don't like the idea of going to the Château in my everyday things, which have been patched up so often, especially at the elbows. I am so terrified of appearing to show off my poverty. You never know what they might think. . . .

Then I should like to be able to eat—just enough not to attract attention. But it's impossible to anticipate how I shall feel, my inside is so capricious! At the slightest provocation, back comes the little pain in my right side, it is as though something had snapped inside me, a sort of spasm. My mouth dries up at once and I can't swallow another thing.

These are mere discomforts, nothing more. I can put up with them all right, for I'm no mollycoddle really; I take after mother. 'Your mother was a tough one,' my uncle Ernest is always saying. Among the poor I think that means a relentless housewife, never ill, and dying without costing much.

M. le Comte is certainly more like a peasant of my description, than many a rich business man that I have come into contact with in the course of my work. He made me feel at ease in a couple of words. Surely some magic of breeding, for these people hardly appear any different from others, yet do nothing in the same way. The slightest show of respect always embarrasses me, but *they* were able to go as far as deference without ever allowing me to forget that this was mere regard for my cloth. Mme la Comtesse was perfect throughout. She was dressed very simply in a house-frock, with a sort of mantilla over her grey hair which so reminded me of the one poor dear mother used to wear on Sundays. I couldn't help telling her so, but I expressed myself so badly that I am wondering if she understood.

We all had a good laugh over my cassock. Anywhere else there would doubtless have been some pretence not to notice it, and I would have been in agony. These aristocrats have such a free way of talking about money and all matters concerning it—such discretion and grace. . . . There is even a feeling that true authentic poverty lets you right into their confidence, creates some kind of sly, unspoken understanding. I was most aware of this when M. and Mme Vergenne (he is an extremely wealthy retired flour-merchant who bought the Château de Rouvroy last year) called in for coffee. When they had gone M. le Comte smiled a little ironically and his meaning was unmistakable: 'Well, bye-bye; now we can have a chat between ourselves.'

And yet there is much talk of Mlle Chantal and the Vergenne boy getting married. . . .

Still, I think there must be something other than mere politeness, however sincere, in this approach which I describe so badly. Good manners hardly explain everything.

Naturally I wish M. le Comte could have displayed rather more enthusiasm about the Young Men's Guild or Sports Club which I have in mind. He may wish to take no personal part, but why not let me have the use of a small field and that old barn which nobody wants and could easily be turned into a pavilion for indoor games, lectures, lantern-slides and so on. I do realize that I am as awkward in my requests as in my gifts, people like time to think things over, and I am for ever anticipating an immediate heartfelt response.

I left the Château late—far too late. I am also very bad at taking my leave. Each time the clock goes round I make a tentative move, calling forth much polite protestation which I have not the courage to resist. It might go on for hours! At last I managed to get away, not knowing in the least what I had been talking about, and yet buoyed up with a kind of confidence, the joyous sensation of good news, very good news, which I should have liked to go straight and tell a friend. I felt like running all the way home.

Nearly every day I plan my rounds so as to come back to the presbytery by the Gesvre road. At the top of the hill, whether it be raining or blowing, I sit down on the trunk of a poplar, forgotten these many winters ago, nobody knows why, and rotting with age. Parasitic climbers have enveloped it in a kind of sheath which by turn seems hideous or beautiful according to my mood and the hues of the weather. It is here that the idea of this diary first occurred to me, and I don't feel I could have thought of it anywhere else. In this country of woods and pastures, streaked with quickset hedges and all grown over by apple-trees, it would be hard to find such another place from which to overlook the whole village, gathered together, as it were, in the palm of a hand. I look down, but it never seems to look back at me. Rather does it turn away, cat-like, watching me askance with half-shut eyes.

What does it want of me? Does it even want anything of me? Anyone else sitting here, a rich man for instance, could estimate the value of those hovels, calculate the exact area of those fields and pastures, and could daydream he had paid up just what it was all worth, and owned the village. But I can't think along those lines.

Whatever I were to do, were I to pour out my last drop of blood (and indeed sometimes I fancy the village has nailed me up here on a cross and is at least watching me die) I could never possess it. Although it looks fresh and white enough just now (they've been washing down their walls for All Saints with milk-of-lime and household starch), I can never forget it has been there for centuries, and its age frightens me. Long, long before this little fifteenth-century church, through which I am merely a passer-by, *it* was there, patiently enduring heat and cold, rain, wind and sun, now thriving, now starving, fastened like a limpet to this strip of land, sucking in life and yielding up its dead.

How profound, how secret such experience of life must be! I shall be swallowed up with all the rest, and quicker than most, surely.

There are some thoughts which I never dare confide, though they don't seem mad to me—far from it. I wonder what I should become if I resigned myself to the part which many Catholics would have me play—those that are so preoccupied with social preservation, which really means their own preservation. Oh, I don't accuse these people of hypocrisy, I believe them to be sincere. So many of us, supposedly standing for law and order, are merely clinging on to old habits, sometimes to a mere parrot vocabulary, its formulae worn so smooth by constant use that they justify everything and question none. It is one of the most mysterious penalties of men that they should be forced to confide the most precious of their possessions to things so unstable and ever changing, alas, as *words*. It needs much courage to inspect the key each time and adapt it to one's own lock. It is far easier to force up the latch with the nearest and handiest—so long as the Yale works somehow. I wonder at revolutionaries who strive so hard to blow up the walls with dynamite, when the average bunch of keys of law-abiding folk would have sufficed to let them in quietly through the door without wakening anyone.

Received this morning another letter from my old friend—even stranger than the first. Finishing thus:

'My health is not good, and that is my only real source of worry, for I should hate to die now when after so many storms I am at last reaching the harbour. *Inveni portum.* All the same I don't regret having been ill, for leisure has thus been possible which I could never have had otherwise. I have spent the last eighteen months in a sanatorium, which enabled me carefully to turn over in my mind the problem of life. If you thought things out, I believe you'd come to the same conclusions. *Aurea mediocritas.* These two words are proof of my claims being very moderate, that I am no rebel. In fact I am still very grateful to our teachers. The real trouble doesn't lie with what they taught so much as with the education they had been given and passed on simply because they knew no other way of thinking and feeling. That education made us isolated individualists. Really we never escaped from childhood, we were always playing at make-believe; we invented our troubles and joys, we invented life, instead of living it. So before daring to take one step out of our little world, you have to begin all over again from the beginning. It is very hard work and entails much sacrifice of pride; but then to be alone is harder still, as you'll realize some day.

'You'd better not discuss me with your friends. A busy, healthy life, *normal* in every way' (the word *normal* underlined three times) 'should contain no mysteries. But unfortunately our society is such that happiness always seems a trifle dubious. I think a certain type of Christianity, far removed from the spirit of the Gospels, has something to do with this prejudice, equally shared by believers and unbelievers. Out of respect for the freedom and feeling of others, I have so far preferred not to say anything. But now, after careful thought, I feel I must speak for the sake of a lady who has a right to the greatest consideration. Although my health may have greatly improved during the last few months, there is still cause for grave anxiety which I will explain when I see you. Come quickly.'

Inveni portum. . . . The postman handed me this letter as I was going out this morning to my catechism class. I read it in the churchyard, a few steps from where Arsène was starting to dig a grave for Mme Pinochet, who is being buried to-morrow. He, too, was 'turning over life.' . . .

'Come quickly'—it went straight to my heart. That child's cry at the end of his pathetic, solemn screed, so carefully phrased (I could just see him scratching his forehead with his penholder, as he used to do)—he couldn't keep it back, it had to come out. At first I tried to persuade myself that I was imagining things, that no doubt he was being looked after by some relative. Unfortunately I happen to know he has only a sister, a barmaid at Montreuil. It could hardly be she who 'had a right to the greatest consideration.'

No matter, I shall certainly go.

M. le Comte has called to see me. Very pleasant, respectful, yet at the same time friendly, as he always is. He asked my permission to smoke his pipe, and left two rabbits which he had shot in the Sauveline woods.

'Mme Pégriot'll cook them for you to-morrow. She knows all about it.'

I didn't dare tell him that my inside will only stand dry bread for the moment. His stew will cost me a half-day's wages, and my char won't even enjoy them herself as the gamekeeper's entire family are sick to death of rabbits.

Of course I could get the choirboy to take some round to my old bell-ringer, at night though, so as not to attract any attention. My bad health is over-discussed as it is.

[43]

M. le Comte doesn't altogether endorse my plans. He is particularly anxious to warn me against the maliciousness of the villages who, according to him, have had far too much done for them ever since the War, and had better be left to stew in their own juice.

'Don't go seeking them out too quickly, don't be at their beck and call, let them come to you first.'

He is the nephew of the Marquis de la Roche-Macé, whose estate lies only five miles from my native village. He used to spend part of his holidays there at one time, and he remembers poor darling mother very well; she was housekeeper at the Château in those days and would stuff him on the sly with great slices of bread and jam, as the late marquis was very mean. I had begun asking him about her, somewhat impulsively, and he answered me at once, so kindly, without the slightest embarrassment. Sweet mother! Even when she was so young and so poor, she knew how to inspire respect and sympathy.

If ever these pages were to be seen by indifferent eyes, I would certainly be thought very credulous. And no doubt I am, for there can surely be nothing abject in the strange regard which I feel towards this man, whose approach is so simple and at times so playful, like an eternal schoolboy on eternal holiday. I don't consider him particularly intelligent, and he is said to be rather hard on his farmers. And he isn't an exemplary parishioner, for though he comes to low mass every Sunday, I have never yet seen him at the altar rails. I am wondering if he will come to Holy Communion at Easter. For what reason then should he suddenly have assumed in my life the place—alas, so often empty—of a friend, an ally, a close companion? Maybe because I seem to find in him a natural simplicity for which I seek in vain elsewhere. Not all his conscious superiority, his inherited instinct to command, not even his age, have succeeded in marking him with that air of pompous self-assurance, of funereal gravity which the privilege of money alone bestows on the smallest of small shopkeepers. These, I believe, are for ever anxious to keep 'other people in their places' (as they express it) whereas he knows *his* place and keeps it. I'm well aware there is much vanity—and I prefer to think it is unconscious—in that laconic gruffness of manner which never attempts to condescend, and yet could make nobody feel small, since it arouses in the poorest no sense of subjection, but rather of discipline freely accepted—military. Much vanity, I fear. And pride, too. All the same it does me good to hear it. And when I talk about the interests of the parish, of souls, of the church, and he answers 'we,' as though he and I could only serve a common cause, it seems natural and I dare not contradict him.

M. le Curé de Torcy dislikes him heartily. He will keep calling him 'the little count,' 'your little count.' It gets on my nerves. 'Why "little count"?' I asked. 'Because he's an ornament. A pretty little period gadget—that's all. He looks rather effective on a farmer's mantelpiece. But if you were to see him in a curio-shop or an auction-room, one day when they were knocking down a big collection, why, you wouldn't even notice he was there.' And when I admitted that I still hoped to awaken M. le Comte's interest in my boys' guild, he only shrugged: 'A pretty little porcelain money-box, your little count—but he's unbreakable.'

And I must say I don't think he's very generous. He never gives the impression of being ruled by money, as so many do, but he certainly doesn't like parting with it.

I tried to put in a word about Mlle Chantal, whose depression worries me. He closed up at once and then suddenly became hearty—but his gaiety seemed a little constrained. Any mention of Mlle Louise seemed to rile him. I held my tongue.

My old professor Canon Durieux once said to me: 'You have a gift for making friends. But mind you don't let it become a passion. It's the only one of them all that can't be cured.'

We preserve. No doubt. But we only preserve in order to save, and the world can never realize that, for the world asks only to survive. And mere survival suffices no longer. The ancient world might have survived. It might have lasted a very long time. It was made to last. It was terribly heavy, its huge bulk was clamped to the earth. It was reconciled to injustice. It used no guile against the unjust, but swallowed injustice whole, without any repugnance, made of it a mere institution like any other: slavery. No doubt it would still have been afflicted by the curse of Adam, whatever degree of perfection that civilization might have attained. Of that the devil was well aware, he knew it better than anyone else did. All the same it was not so easy to load the shoulders of human cattle with almost the full weight of such malediction; they might have reduced the burden by just so much. The greatest possible sum of revolt, ignorance and despair, reserved for a race of scapegoats, a sacrificed race, a nameless people without history, dispossessed and without allies—at least none that could be named—without family—that could be legally recognized—anonymous and without gods. What an easy way out of the social problem, what a simplification of government!

Yet that institution which seemed so unshakable was really brittle in the extreme. It took only a century to destroy it for ever. Perhaps one day would have been enough. Once the castes had begun to mingle, once the race of scapegoats had been dispersed, what power could ever compel it back under the yoke? Slavery as an institution is dead, and with it crumbled the antique world. Men believed, or pretended to believe in its necessity, they recognized and accepted it. It will never be reestablished. Humanity will never dare run the horrible risk again, the danger is too great. The law may condone injustice, be secretly on its side, but will never sanction it openly. Injustice can never be 'lawful' again, that is finished and done with. But none the less all over the world its scattered fragments still persist. And the social body, no longer daring to use it to maintain the privilege of the few, is thus condemned to cleanse itself of these germs, this disease which, though purged out by the laws, ran rife again in our customs almost immediately, renewing from below its indefatigable onslaught, the same old circuit engendered of hell. Willy-nilly, the social order must henceforth share the natural burden of humanity, embark on the same divine adventure. In the past alike indifferent to good and evil, knowing only the laws of its own power, society has found a soul in Christianity, a soul to lose or to save.

I gave the above to M. le Curé de Torcy to read, but I did not dare tell him that I had written it. He is so shrewd, and I'm such a pitiful liar that I still wonder if he believed me. He handed me back the paper with a smirk, a glint in his eye to which I'm accustomed, and that bodes no good. At last he said:

[47]

'Your friend seems to write rather well, rather too well, if you ask me. Generally speaking, it's always a good thing to think objectively, and that's about as far as one need go. You see a thing just as it is, without setting it to music, and so there's no risk of making a great song and dance about it for oneself alone. If ever you glimpse the passing truth, take a good look at her, so as to be quite sure you'll know her again; but don't expect her to make eyes at you. Gospel truth makes eyes at nobody. And it's dangerous to get into conversation with any other sort of truth, because you never know where that particular lady mayn't have been gadding around before she met you. I don't want to set myself up as an example, a great lout like me—but I know that when I happen to strike an idea—the kind of notion that might be of use in saving souls, because of course, any other kind—! Well, I do my best to show God what I've seen, I put it into my prayers at once. It's marvellous how different it looks. Sometimes you'd scarcely recognize it. . . .

'Still, your friend's not wrong. The modern world may deny its Master, but it's been redeemed just the same; present-day society is no longer content merely to administer our common patrimony, so whether it wants to or doesn't, it's got to set out and seek the Kingdom. And that Kingdom is not of this world. Which means they'll never find it. Yet they'll never be able to give up the search. "Save yourself or die," there's no getting away from it. And what your friend says about slavery is perfectly true. The ancient law tolerated slavery and the apostles endorsed that toleration. They didn't say to the slave: "Be free of your Master," though for instance they did say to the lecher: "Free yourself from the flesh and look sharp about it!" It's a fine distinction. And why was that, d'you suppose? Because I should think they wanted to give the world a chance to breathe before launching it into a fresh superhuman crusade. And believe me, a great fellow like St. Paul wasn't kidding himself. Doing away with slavery wasn't going to put an end to the exploitation of man by man. Come to think of it, a slave cost something to buy, so his master was bound to spare him in some ways. Whilst I remember a filthy old glass-blower when I was young who used to get lads of fifteen to blow down his tubes, and when their poor little lungs were nearly done for, the swine could get as many more as he wanted; I'd a hundred times rather have been the slave of a good solid Roman citizen, who'd be bound to look a penny on both sides. No, St. Paul wasn't kidding himself. He simply knew Christianity had let loose a truth in the world that nothing would ever stop again because it was already there, right down in the depths of human consciousness, and man had instantly seen himself mirrored in it; God saved each one of us and each one of us is worth the blood of Our Lord. You can translate that any way you like, even into rationalism—the silliest talk of the lot—it makes you shove words together that fuse when they touch. Let future society try and sit on that lot! Her behind'll catch fire, that's all.

'All the same the poor old world goes on dreaming of that ancient contract with the Fiend which seemed to promise a quiet life. The subduing of a quarter or a third of the human race to the level of cattle—the best cattle, mind you—was perhaps not too high a price to pay for the advent of the supermen, the thoroughbred, the real Kingdom on earth. . . . That was the idea, though no one

[49]

dare say so. But Our Lord took poverty as his bride, and invested the poor man with such dignity that now we'll never get him off his pedestal. He gave him an ancestor—and what an ancestor! A name, and what a name! And now the revolt of the poor man inspires us more than his resignation, he seems to be already part of the Kingdom of God, where the first shall be last; he is like a spectre at the King's Feast, in his wedding garment. . . . And so the state has begun to make the best of a bad job; looking after kids, bandaging cripples, washing out dirty linen, hotting up soup for the disabled, de-lousing decrepit old men—but with one eye on the clock, wondering when there'll ever be a chance to attend to its own business. No doubt still hoping to replace the slaves by machines. What a hope! The machines keep going round and round and the ranks of unemployed keep swelling and swelling, as though the machines were just manufacturing unemployed, see what I mean? Ah, the poor take some getting rid of! Well, they're still having a last try in Russia. . . . Mind you, I don't think the Russians are any worse than the rest— they're all mad, mad dogs, the people of to-day—but those Russian bastards have got some guts. They're the Flemish of the far North, those blokes are! They can stomach anything. Give 'em another century or two and they'll be able to swallow a polytechnic engineer—and keep him down!

'After all, theirs isn't such a fool's plan. Get rid of the poor—that's always been the idea, since the poor man bears witness for Jesus Christ, the heir of Jewry, isn't that it?—but instead of making him a beast of burden or wiping him off the face of the earth, they've got the notion of turning him into a small *rentier* or even

—supposing things should really go ahead—into a low-grade government official. Quite the easiest thing to manage, the most orderly and submissive!'

I, too, often find myself thinking about the Russians. My friends in the seminary used to argue about them without really knowing, I think. Mostly to rile the professors. Our democratic colleagues are very pleasant and full of zeal, but I find them just a little—how shall I put it?—a little *bourgeois*. And they are not really liked by the people. No doubt because they are not understood. Anyway I often think of the Russians with a strange sort of inquisitiveness and tenderness. If one has known real poverty, its joys, mysterious, incommunicable—Russian writers can brings tears to the eyes. The year father died, mother had to be operated on for a tumour, she was kept at the hospital of Berguette for four or five months. An aunt took me in. She kept a little pub. just outside Lens, a horrible wooden shanty where they sold gin to miners who were too poor to go anywhere else. The nearest school was a couple of miles away, and I used to do my homework squatting behind the bar on the floor—that is to say a few rotting boards. The dank reek of earth came up between them, earth which was always wet, the reek of mud. On pay-nights our customers didn't even go outside to relieve themselves; they would pass water where they stood, and I was so terrified, crouching behind the bar, that in the end I'd fall asleep. But the teacher was kind to me, lending me books. It was there I read the childhood memories of Maxim Gorki.

Of course there are many distressed areas in France. Little islands of extreme poverty. Never large enough to enable the poor to live their own life, the true life of poverty. And wealth itself is too finely graded—too humane is perhaps the word—ever to permit that relentless glare, the full glitter of money, its blind power and cruelty. But I fancy these Russians were really poor people, a country of authentic paupers, that they must have known the mad stupor and clutch of poverty. If the church could make saints out of whole nations, and had chosen this one, she would have made Russia the patron saint of Want. It seems M. Gorki has now made a great deal of money, that he lives in luxury somewhere on the Mediterranean, at least, I saw something about it in the paper. Even if that is so—more especially if it is so—I am glad to have prayed for him every day for so many years.

I dare not say I knew nothing of God when I was twelve years old, because mingled with so many other calls like thunder and rushing water sounding through my poor little head, already I could recognize His voice. Nevertheless the first realization of misery is fierce indeed. Blessed be he who has saved a child's heart from despair! It is a thing most people know so little about, or forget it because it would frighten them too much. Amongst the poor, as amongst the rich, a little boy is all alone, as lonely as a king's son. At all events in our part of the world, distress is not shared, each creature is alone in his distress; it belongs only to him, like his face and his hands. I don't think I had any perception of that loneliness, or perhaps I had no clear notion of it at all, but merely submitted to this law of my life, without understanding. In the end I should even have loved it. There is nothing harder to break down than the pride of the very poor, but suddenly this book of Gorki's, come from so far, from those vast stretches of land, gave me a whole people for my companions.

I lent that book to a friend, who, of course, never returned it. I don't really want to read it again, there is no need to. Sufficient to have once heard—or thought I heard—the cry of a people, a cry different from that of any other nation, even unlike the cry of the Jews, mortified in their pride, like the dead in spices. Really it isn't a cry, but a chant, a hymn. Oh, not a church hymn, nothing that could be called a prayer. There's some of everything in it, as they say. The howling of a moujik under the rods, the screaming of a beaten wife, the hiccup of a drunkard, and the growlings of animal joy, that wild sigh from the loins—since, alas! poverty and lust seek each other out and call to each other in the darkness like two famished beasts. No doubt I should turn from all this in disgust. And yet I feel that such distress, distress that has forgotten even its name, that has ceased to reason or to hope, that lays its tortured head at random, will awaken one day on the shoulder of Jesus Christ.

So I took up the cudgels.

'But suppose they managed to pull it off after all?' I said to M. le Curé de Torcy.

He thought for a while.

'You may be sure I wouldn't advise the poor devils to go straight and give the boss their meat-tickets back. It 'ud last as long as it lasted. . . . But you see, *we're* here to teach the truth. It can never shame us.'

His hands were shaking a little on the table, not much, yet I knew my question had awakened in him the memory of terrible struggles, in which his reason and courage had almost failed, and perhaps his faith. Before answering, he squared his shoulders like a man who finds his way barred, yet means to get past. He'd have brushed me aside soon enough.

'Teaching is no joke, sonny! I'm not talking of those who get out of it with a lot of eyewash: you'll knock up against plenty of *them* in the course of your life, and get to know 'em. Comforting truths, they call it! Truth is meant to save you first, and the comfort comes afterwards. Besides, you've no right to call that sort of thing comfort. Might as well talk about condolences! The Word of God is a red-hot iron. And you who preach it 'ud go picking it up with a pair of tongs, for fear of burning yourself, you daren't get hold of it with both hands. It's too funny! Why, the priest who descends from the pulpit of Truth, with a mouth like a hen's vent, a little hot but pleased with himself, he's not been preaching: at best he's been purring like a tabby-cat. Mind you that can happen to us all, we're all half asleep, it's the devil to wake us up, sometimes—the apostles slept all right at Gethsemane. Still, there's a difference. . . . And mind you many a fellow who waves his arms and sweats like a furniture-remover isn't necessarily any more awakened than the rest. On the contrary. I simply mean that when the Lord has drawn from me some word for the good of souls, I know, because of the pain of it.'

He was laughing, but it was a laugh I couldn't recognize. A very valiant laugh, yet broken.

I dare not allow myself to judge a man so greatly my superior in every way, and I am going to speak of an attribute foreign to me, and to which I was never inclined either through birth or education. There is no doubt that certain people consider M. le Curé de Torcy something of a lout, almost vulgar or—to quote Mme la Comtesse—definitely *common*. But I can write what I please here, without the risk of offending anybody. Well, what seems to me—from the human standpoint, anyhow —the main feature in that erect presence, is pride. If M. le Curé de Torcy is not a proud man, then that word has no meaning, at least I could no longer find it one. He was suffering in his pride at this moment, I know —the pride of a very proud man. And I suffered with him. I did so long to do something useful, effective. I began rather ineptly:

'Well, I think I must purr a good deal, because—'

'Hold your tongue,' he replied, and I was struck by the sudden softness of his voice. 'You don't expect a poor little ragamuffin like yourself to attempt any more than just saying his lesson, do you? But the Lord must have blessed your lesson, all the same, because you haven't that prosperous look of a special preacher at low mass.'

He began to walk about the room, his arms plunged deep into the pockets of his cassock. I wanted to rise as well, but he made me sit down again with a jerk of his head: I felt he was still hesitating, still trying to judge me, size me up for the last time before telling me what he had perhaps never told before—in the same terms, at all events. He was obviously doubting me, but I swear there was nothing humiliating in that doubt. He could never humiliate a soul. His eyes were very gentle, now, and— this seems absurd when speaking of a man almost blatant in his strength and health, with such great experience of life and living creatures—strangely, indefinably pure.

'One should consider very carefully before speaking

of poverty to the rich. Or we should render ourselves unworthy of teaching it to the poor. And how could we then dare to stand in the presence of Jesus Christ?'

'Teach it to the poor?' I whispered.

'Ay, to the poor. God sends us to them first, and what is our message? Poverty. They were expecting something different. They were hoping for the end of their distress, and God takes Poverty by the hand and says: "Here is your Queen, recognize her, swear to honour her and be faithful." What a blow, my children! Remember that's been more or less the story of the Jewish people and their Kingdom on earth. The poor are also a wandering people, searching through every nation for the realization of their carnal hopes; they are a disappointed people—disappointed to the marrow.'

'And yet—'

'And yet that's how things are, no getting away from it. Oh, a coward might skirt round the difficulty. The poor are an easy audience to gull, when you know how to go about it. Go and talk cures to an incurable, he'll be only too anxious to believe you. Nothing easier, come to think of it, than to make them feel poverty as a shameful illness, unworthy of a civilized country, that we're going to get rid of the filthy thing in no time. But which one of us would dare to speak thus of the poverty of Jesus Christ?'

He was staring me straight in the eyes, and I still wonder if he was really able to distinguish me from all the familiar things around him, his habitual silent friends. No, he couldn't see me. Mere intention of convincing me would not have put such tragedy into his eyes. He was battling with himself, against another self, crushed a hundred times, vanquished a hundred times, still in rebellion; he was drawn up to his full height, to his greatest strength, as though fighting for his life. How deep the wound must have been! He was as though tearing himself with his own hands.

'See here,' he said, 'I shouldn't mind preaching rebellion to the poor—not in the least. Or rather I wouldn't preach anything at 'em. I'd just get hold of some of those tub-thumping militants, those pottering little sedition-mongers, and I'd make 'em take a look at a real Flemish rebel. We have revolt in *our* blood, you know. Remember our history! We've never been scared of our nobles, our rich. Thanks be to God—no harm in saying so now—hefty and strong as I am, the Lord never allowed my flesh to be sorely tempted. Whereas injustice and misery —that makes my blood boil! Anyway, it's all over now, you don't realize; how could you? . . . For instance, that famous encyclical of Leo XIII, "Rerum Novarum," *you* can read that without turning a hair, like any instruction for keeping Lent. But when it was published, sonny, it was like an earthquake. The enthusiasm! At that time I was curé de Norenfontes, in the heart of the mining district. The simple notion that a man's work is not a commodity, subject to the law of supply and demand, that you have no right to speculate on wages, on the lives of men, as you do on grain, sugar or coffee—why it set people's consciences upside-down! I was called a "socialist" for having explained it in the pulpit to my mining fellows, and the pious peasants had me sent off to Montreuil in disgrace. Not that I cared two hoots for the disgrace, mind! But at the time—'

Trembling, he said no more. His eyes rested on me and I was ashamed of my little troubles; I could have kissed his hands. When I dared look up he was turning his back on me, staring out of the window. And after another long silence he went on in a more muffled tone, still full of pain.

'You see, Pity is like an animal. An animal from which one can make great demands—but must not ask too much. The best of dogs can go mad. Pity is powerful and devouring. I don't know why we always think of it as something rather snivelling and silly. One of the strongest passions of man—that's what it is. At that time I thought I should be eaten up by it. Pride, envy, anger, even lust, the seven deadly sins, were just a chorus howling their pain. Like a pack of wolves with petrol poured over them and set alight.'

Suddenly I felt his hands on my shoulders.

'Well, I've had my troubles like everyone else. The worst of it is nobody understands you. To the outside world you are just a little democratic parson, vain and pretentious. Perhaps as a general rule democratic priests haven't such deep feeling, but I think *I'd* got rather more feeling that was good for me. Why at that time I knew what Luther was driving at. He could feel things, too. And in that dead-alive monastery at Erfurt, I'm certain he was madly thirsting for justice. . . . But Almighty God doesn't like us to meddle with His justice, and His wrath is rather too much for poor devils like us. It intoxicates, makes us worse than beasts. So after he'd made the cardinals shake in their shoes, in the end old Luther took his mash round to the trough of the German princes, and a nice lot *they* were. . . . Take a look at Luther's deathmask. Nobody would believe that bloated old fellow with a fat under-lip had once been a monk. Even though in essentials he was just, his ire had poisoned him by inches; it had turned to unhealthy fat, that's about all.'

[58]

'Do you pray for Luther?' I asked.

'Every day,' he answered. 'And besides my name is also Martin.'

Then a very strange thing happened. He shoved a chair close up against me, sat down on it, and took my hands in his without ever turning his eyes from my face, his magnificent eyes full of tears and yet more imperious than ever, eyes that would make death simple, an easy matter.

'I'm always calling you a ragamuffin,' he said, 'but I respect you. Take the word for what it's worth. It's a great word. As far as I can see, there's no doubt about your vocation. To look at you, you're more like the stuff that monks are made of. No matter. You may not have very broad shoulders, but you've got grit. You deserve to serve with the foot-sloggers. But remember this: you mustn't fall out. If once you report sick, you'll never set off again. You weren't built for wars of attrition. Keep marching to the end, and try to land up quietly at the road-side without shedding your equipment.'

I am well aware I don't deserve his confidence, but once it is given I don't think I shall betray it. Therein lies my whole strength, the strength of children and weaklings.

'Experience of life comes sooner or later, but in the end we all experience it, according to individual capacity. You can't get more than your share. A half-pint pot can never hold so much as a pint. But each has his taste of injustice. . . .'

I felt my face tauten against my will, since that word always hurts. I was about to reply. . . .

'Shut up. You don't know what injustice is. You'll know soon enough. You're the kind of man that injustice can smell a mile off, and waits for patiently till the day. . . . You mustn't let yourself be mauled. Above all don't go thinking you can make it turn tail by staring it straight in the face like a lion-tamer. You'd never escape its fascination, its power to hypnotize. Never look at it more than you actually need, and never without saying a prayer.'

His voice was becoming a little unsteady. God knows what pictures, what memories passed at that moment behind his eyes.

'Ah, lad, you'll often find yourself envying the little nun who sets out betimes in the morning to her ragged schoolchildren, her beggars, her drunken navvies, and works her fingers to the bone all day for 'em. You see she doesn't give two hoots for injustice. She'll sponge and scrub and bandage her ragged regiment, and in the end she'll bury 'em. God did not confide His word to her. The word of God! Give me back my Word, the Judge will say on the last day. When you think what certain people will have to unpack on that occasion, it's no laughing matter, I assure you!'

He stood up again, and again faced me. I too stood up.

'Have we kept God's word intact: *the poor you have always with you?* Does that sound like the slogan of a demagogue? But it's God's word and we have received it. All the worse for the rich who pretend to believe it justifies their selfishness. All the worse for us whom the powerful use as their hostages each time the army of paupers returns to the assault. It is the saddest saying in the Gospels, the most burdened with sadness. And firstly it is addressed to Judas. Judas! Saint Luke relates that he was the purse-bearer and didn't always keep his books very accurately. That may be so. But after all he was banker to the twelve, and I've never yet heard of a bank with all accounts strictly in order. No doubt he kept his commission fairly high, like most people. Judging by that last deal of his, he'd hardly have made a first-rate broker's clerk, old Judas wouldn't. . . . But Our Father takes our poor world as it is, not like the charlatans who manufacture one on paper and keep on reforming it, still on paper. Fact is Our Lord knew all about the power of money: He gave capitalism a tiny niche in His scheme of things, He gave it a chance, He even provided a first instalment of funds. Can you beat that? It's so magnificent! God despises nothing. After all, if the deal had come off, Judas would probably have endowed sanatoriums, hospitals, public libraries or laboratories. Remember he was already interested in the pauper problem, like any millionaire. *The poor you have always with you, but me you have not always with you,* answered Our Lord. Which amounts to this: don't let the hour of mercy strike in vain. You'd do far better to cough up that money you stole, at once, instead of trying to get My apostles worked up over all your imaginary financial deals in toilet waters, and your charitable enterprises. Moreover you think you're flattering My notorious weakness for down-and-outs, but you've got hold of the wrong end of the stick. I'm not attached to My paupers like an English old maid to lost cats, or to the poor bulls in the Spanish bull-ring. I love poverty with a deep, reasoned, lucid love—as equal loves equal. I love her as a wife who is faithful and fruitful. If the poor man's right was derived only from strict necessity, your piddling selfishness would soon reduce him to a bare minimum, paid for by unending gratitude and servility. You've been holding forth against this woman to-day who has just bathed My feet with very expensive nard, as though My poor people had no right to the best scent. You're obviously one of those folk who give a ha'penny to a beggar and then hold up their hands in horror if they don't see him scurry off at once to the nearest baker's to stuff himself with yesterday's stale bread, which the canny shopkeeper will in any case have sold him as fresh. In his place those people would do just as he did: they'd go straight to the nearest pub. A poor man with nothing in his belly needs hope, illusion, more than bread. You fool! What else is that gold, which means so much to you, but a kind of false hope, a dream and sometimes merely the promise of a dream? Poverty weighs heavily in the scales of My Heavenly Father, and all your hoarded smoke won't redress the balance. The poor you have always with you, just because there will always be rich, that is to say there will always be hard and grasping men out for power more than possession. These men exist as much among the poor as among the rich, and the scallywag vomiting up his drink in the gutter is perhaps drunk with the very same dreams as Caesar asleep under his purple canopy. Rich and poor alike, you'd do better to look at yourselves in the mirror of want, for poverty is the image of your own fundamental illusion. Poverty is the emptiness in your hearts and in your hands. It is only because your malice is known to Me that I have placed poverty so high, crowned her and taken her as My bride. If once I allowed you to think of her as an enemy, or even as a stranger, if I let you hope that one day you might drive her out of the world, that would be the death-sentence of the weak. For the weak will always be an insufferable burden on your shoulders, a dead weight which your proud civilizations will pass on to each other with rage and loathing. I have placed My mark upon their foreheads, and now you can only confront them with cringing fury; you may devour one lost sheep, but you will never again dare attack the flock. If My arm were to be lifted for only an instant, slavery —My great enemy—would revive of itself, under one name or another, since your law of life is debit and credit, and the weakling has nothing to give but his skin.'

His huge hand was trembling on my arm, and the tears which I fancied I could see in his eyes seemed to be slowly scorched up by the fixed look which still confronted me. I could not weep. Dusk had gathered without my perceiving it, and now I could scarcely make out his face, as quiet and noble, as pure, as peaceful, as the appearance of death. In that same instant we heard the first bell of the angelus, come from who knows what vertiginous peak in the sky, as though from the topmost point of evening.

3

SAW THE DEAN OF BLANGERMONT yesterday, who—very
paternally but also at great length—impressed it upon me
how necessary it is for a young priest to keep strict accounts. 'Above all no running into debt, I never allow it,'
he concluded. I admit that I was rather taken aback and
I stood up clumsily to take my leave. He asked me to
sit down again (no doubt he mistook it for bad temper).
In the end I gathered that Mme Pamyre had been com-
plaining about her bill not having been paid yet—those
bottles of elderberry wine! Besides, it seems I owe fifty-
three francs to Geoffrin the butcher, and one hundred
and eighteen to Delacour the coal merchant. M. Delacour is on the town council. These two gentlemen, however, haven't been lodging any complaints, and the dean
was obliged to admit that he had heard all about it from
Mme Pamyre. She bears me a grudge for getting my
groceries from Camus, a stranger in these parts, with a
daughter who has just been through the divorce courts,
they say. The dean is the first to laugh at this ridiculous
gossip which he despises, but he showed a certain annoy-
ance at my determination never to set foot again in Mme
Pamyre's shop. He reminded me of certain remarks of
mine, ir the course of one of our quarterly meetings at
the house of the Curé de Verchocq, when he had not

been present. It appears that I spoke in his opinion far too acidly of business and business people.

'Get this well into your head, dear boy, that anything said by a callow young priest like you will always be noticed by his elders, whose duty it is to form an opinion of their new colleagues. At your age these outbursts are not allowed. In a small community like ours there is no harm at all in such mutual criticism, and it would be most unsporting not to accept it in good part. I agree that business integrity is not what it used to be, and some of our best families are much to blame for their indifference in this matter. But the present terrible economic crisis is a severe test, no getting away from it. I remember the time when that class of small hard-working thrifty shopkeepers, who are still the backbone and greatness of our dear France, was almost entirely guided by an atheist or liberal Press. But now they can see the fruits of their labour being threatened by the forces of disorder, and they realize the time for such generous illusions is past, and that the social order has no surer prop than our Holy Church. Is not the right of possession set down in the Gospels? Oh, of course one must always know how to discriminate, there are exceptions, and in the confessional you should draw the penitent's attention to the duties which such rights entail, but all the same—'

My petty ailments have made me horribly bad-tempered. I could not hold back the words which sprang to my lips; and to make matters worse I spoke them in a trembling voice the inflections of which astonished me.

'One doesn't often hear a penitent accusing himself of cooking accounts.'

The dean glared at me, but I did not turn my eyes

away. I was thinking of the Curé de Torcy. The most righteous indignation is always too suspect an emotion for a priest to indulge in: and besides I feel there is always something else beyond wrath in me when I am compelled to speak of the rich—the real rich, rich in cunning, were they to have but a farthing in their pockets, moneyed men as they are called. . . . Moneyed men!

The dean said dryly: 'I am rather surprised to hear you take this line. I seem to sense some spite, some lack of charity.' His voice became softer: 'My dear lad, I am afraid the academic successes of your boyhood may perhaps have distorted your judgement. The seminary is not the world you know—real life is not like that. I don't think it would need much to turn you into an intellectual, that is to say a rebel, systematically in revolt against every form of social superiority except those derived from the intellect. The church has a body and a soul: she has to attend to the needs of her body. A sensible man is not ashamed of eating. Let us see things as they are. We were talking of shopkeepers just now. From where does the state get its most important revenue? Surely from those very lower-middle classes, who are so greedy of gain, hard as nails in their dealings with the poor as with each other, mad on economy. Modern society is their creation.

'Of course, nobody's asking you to modify your principles in any way, and in no diocese, as far as I know, has the fourth commandment been tampered with. But can we go poking our noses into their ledgers? They may be more or less amenable to our teaching as far as, for instance, the errors of the flesh are concerned—in their worldly prudence they can see where such disorders lead: they consider they're wasteful, though usually in no higher sense than as a risk, as money thrown away; but what they call "business" appears to these industrious folk their special preserve, where hard work excuses everything, since to them work is a kind of religion. "Each for himself and the devil take the hindmost," is their rule of life, And we are helpless, it will take years, centuries maybe, to enlighten their minds and rid them of the feeling that business is in the nature of "war," with all the rights and privileges of real war. A soldier on the battlefield does not consider himself a murderer. Nor does a business man who draws excessive profit from his activities consider himself a thief, since he knows he can never bring himself to take sixpence from another man's pocket. Men are men, my dear boy, what else do you expect? If some of these business men were ever to take it into their heads to follow strict theological precepts on the subject of lawful profit, they would certainly end up in the bankruptcy court. And is it wise to class as inferior, industrious citizens who have struggled so hard to rise socially, and constitute our strongest support in a materialistic world, who take their share of the burden of church expenses, and who—now that in the villages vocations have almost ceased—even give us priests? Big business exists only in name to-day, it has been absorbed by the banks, the aristocracy is dying out, the proletarian slips through our fingers, and yet you'd like to get the middle classes to provide an immediate and spectacular solution to ethical difficulties which need endless time, prudence and tact to unravel. Was not slavery an even more flagrant breach of God's laws? And yet the Apostles— At your age we like to be intolerant. Be on your guard against that fault. Don't think in abstractions, see men as they are. Why these very

Pamyres we were talking about might serve to illustrate what I've just been saying. The grandfather was simply a working mason, notoriously anticlerical, quite a socialist. Our venerable colleague de Bazancourt remembers seeing him stand outside his house and jeer at the sight of a procession. He started by buying a small wine and spirit business which had rather a bad name. Two years later his son, who'd been reared at the board-school, married into a respectacle family, the Delannoys; they had a nephew who was a priest in the Brogelonne district. The daughter opened a grocery shop—she had her head screwed on the right way. Of course the old man took a hand in it. You could meet him any time of the year racing over the roads in his dog-cart. It was he who paid for his grandchildren's schooling at the Diocesan College of Montreuil. It tickled his vanity to see them rubbing shoulders with gentlemen: he'd long since ceased to be a socialist, you see. His assistants were scared to death of him. At twenty-two Louis Pamyre has just married the daughter of Delivaulle, the solicitor, His Excellency's legal advisor; Arsène is looking after the shop, Charles is studying medicine at Lille, and Adolphe, the youngest of the lot, is preparing for the priesthood at Arras. Oh, everybody knows that although those people may be hard workers, they are not easy to deal with, and they've skimmed the district for all the cream they can get. But after all, though they may rob us, at least they respect us. That makes for a kind of social solidarity between ourselves and them—deplore it or not, it exists, and everything that exists should be used for some good purpose.'

He paused, a little red in the face. I always find it difficult to follow this kind of conversation, for my

mind is inclined to wander when some vague and secret
understanding prevents me from passionately forestall-
ing the other man's conclusions, and so I get 'left behind,' as my old teachers used to say. How expressive is
the popular way of putting it: 'Something you can't get
off your chest.' My unspoken words were like a stab of
ice inside me, and prayer alone, I felt, stood a chance of
melting it. . . .

'I may have spoken rather harshly,' pursued the Dean
of Blangermont. 'It's for your own good. When you've
lived longer you will understand, but you'll have to
live. . . .'

'Have to live!' I answered without thinking. 'An awful thought—isn't it?'

I expected an outburst, for I had spoken in the voice
of my worst moods, a voice I know well—'Your father's
voice,' my mother used to say. . . . The other day I
heard a tramp answering a policeman who was asking for
his papers. 'Papers? Where d'you expect me to get 'em?
I'm the bleedin' son of the Unknown Warrior.' He had
a voice somewhat the same.

The dean merely gave me a slow attentive stare: 'I
suspect you of being a poet,' he said. (He pronounced
it po-ate.) 'Fortunately you're going to be kept pretty
busy with your double parish to look after. Work'll put
you right.'

Last night my courage failed me. I would like to have
summed up that conversation. What was the use? I
must allow for the dean's disposition, for the obvious
satisfaction he seems to derive in going against me, humiliating me. He used to be well known for his zeal in
attacking democratic young priests, and no doubt he
takes me for one of them. A very natural mistake; my

extremely humble extraction, my unhappy and neglected childhood, the contrast, of which I am becoming more and more aware, between an education that was very inadequate, not to say rough, and a certain sensitiveness of mind which makes me realize many things—all this places me in a category of naturally undisciplined people whom my superiors have every reason to mistrust. What should I have become if—? At all events my feeling with regard to what is called social order is very undefined. . . . In spite of the poverty of my birth, indeed, perhaps because of it, who knows—? I can only really appreciate the superiority of race, of blood. Were I to confess it I should be laughed at. For example, it seems to me I would willingly have served an authentic master—a royal prince or a king. You can put your two hands folded within those of another man and swear faith as a vassal, but no one would dream of going through such a ceremony at the feet of a millionaire, just because he was a millionaire, it would be idiotic. The idea of money and that of authority cannot so far be confused, for the former is abstract. Of course it's easy enough to say that many a feudal lord in the past owed his heritage to the money-bags his miserly father had left him, but whether he won it or not at the point of the sword, he had to defend it with the sword as he would have defended his life, for such a man and his heritage were identified even to the very name which stood for both. Is not this mystic identification also a sign of royalty? And a king in Holy Writ was very near to a judge. Of course a millionaire holds more human lives locked away in his safe than any monarch, but his power is like that of graven images, without eyes or ears. He can kill and that is all, without even knowing what he kills. This privilege may also be that of evil spirits.

Sometimes I think of Satan as trying to get hold of the mind of God, and not merely hating it without understanding, but understanding it the wrong way round; thus unknowingly struggling against the current of life, instead of swimming with it; wearing himself out in absurd terrifying attempts to reconstruct in the opposite direction, the whole work of the Creator.

The governess came to see me this morning in the sacristy. We had a long talk about Mlle Chantal. It seems the child is becoming more and more bitter, that her presence in the Château is unbearable and that it would be advisable to send her away to a finishing school. Mme la Comtesse has not quite made up her mind to this. And it appears I am expected to approach her on the matter, and am to dine at the Château next week.

Obviously mademoiselle won't say all she knows. Several times she looked me straight in the face, so insistently that it made me uneasy, and her lips were trembling. I walked with her as far as the back gate of the cemetery. There she stopped and excused herself—in the quick, flurried 'confessional voice' with which one brings out some humiliating admission—for having to ask my help in such a dangerous and delicate matter.

'Chantal is a queer, unbalanced girl. I shouldn't say she was *really* wicked. Young people of her age nearly always give way to the wildest fancies. And, of course, it was some time before I could bring myself to tell you to be on your guard against a child that I'm very fond of and awfully sorry for, too. But really, you know, she might do *anything*. . . . And, of course, with you being a newcomer to this parish it would never do and be quite useless—supposing anything were to happen—to let your kindness run away with you and appear to encourage her to tell you things which—well, M. le Comte would not allow it, anyhow,' she concluded in a manner I disliked.

Certainly I have no real reason to suspect her of being biased and unfair, and when I bowed as frigidly as I could without even offering her my hand, she had tears in her eyes, real tears. And anyway Mlle Chantal has a manner which I dislike, she has the same hard fixed expression that I notice very often on the faces of many young village girls; I still don't know, and no doubt never shall, exactly what there is behind it. Since even on their deathbeds they give you scarcely more than a glimpse. The boys are very different! I don't really believe in sacrilegious confessions at such a time, since the dying girls of whom I speak showed plainly how they repented of their sins. Yet it was only after death that their poor sweet faces managed to recapture that serene look of the little children which they almost were. . . . An indefinable air of confidence and wonder, that limpid gaiety. The devil of lust is a dumb fiend.

All the same, I can't help feeling that this overture from mademoiselle is slightly suspect. I am obviously far too lacking in experience, in authority, to act as go-between in such a very delicate family matter, and it would have been wiser to keep me right out of it. But since it is considered expedient to involve me, why this sudden prohibition to judge for myself? 'M. le Comte would not allow it. . . .' That was going too far.

Another letter yesterday from my friend; only a few lines, asking me to be so good as to put off my journey to Lille for a few days since he has to go to Paris himself on business. His letter ends: 'You have realized for some time that I have now "unfrocked" myself, as they call it. But I am the same at heart; it is merely that my view of life is more humane and *consequently* more generous. I am earning my living—a big saying and a big thing. To earn one's living! The habit which begins in the seminary of receiving our daily bread or dish of daily beans from the hands of our superiors, like a dole, makes schoolboys of us, children to the very end of our lives. I was, as you no doubt still are, entirely ignorant of my social value. I would scarcely have dared to offer myself for the humblest employment. Well, although the poor state of my health has prevented me from taking all the necessary steps towards obtaining it, I have already received a number of extremely flattering offers, and when it comes to the point, I shall merely have to choose between half a dozen very well-paid jobs indeed. Even by the next time you come to see me I hope to have the pleasure and satisfaction of being able to welcome you in more suitable surroundings, since our home up to now has been run on very simple lines.'

I know this is all mainly puerile showing-off, and only merits a shrug of the shoulders. But I can't shrug mine. There is a certain silliness, a certain inflection of silliness in which, as soon as I encounter it, I perceive with a shock of humiliation, sacerdotal pride; but pride denuded of all supernatural character, pride turned into foolery, as milk turns. How vulnerable we are before mankind and life itself! What ridiculous childishness!

And yet this schoolfellow was considered one of the best and most gifted pupils at the seminary. He did not even lack a kind of precocious, slightly ironic intuition of other people, and he was able to sum up some of our professors with sufficient insight. Why then to-day should he try to impress one with this miserable bragging which, I presume, doesn't even take *him* in? Like so many others he will end up in some office where his bad temper and morbid touchiness will put him on the wrong side of the other clerks, and no matter how much he tries to hide the past from them, I doubt he'll ever make many friends.

We pay a heavy, very heavy price for the superhuman dignity of our calling. The ridiculous is always so near to the sublime. And the world, usually so indulgent to foibles, hates ours instinctively.

Feminine silliness is sufficiently irritating, clerical silliness even more irritating, and in some mysterious way seems to emanate from the former. It may be that the real reason why so many of the poor keep the priest at arm's-length—their deep dislike of him—does not only arise, as people would have us believe, from a more or less conscious rebellion of natural appetite against the law and its representatives. . . . Why deny it? It is not necessary to have a very clear idea of beauty in order to feel repelled by ugliness. The mediocre priest is ugly.

I am not speaking of bad priests. Or rather the bad priest is the mediocre one. The other is monstrous. Monstrosity rejects all common norms. Who can know God's intentions with a monster? What is his use? What is the supernatural meaning of so amazing a deformity? Try as I may I cannot for example believe that Judas belonged to this world—to this world for which Jesus so mysteriously refused his prayer. . . . Judas is not part of that world. I am convinced my unfortunate friend doesn't deserve to be called a bad priest. I should even think he is really attached to this woman, for I remember he used to be rather sentimental; a mediocre priest, alas, is nearly always sentimental. Vice is perhaps less dangerous to us than a cerain staleness. There is softening of the brain. Softening of the heart is worse.

As I was walking home across the fields this morning from my second parish, I caught sight of M. le Comte putting his dogs to a scent round the Linieres wood. He waved to me from a distance, but didn't look as though he wanted to speak to me. I think he knows in some way that mademoiselle has been approaching me. I must act with great discretion and prudence.

Yesterday I heard confessions. Children from three to five. Of course I began with the boys.

May Our Lord love and protect these little ones! Anyone but a priest would be sent to sleep by the sound of their droning voices, too often a mere repetition of phrases, picked out of the prayer-book Examination of Conscience and mumbled over every time. And if he were really out to understand, and questioned them at random from sheer curiosity, I don't think he could avoid being disgusted. Such scarcely veiled animality! But after all—

What do we know of sin? Geologists teach us that the very ground which seems so solid is in reality only a thin film over an ocean of liquid fire, for ever trembling like the skin on milk about to boil. . . . How far down would one need to dig to rediscover the blue depths? . . .

I am seriously ill. Yesterday I was suddenly sure of it —the knowledge seemed to light up my mind. The time

when I knew nothing of this relentless pain which sometimes appears to slacken without ever really loosening
its hold, suddenly seemed to slip away into the past, to
slip away into an almost dizzy remoteness, right back to
childhood. . . . It is just six months ago that I felt the
first warnings of this trouble, and now I can hardly remember those days when I ate and drank like everybody
else. A bad sign.

Yet the most acute pains are disappearing. I have no
more of them. I have deliberately cut out meat and vegetables, and now live on bread soaked in wine, taken in
very small quantities every time I feel slightly giddy.
Fasting really suits me very well. My head is clear and
I feel stronger than I did three weeks ago, much stronger.

Nobody bothers about my discomforts now. The fact
is I too am getting used to my sorry countenance: it can
get no thinner, and somehow retains a quite unaccountable air of youth, I dare not say—health. At my age a
face doesn't sink in, the skin, taut over the bones, remains elastic, which is something.

I am reading over these lines which I wrote yesterday
evening. I've had a good, restful night and feel full of
courage and hope. Providence has answered my jere-
miads, a very gentle reproof. I have often perceived or
thought I had become aware of—this imperceptible irony.
(Unfortunately I can think of no other word.) Something like a watchful mother shrugging her shoulders at
the first clumsy steps of her little child. Ah, if we only
knew how to pray!.

Mme la Comtesse now only returns my greeting with
a cold, very distant nod.

Saw Dr. Delbende to-day; he is an old G.P. who is considered rather rough and doesn't practice much now, for his colleagues are only too anxious to make fun of his corduroy breeches and dirty gaiters which stink of stale leather. The Curé de Torcy had told him I was coming. He made me lie on his sofa and prodded my stomach at great length with his long hands that certainly weren't very clean. (He'd been out shooting.) While he was examining me his big dog, lying across the threshold, followed each of his movements with extraordinary eyes, full of adoration.

'You're not up to much,' he said. 'Take a look at that' (he seemed to be calling his dog to witness), 'and it's easy enough to tell you've not always eaten as much as you wanted, now have you?'

'At one time perhaps not, but now—'

'Now it's too late. And drink? What about that? Oh, not the drink you've had, sure enough! All the drink that's been supped for you, long before you came into the world. Come back and see me in a fortnight. I'll give you a note to take to Dr. Lavigne in Lille.'

Heavens! I realize heredity must weigh heavily on shoulders like mine, but the word 'drink' is hard to stomach. I caught sight of myself in the mirror as I got dressed, and my face drawn and more yellow each day, with its long nose and double furrows descending on either side of the mouth, its bristly chin which a bad razor cannot deal with, suddenly seemed hideous to me.

No doubt the doctor noticed my glance, for he burst out laughing. The dog barked to hear him and then jumped for joy.

'Down, Fox, down, you rascal!'

Finally we went into the kitchen. All this din had

cheered me up, I don't know why. The deep fireplace, piled up with logs, was blazing like a hayrick.

'When you're feeling too fed up for words, you come round and see me. I wouldn't say that to anybody. But the Curé de Torcy has talked to me about you, and you've got the kind of eyes I like. Faithful eyes, dog's eyes. I've got dog's eyes too. It's rather rare. Torcy, you and I, we're the same sort, a queer sort.'

The idea of being the same sort as those two strong broad-shouldered men would certainly never have occurred to me. Yet I knew he was serious.

'What sort?' I asked.

'The sort that isn't got down. And why isn't it got down? Nobody knows exactly. By the grace of God, you'll say. But you see, my dear fellow, I don't believe in Him. All right, you needn't trouble to tell me, I know it by heart: "The wind bloweth where it listeth, I am part of the spirit of the Church"—rubbish! Why not be got down? Why not sit down or lie down? The physiological explanation is no good. It's impossible to bolster up with facts the theory of some physical predisposition. Athletes are mostly peaceful citizens, law-abiding as hell, and they only go in for the effort that *pays*—not ours. Of course you people invented paradise. But I was only saying to Torcy the other day: "Now, admit you'd stick it out, with or without paradise." Besides, between ourselves, we all get into your paradise, don't we? Labourers of the eleventh hour and all. When I've been working too much—I say "working too much," as one might say "drinking too much"—I wonder if it's not just pride at the root of us all?'

Although he laughed so noisily, his laughter jarred and one would have said the dog felt as I did: it suddenly ceased capering, and humbly, its belly along the ground, raised his soft eyes to his master: a quiet look seemingly detached from all things, even from the dim hope of understanding the pain awakened in the very depths of its being, in every fibre of its sensitive dog's body. And with the point of its nose carefully resting on folded paws, eyes blinking, strange shivers running down its long spine, it began to growl softly as though scenting some enemy.

'I want to know just what you mean by "not being got down"?'

'It's rather long to explain. Let's say, to cut it short, that to stand up straight is a privilege of the powerful. A sensible man waits—before daring to stand—till he has power, power or the sign of power, authority, money. Well, I didn't wait. When I was in the third form at Montreuil College, the head asked us each to choose a motto. D'you know what mine was? "Face up to it." Face up to *what*, I ask you, a kid of thirteen?'

'Injustice, perhaps. . . .'

'Injustice? Yes and no. I'm not the sort that always keeps blabbing about "Justice." To start off with, I honestly don't insist on it myself. Where the hell am I to go asking for it, since I don't believe in God? Suffering injustice is the natural condition of mankind. Why, ever since my colleagues have put it about that I've no notion of aseptic precautions, the practice has gone phut; and now I've only a handful of village idiots left who pay me with a chicken or a basket of apples and take me for a fool into the bargain. In a way, compared with rich folk, those blighters are victims. Well, you know, Father, I lump 'em together with their exploiters, they're scarcely any better. They swindle me till it's their turn

[79]

to do some exploiting.' He scratched his head, watching me round the corner of his eye without seeming to do so. And I saw how he blushed—that blush on his old face was rather beautiful. 'But there's a difference between suffering injustice and having to submit to it—they submit. It degrades them; I hate to see that. It's a feeling you can't control, eh? When I'm at the bedside of a poor devil who won't die in peace—it rarely happens, but you see it now and then—I find myself just itching to say: "Get out, you fool, I'll show you how to do that decently." Pride again—always pride. In a way, my dear chap, I'm no friend of the poor. I'm not out for a new world. I'd rather they settled it without me—had it out with the powerful. But they don't know how to begin, they make me ashamed of them. Remember it's always a misfortune to be on the side of a parcel of ninnies who medically speaking are mostly fit for the scrapheap. Probably it all boils down to race. I'm a Celt—Celt to my finger-tips. Ours is a sacrificial race. A mania for lost causes, eh? As a matter of fact I think humanity is divided into two categories, according to one's idea of justice. For some it is a balance, a compromise. For others—'

'For others,' I said, 'justice is a flowering of charity —its triumphant realization.'

The doctor stared for a long while with a look of surprise and hesitation that was most embarrassing for me. I think the phrase had annoyed him. It was only a phrase after all.

'Triumphant! Triumphant! I don't think much of your triumph, my boy! You'll say the Kingdom is not of this world. Right. But it wouldn't hurt to give the hands of the clock a little shove all the same. My grouse against you people isn't that poverty still exists—oh, no! And I'll even grant you this much. I'll agree that it's the job of old fools like me to feed and clothe and look after them and keep them clean. But since they're really your responsibility I cannot forgive you for sending them to us so dirty. See what I mean? Why, damn it all, after twenty centuries of Christianity, to be poor ought not still to be a disgrace. Or else you have gone and betrayed that Christ of yours! There's no getting away from that, good God Almighty! You have every means of humbling the rich at your disposal, for setting their pace. The rich man wants to be well thought of, and the richer he is the more he wants it. If you would only have the pluck to make them take the back seats in church round the Holy Water stoup, or even out on the steps—why not? It would have made them think. They'd all have had one eye on the poor men's seats, I know 'em! The first everywhere else, but here in the House of God, the last! Can you see that happening? Oh, of course I know the thing wouldn't be easy. If the poor man really is the living image of Jesus—Jesus Himself—it's awkward to have him sitting there in the front row, displaying his obscene misery, his face from which in two thousand years you haven't yet been able to wipe the spittle. Because first and foremost the social problem is a matter of honour, it is the unjust humiliation of poor men which makes your pauper. Nobody's asking you to fatten up people who from father to son have in any case lost the habit of getting fat, who'd probably always be thin as laths; and at a pinch, to make the thing look a bit more decent, there's no reason why you shouldn't eliminate freaks, unemployables, drunkards, anything too uncomfortable to look at. The fact remains that a poor man, a real poor man, an honest man, goes of his own accord to what he considers his proper place, the lowest in the house of the Lord. And you've never seen and never will see a beadle dressed up like a hearse come down to look for him, at the very back of the church, to lead him to the altar rails with all the ceremony due to a prince—a prince in the order of Christianity. That notion usually makes your colleagues smirk. Vanity, rubbish. . . . But why the devil must they always show such respect to the powerful of this earth, who revel in it? And if such respect is vain and empty, why is it always so expensive? We should have people laughing at us, they say—a tramp sitting in the choir would soon become comic. All right. But when the tramp has definitely changed his rags for a plain deal box, when you're sure—absolutely certain—there's no more danger of his wiping off the snot with his fingers or spitting on your lovely carpets, what do you do with the fellow then? Get along with you! You can think me a fool, but I've got hold of the right end of the stick; the Pope himself wouldn't change my mind, and I'm only saying what your own saints practised, my dear fellow, so it can't be so foolish as all that. On their knees to paupers and cripples and lepers, that's the idea we get of your saints. Queer sort of army yours must be where a mere passing corporal need only give the royal Host a patronizing tap on the shoulder, while field-marshals are grovelling at his feet.'

He paused, a little uneasy at my silence. I know I have very little experience, yet I seemed instantly to recognize a certain inflection betraying some profound spiritual hurt. Others perhaps might then be able to find the right words to appease and persuade. I don't know such words. True pain coming out of a man belongs primarily to God, it seems to me. I try and take it humbly to my heart, just as it is. I endeavour to make it mine—to love it. And I understand all the hidden meaning of the expression which has become hackneyed now: to commune with. Because I really 'commune' with his pain.

The dog came and laid its head on my knees.

(During the last two days I have been reproaching myself for not having answered this kind of indictment; and yet after much searching within myself I cannot see that I was wrong. Besides, what could I have said? I am no philosopher—Deity's mouthpiece, I am the servant of Jesus Christ. And I fear the only defence which would have sprung to my lips would have been powerful in one way, is yet so weak in another that I have long been convinced by it, yet never really at peace.) *There is no Peace save in Jesus.*

The first half of my programme is on the way to being achieved. I have undertaken to visit each family once every three months at least. My colleagues consider this excessive, and indeed such a promise will be hard to keep, since first and foremost I must not neglect a single duty. People who set themselves up to judge us from some remote distance, sitting in a comfortable office where they do the same routine tasks every day, cannot begin to realize how 'untidy,' how scattered our daily work can be. We can barely manage our ordinary parochial round, the kind of thing which—when it is strictly carried out—makes a superior exclaim: 'There's a nice well-kept parish!' There remains the unforeseen. And the unforeseen is never negligible. Am I where Our Lord would have me be? Twenty times a day I ask this question. For the Master whom we serve not only judges our life but shares it, takes it upon Himself. It would be far easier to satisfy a geometrical and moralistic God.

This morning, after high mass, I announced a meeting for the evening after vespers, for all young men in the parish who wanted to form a sports club. This decision was not taken in a hurry. I carefully ticked off in the parish books the names of all probable members, possibly fifteen, at least ten. M. le Curé d'Eutichamps approached M. le Comte on my behalf; he is a frequent guest at the Château. M. le Comte did not actually refuse to give us a playing-field, but he wants us to rent it— three hundred francs a year for five years. On termination of this agreement, if no further arrangement is entered into, the said grounds would revert to him, and all eventual amenities and constructions thereupon would become his property. The truth is he probably doesn't expect the idea to succeed. I even think he must be trying to discourage me by such haggling, which seems hardly in keeping with his standing and disposition.

He spoke somewhat severely to the Curé d'Eutichamps, saying that certain people might no doubt be full of rather muddled good intentions, which constituted a public danger, but that, speaking personally, he wasn't the sort to commit himself to any vague scheme, that I must show there was something in it by getting a move on, and letting him have a look at what he called my 'suckers in sweaters' as soon as possible.

I had only four applicants. Not too good. I hadn't realized there was already a sports club at Héclin, munificently endowed by M. Vergnes, the shoe-manufacturer who keeps seven parishes employed. To be sure Héclin is twelve kilometres away, but the village boys can do that easily on their bicycles.

Still, we did manage to exchange a few stimulating ideas. I think the poor lads are kept at arm's-length by some of their more coarse-grained fellows who haunt dance-halls and run after girls. As Sulpice Mitonnet, the son of my former bell-ringer, so aptly put it: 'The pub makes you sick and costs too much.' Meanwhile, till something better turns up and our membership increases, we intend no more than to found a very modest 'study-circle' with a library to be used for games, and a few newspapers.

I had never really noticed Sulpice Mitonnet. A very delicate lad who has just finished his military service (after having been rejected twice). Now he picks up what money he can by practising his trade as a sign painter, and is considered lazy by the village.

I think his real trouble is that he shrinks from the coarseness of the surroundings he is forced to live in. Like so many others of his sort, he longs to get a job in town, for his signs are neatly done. But, alas, although it may be different, the gross ugliness of big towns is equally to be dreaded, I feel. It is probably more insidious, more catching. A weak man stands no chance against it.

After the others had left we had a long talk. His eyes, vague and shifty in their expression, have in them that look which moves me so deeply, of those born to be alone, never to be understood. Mademoiselle has much the same expression.

Yesterday Madame Pégriot told me that she did not mean to come back to the presbytery. She would be ashamed, she says, to go on taking money and doing so little for it. (Certainly my rather frugal diet and the state of my under-clothes must leave her plenty of free time.) 'And, anyway,' she added, 'I was never a one to waste me time for nothin'.'

I tried to pass it off as a joke but couldn't manage to make her see it. Her small eyes were blinking with fury. No matter how hard I try to quell it, I am seized with almost invincible disgust of that round soft face with its low forehead pulled backwards towards the top of the head by hair wisps combed into a bun, and especially of that fat neck striped with horizontal weals, shiny with eternal perspiration. Such impressions are outside our control, and I so much dread giving myself away to her, that doubtless she sees what is in my mind. She ended up with an obscure reference to 'certain people' whom she'd 'rather not have to be meetin' here.' What does she mean?

This morning the governess came to confession. I happen to know that her regular confessor is my colleague, the Curé de Heuchin, but I could not refuse her as a penitent. Those people who think the Sacrament gives us instant power to read the hidden places of a soul are indeed credulous! If only we could ask them to try for themselves! Used as I am to the confessions of simple seminary students, I still cannot manage to understand what horrible metamorphosis has enabled so many people to show me their inner life as a mere convention, a formal scheme without one clue to its reality. I should imagine that once they have ceased to be adolescents, few Catholics go in mortal sin to communion. It's so easy not to go to confession at all. But there are worse things. Petty lies can slowly form a crust around the consciousness, of evasion and subterfuge. The outer shell retains the vague shape of what it covers, but that is all. In time, by sheer force of habit, the least 'gifted' end by evolving their own particular idiom, which still remains incredibly abstract. They don't hide much, but their sly candour reminds one of a dirty window-pane, so blurred that light has to struggle through it, and nothing can be clearly seen.

What then remains of confession? It barely skims the surface of conscience. I don't say dry rot has set in underneath; it seems more like petrification.

A terrible night. No sooner had I shut my eyes than desolation came upon me. I can find no other word to describe this indefinable exhaustion, as though my very soul were bleeding to death. I awoke with a start, with a loud cry ringing in my ears. But was it really a cry? Is that the word for it? No, obviously.

As soon as I had shaken off my drowsiness, the instant I could fix my mind on something, peace returned all at once. The continuous check I put on myself to control my nerves is probably far more exhausting than it seems. Such thought is balm after the agony of those last hours, for this effort of which I am scarcely aware, and which therefore gives my pride no satisfaction, is gauged by Almighty God.

How little we know what a human life really is—even our own. To judge us by what we call our actions is probably as futile as to judge us by our dreams. God's justice chooses from this dark conglomeration of thought and act, and that which is raised towards the Father shines with a sudden burst of light, displayed in glory like a sun.

All the same, this morning I felt so weak and ill that I

would have given anything for one word of human pity, of tenderness. I wanted to hurry along to Torcy. But I had to take the children's catechism at eleven o'clock. Even on my bicycle I couldn't have got back in time.

My best pupil is Sylvestre Galuchet, a rather grubby little boy (his mother is dead, he is being brought up by a not very sober old granny). And yet he is a strangely beautiful child who gives me the almost poignant feeling of innocence, an innocence previous to all sin, the sinlessness of an innocent beast. Since this was my day for distributing rewards he came with me into the sacristy to take the picture of a saint, and I felt that in his quiet attentive eyes I could read the sympathy I craved. My arms closed round him for an instant, and I sobbed with my head on his shoulder, foolishly.

First official meeting of our 'Study-Circle.' I had thought of suggesting Sulpice Mitonnet as president, but the rest seem rather to cold-shoulder him. So naturally I did not press the matter.

In any case we only drew up a formal scheme of what, considering our resources, will have to be a very modest programme. These poor lads have obviously little imagination and still less enterprise. As Engelbert Denisane admitted, they dread 'having people laugh at us.' I feel that they have only come to me because they had nothing else to do, and just to see what I was up to.

Met M. le Curé de Torcy on the road to Desvres. He drove me right back to the presbytery in his car, and even accepted a glass of my famous Bordeaux. 'Do you like this wine?' he asked. I told him that the ordinary red wine which I get from the 'Four Lime-Trees Grocery' was quite good enough for me—and that seemed to re-assure him.

I got a very definite impression that something or other was on his mind which he'd decided already to keep to himself. He only half listened to what I was saying, and against his will his eyes kept asking me some question which I should have found very hard to answer, since his own mind refused to formulate it.

I began chattering at random as I usually do when I feel uneasy. There are silences which draw you out—fascinate you, till you long to throw in any words, anything to break them. . . .

At last he said: 'You're a queer specimen! I shouldn't think there's another softy like you in the whole diocese! And you work like a cart-horse, sweating your guts out.
. . . Really His Grace must have been very hard up for priests to have given you the handling of a parish. Luckily a parish is solid enough—or you might break it.'

I knew instinctively that his pity for me was making him joke about something he had seriously considered and deeply felt. He saw at once what I was thinking.

'I might overwhelm you with good advice, but what use would it be? When I taught mathematics at Saint Omer I had some really astonishing pupils. They could solve the most abstruse problems without ever using the ordinary rules—out of sheer spite. And besides, lad, you aren't my subordinate—you'll have to go your own way, show what you're made of. I've no right to cloud the judgement of your superiors. I'll tell you my system another day.'

'What system?'

He would not answer directly.

'Well, you see, our superiors are right in advising us

to walk circumspectly. I'm circumspect myself, it's the best I can do. I'm that by nature. Nothing could be more idiotic than an impulsive priest always letting himself go, for no reason—just a pose. Yet all the same our way isn't the way of the world. You can't go offering the truth to human beings as though it were a sort of insurance policy, or a dose of salts. It's the Way and the Life. God's truth is the Life. We only look as though we were bringing it to mankind; really it brings us, my lad.'

'Where have I been wrong?' I asked. My voice was trembling. It required two efforts to speak the words.

'You're too restless. You're like a hornet in a bottle. But I believe you have the spirit of prayer.'

I thought he was going to advise me to be off to Solesmes and become a monk. He read my thoughts a second time. (I don't suppose it was very difficult.)

'Monks are even shrewder than we are, and you haven't an atom of common sense. Your wonderful schemes won't bear looking into. As to what you know about people—ah, well, least said soonest mended. Why, you take our little count for a great gentleman, the guttersnipes in your catechism class for young poets after your sort, and your dean for a socialist. There you are, with your brand new parish, and a queer enough way of setting about it, it seems to me. With all due respect, you remind me of some young fool of a husband who makes a point of "studying his wife," while she's had him taped from the word go!'

'Yes—and—?' (I could scarcely speak, I was dumbfounded.)

'And? Well, go on doing it! What else did you expect me to say? You haven't the least shadow of pride, and it isn't easy to judge your experiments, because you push them so far. You risk yourself. Of course it is never wrong to act according to human prudence. You remember Ruysbroeck, the Admirable—another Fleming by the by: "Though you be caught up in the very rapture of God and there come a sick man to demand of you a bowl of broth, descend again from your seventh heaven and give him that which he comes to ask." There's a sound bit of advice! Yes, but it mustn't be made an excuse for laziness. There's a kind of supernatural laziness which comes with age, disappointment, experience.' He sighed. 'Old priests are hard as nails! Prudence is the final imprudence when by slow degrees it prepares the mind to do without God. Some old priests are really horrible.'

I give his words as best I can, not very well. For I wasn't really listening; I was guessing so many things. I have no self-confidence, and yet I have so much goodwill that I always fancy it must be obvious to all, and that people are bound to judge me by my intentions. What crazy stupidity! I imagined myself to be still on the threshold of this small world, when really I had long since entered into it alone—and now, no retreat, the way back is barred. I still do not know my parish and my parish have pretended not to see me. Yet even now my parishioners' notion of me is all too definite, too exact. I shall never be able to modify it except by a very great effort.

In my foolish face, M. le Curé de Torcy read consternation, and I am sure he understood that for the moment any attempt to reassure me would have been in vain. He held his peace. I tried to smile. I think I even succeeded in smiling, but it wasn't easy.

A restless night. At three o'clock in the morning I took my lantern and went into church. I looked about everywhere for the key of the little side-door, but could not find it, so I had to open the big centre door. The scraping of the lock made a huge din under the vaultings.

I fell asleep on a bench with my head resting between my hands, and slept so soundly that the early-morning rain awakened me. It came sprinkling in through a broken window-pane. On my way out of the churchyard I ran into Arsène Miron—I could only just see who it was—and he growled a surly 'good morning.' I must have been a strange sight, my eyes still puffy with sleep, and my damp cassock.

I have to keep struggling against my impulse to run and see Torcy. It's the idiotic frenzy of a gambler who knows perfectly well that he has lost, and yet is never tired of hearing it. And besides, in my present state of nerves I could only keep stammering apologies. What is the use of discussing the past? The future is all that matters, and that I am still unable to face.

Probably M. le Curé de Torcy feels just as I do. There can be no doubt that he does. This morning, while I was putting up the hangings in preparation for Marie Perdrot's funeral, I thought I heard his footsteps come up the aisle, such firm, rather heavy steps! It was only the grave-digger, who'd come to tell me the grave was finished.

So great was the shock of disappointment that I thought I should tumble off the step-ladder. . . . Oh, no, I'm in no state to go to him.

I ought to have said to Dr. Delbende that the Church is not only, as he supposes her, a kind of sovereign state with laws, officials, armies—a moment, as glorious as you please, in human history. The Church is on the march through time as a regiment marches through strange country, cut off from all its ordinary supplies. The Church lives on successive régimes and societies, as the soldiers would from day to day on the inhabitants.

How then could she ever give the poor, God's legitimate heirs, a kingdom which is not of this world? She is in search of the poor—she calls them to her from all the byways of the earth. And the Poor Man for whom she seeks eternally, is always there at the same place, on the topmost summit of the mountains, that giddy peak where he stands confronting the Prince of Darkness, having harkened now for twenty centuries to the same words repeated incessantly in the same voice, an angel's voice, a sublime voice, the voice of prodigies: 'All these things will I give thee, if thou wilt fall down and worship me.' Such may be the divine explanation of the strange patience of the multitude. The Poor Man could so easily seize power, but he does not know, or seems not to know it. He stands there with eyes downcast, his Tempter awaiting from second to second the word which would give him power over humanity, that word which will never be spoken by those consecrated lips, sealed by God Himself.

Insoluble problem: to give back his rights to the Poor Man without investing him with power. But if the impossible were to happen? If some merciless dictatorship with its hordes of bureaucrats, experts, statisticians—themselves defended by millions of police and spies—should succeed in curbing simultaneously, all over the world, those fierce and cunning brutes formed only to prey upon their fellows, the sharp wits that feed on human flesh, the race of men which has its teeth into humanity (since doubtless their eternal itch for gain is no more than a veiled, hypocritical, perhaps unconscious form of the horrible craving, too base to admit, which still obsesses them)—even then, that golden mediocrity, which such a state of things had made the rule, might soon weary humanity so profoundly that everywhere poverty, self-imposed, would blossom forth in a new spring.

No community will ever get the better of its poor. Some live by their neighbour's stupidity. Some by his vanity or his vices. The poor man *lives by charity*. A great saying!

I don't know what happened last night. I must have been dreaming. About three this morning (I had just warmed myself some wine and was dipping my bread in it as usual) the garden gate began banging to and fro so loudly that I had to go down. I found it shut, and this did not really surprise me, at least not from one point of view, since I knew quite well I had locked it as usual that night. Then, about twenty minutes later it began crashing to and fro again and even louder than the first time (there was a high wind, a real hurricane). An absurd business. . . .

I have started on my rounds again—by the grace of God. M. le Curé de Torcy has made me cautious, and I now endeavour to ask very few questions, and these I make as discreet as possible—as commonplace, at least in form. According to the reply forthcoming, I try to raise our talk on to a slightly higher plane, though not too high, until we discover some truth together—a very carefully selected, simple truth. . . . But discreet truths do not exist. However cautious I may be, even when my lips avoid the sound of it, still God's name seems to shine out suddenly in the midst of the thick stifling atmosphere, and faces that were just awakening close in once again. More precisely, they darken, they cloud over.

Revolt which spends itself in insult, is blasphemy—perhaps, after all, that is harmless enough. . . ? Hatred against God always makes me think of possession by devils. 'And then the devil entered into him.' (Judas.) Yes, it is 'possession,' madness. Whereas that shifty fear of the Divine, that oblique flight through life, as of a man in the shadow of a wall, while the whole earth is bright with sunshine. . . . It puts me in mind of some wretched animal, dragging itself back into its hole, having served as the plaything of cruel children. How much more of mystery there is in the fierce inquisitiveness of devils, their horrible solicitude for humanity. . . . Ah, if we could view with angelic sight these maimed human beings!

4

I FEEL MUCH BETTER. The bouts of pain come at longer
intervals, and at times I seem to become aware of something vaguely like an appetite. In any case I can now
prepare a meal without any feeling of nausea—always
the same meal, bread and wine. Only now I sugar the
wine plentifully, and keep my bread for several days
until it becomes so stale and hard that I often have to
break it up instead of cutting it. The chopping-board is
very useful for this, and the bread is much easier to
digest.

Owing to this diet, I manage to get through my work
without too much fatigue, and I've even begun to regain
a little self-confidence. Perhaps on Friday I might go
and see the Curé de Torcy. Sulpice Mitonnet comes
round every day. He certainly isn't very bright, yet full
of consideration and tact. I've given him the key of the
bakehouse, and when I'm out he comes in and potters
about. Thanks to him my poverty-stricken dwelling
looks quite different. He says wine upsets his stomach,
but he loves stuffing himself with sugar.

He nearly cried as he told me how he was being
sneered and laughed at for his frequent visits to the presbytery. Really, I think the kind of life he leads is too
much for our very hard-working peasants, and I talked

to him seriously about his idleness. He promised me he would look for work.

Mme Dumouchel came into the sacristy for a talk. She was vexed with me for having ploughed her daughter in my quarterly exam.

I do my best to say nothing in this diary of certain vexations and trials which I always want to forget immediately, since, alas! they are not of the kind which I find I can accept with joy—and of what use is joyless resignation? It isn't that I exaggerate their importance. No; far from it! I know they are the most usual things in life. The shame with which they always fill me, the nervous fear I find impossible to control, most certainly do me little credit; but I am unable to rid myself of the sheer physical impression, the kind of disgust which they arouse in me. What is the use of denying it? Too early in my life I was forced to see vice as it really is, and though in the very depths of myself I feel compassion for these poor souls, the vision their misfortune evokes in me is almost too horrible to bear. In a word, I am terrified of lust.

But especially of lust in children. . . . For I know it so well. Not that I mean to take it too tragically. On the contrary, I know how patiently it ought always to be dealt with, since the least imprudence in such matters may have the most terrible results. It is so hard to distinguish the deepest wounds from the rest, and even then so dangerous to probe them! Far better, sometimes, leave them alone to heal themselves—a thriving abscess must not be touched. But that does not lessen my hate of this general silent conspiracy, this foregone determination not to see the obvious, that silly, knowing smirk of grown-ups faced with certain distresses which are called trifling merely because they are too inarticulate for adult words. I knew sorrow, also, too early in my life to feel no disgust with the blind injustice we all are guilty of towards children, whose sorrows are so profound and mysterious. Alas, we have learnt by experience that children may come to know despair. And the demon of agony is essentially I think, a demon of lust.

Therefore I have said very little about Seraphita Dumouchel, though for weeks she has been a perpetual worry. Sometimes I wonder whether she hates me, she shows such precocious skill in tormenting me. Her absurd tricks which once looked like mere heedless stupidity, seem now to betray a certain stubborn concentration which makes it hard for me to class them as merely due to that unhealthy inquisitiveness common to most girls of the same age. To begin with she never indulges in it except in the presence of her classmates; in her attitude to me she then affects an air of knowing complicity which for a long time merely made me smile, so that I have only just begun to feel its danger. Whenever I meet her on the road—and I meet her rather more frequently than I would wish—she greets me staidly, with perfect simplicity. One day I was caught. She stood there quite still waiting for me, with downcast eyes, while I came towards her, talking to her gently. I must have looked like a bird-charmer. She made no movement as long as she was still out of my reach, but just as I came close—her head was drooped so low that now I saw nothing but the stubborn little nape of her neck—she darted away from me, throwing her satchel in the ditch. I was obliged to send it home by one of my altar boys who was given a very rough welcome.

Mme Dumouchel was quite civil. No doubt her daughter's backwardness at her work would sufficiently justify my decision, and yet it would only be a pretext. Besides Seraphita is too intelligent not to get through a second test quite creditably, and I mustn't risk a humiliating contradiction. And so, as discreetly as possible, I tried to make Mme Dumouchel realize that her little girl seemed to me far in advance of her age, so precocious that it would be as well to keep her a few weeks under observation. She would soon catch up with the others and, anyway, the lesson would do her good.

The poor woman reddened with anger as she listened. I saw rage creep up into her cheeks, her eyes. The lobes of her ears were crimson. At last she said:

'My girl is every bit as good as the others. All she asks is to be treated right—see!'

I answered that Seraphita was certainly a very clever girl, but that her conduct, or rather her manners, were not at all what they should be.

'Manners—what d'you mean?'

'She's rather inclined to be coquettish.' This word produced an explosion:

'What d'you mean—coquettish? Anyway, what business is it of yours? You've no business—you a priest and all! Coquettish! Excuse me, M. le Curé, but I think you're a lot too young to be talkin' o' such things—an' with a kid of her age, too!'

Whereupon she left me. The child sat waiting for her mamma, 'as good as gold,' on a bench in the empty church. The door was ajar. I could see the faces of her companions, and hear the sounds of their stifled laughter —they were obviously edging round each other to get a sight of us.

Seraphita, sobbing, flung herself into her mother's

arms. I'm very much afraid it was only play-acting.

What is to be done? Children have a most lively sense of the ridiculous; they can work out a given situation to the very end with surprising logic. Obviously this imaginary duel between their playmate and the Curé was an engrossing sight. If necessary, they would use all their imagination to prolong the story and make it more exciting.

Have I been careful enough in preparing my catechism lessons? This evening I began to wonder whether I hadn't been hoping for too much from what, after all, is only a parochial duty, and one of the most thankless and laborious. Who am I, that I should ask consolation of these little ones? I dreamed of being able to speak quite openly to them, of sharing with them sorrows and joys —oh, of course, I should have been most careful never to hurt them—I wanted my life to pass as gently in this teaching as it does in prayer. . . . That's merely egotism.

In future, therefore, I shall force myself to depend far less on inspiration. Unluckily I haven't much time—it will mean sleeping a little less. To-night I managed quite well, thanks to an extra meal which I found I could digest without any difficulty. I, who once regretted the extravagance of this comforting Bordeaux. . . .

Yesterday a call at the Château which ended disastrously. I decided to go there in a hurry, as soon as I had finished my lunch, which I ate very late, as I had been spending a long time at Berguez with Mme Pigeon, still on her sick bed. It was nearly four and I was feeling 'in good form' as they say, and full of energy. To my great surprise—since M. le Comte is usually in on Thursday afternoons—I only managed to see madame.

How was it that having come there feeling so sociable I suddenly found myself unable to sustain any conversation, or even answer her questions properly? Certainly I had been walking very fast. Mme la Comtesse, with her exquisite tact, at first pretended not to notice, but she was finally bound to inquire about my health. For some weeks now I have made a point of always avoiding such questions, and I feel I am even justified in not always telling the truth. This deception of mine has been quite successful, and I notice how readily people believe me as soon as I say that I feel quite well. Of course I know I'm exceptionally thin (the village boys all call me 'skinny face') but when I say 'it runs in my family,' anxiety is instantly dispelled. Of which I am only too glad. To admit that I wasn't feeling well would be to risk being 'given the boot,' as M. le Curé de Torcy has it. Besides it seems to me that the best I can do—I have so little time for prayer—is to share these small discomforts with Our Lord alone, for as long as possible.

So I told madame that having eaten my lunch very late, I was suffering from slight indigestion. The worst of it was I had to take my leave so hurriedly; I staggered down the steps like a sleepwalker. My hostess was most kind, she escorted me all the way down, and I couldn't even manage to thank her; I kept my handkerchief pressed over my mouth. She eyed me with a strange expression, an indefinable mixture of kindliness, surprise, pity and I think a trace of repugnance. A man who is feeling sick always looks so foolish! Finally I held out my hand which she took saying almost to herself: 'Poor child,' or 'My poor child,' perhaps.

I was so astonished and so moved that I walked across the lawn to get to the drive—right over the beautiful

English turf in which M. le Comte takes so much pride, and that now must be all marked by my clumsy shoes!

Yes, I pray badly and not enough. Almost every day after mass I have to interrupt my act of thanksgiving to see some parishioner—usually ailing and asking for medicine. Fabregarques, my classmate at the junior seminary, now a chemist somewhere near Montreuil, often sends me samples of patent cures. It appears this competition annoys the headmaster who alone used to perform these small services.

How hard it is to avoid offending somebody! And however hard you try, people seem less inclined to use goodwill to their advantage, than unconsciously eager to set one goodwill against another. Inconceivable sterility of souls—what is the cause of it?

Truly, man is always at enmity with himself—a secret sly kind of hostility. Tares, scattered no matter where, will almost certainly take root. Whereas the smallest seed of good needs more than ordinary good fortune, prodigious luck, not to be stifled.

This morning I found among my letters one bearing the Boulogne postmark, written on a cheap squared notepaper of the kind usually kept in workmen's cafés. It was unsigned.

A well-wisher advises you to apply for a change of parish. And the sooner the better. When at last you open your eyes to what everyone else can see so plain, you'll sweat blood! Sorry for you but we say again: 'Get out!'

What can be the meaning of this? I seem to recognize Mme Pégriot's writing—she left an account-book behind her with a list of what she had spent on soap, soda and cleaning materials. I'm evidently not in her good books. But why should she be so anxious for me to leave?

Sent a note of apology to Mme la Comtesse. Sulpice Mitonnet offered to take it. He didn't need much persuading.

Another horrible night, sleep interspersed with evil dreams. It was raining so hard that I couldn't venture into church. Never have I made such efforts to pray, at first calmly and steadily, then with a kind of savage, concentrated violence, till at last, having struggled back into calm with a huge effort, I persisted, almost desperately (desperately! How horrible it sounds!) in a sheer transport of will which set me shuddering with anguish. Yet —nothing.

I know, of course, that the wish to pray is a prayer in itself, that God can ask no more than that of us. But this was no duty which I discharged. At that moment I needed prayer as much as I needed air to draw my breath or oxygen to fill my blood. What lay behind me was no longer any normal, familiar life, that everyday life out of which the impulse to pray raises us, with still at the back of our minds the certainty that whensoever we wish we can return. A void was behind me. And in front a wall, a wall of darkness.

The usual notion of prayer is so absurd. How can those who know nothing about it, who pray little or not at all, dare speak so frivolously of prayer? A Carthusian, a Trappist will work for years to make of himself a man of prayer, and then any fool who comes along sets himself up as judge of this lifelong effort. If it were really what they suppose, a kind of chatter, the dialogue of a

madman with his shadow, or even less—a vain and super-
stitious sort of petition to be given the good things of
this world, how could innumerable people find until
their dying day, I won't even say such great 'comfort'—
since they put no faith in the solace of the senses—but
sheer, robust, vigorous, abundant joy in prayer? Oh, of
course 'suggestion,' say the scientists. Certainly they can
never have known old monks, wise, shrewd, unerring in
judgement, and yet aglow with passionate insight, so very
tender in their humanity. What miracle enables these
semi-lunatics, these prisoners of their own dreams, these
sleepwalkers, apparently to enter more deeply each day
into the pain of others? An odd sort of dream, an unusual opiate which, far from turning him back into
himself and isolating him from his fellows, unites the
individual with mankind in the spirit of universal charity!

This seems a very daring comparison. I apologize for
having advanced it, yet perhaps it might satisfy many
people who find it hard to think for themselves, unless
the thought has first been jolted by some unexpected,
surprising image. Could a sane man set himself up as a
judge of music because he has sometimes touched a key-
board with the tips of his fingers? And surely if a Bach
fugue, a Beethoven symphony leave him cold, if he has
to content himself with watching on the face of another
listener the reflected pleasure of supreme, inaccessible
delight, such a man has only himself to blame.

But alas! We take the psychiatrists' word for it. The
unanimous testimony of saints is held as of little or no
account. They may all affirm that this kind of deepening
of the spirit is unlike any other experience, that instead
of showing us more and more of our own complexity it
ends in sudden total illumination, opening out upon azure

light—they can be dismissed with a few shrugs. Yet when has any man of prayer told us that prayer had failed him?

Literally I can scarcely stand up this morning. Those hours which seemed to me so long have left me with no precise recollection—nothing but the sensation of a blow, directed from nowhere, its force striking me full in the chest, leaving me mercifully half stunned, so that I can still not gauge its seriousness.

We never pray alone. Doubtless my sorrow was too great. I wanted to have God to myself. He did not come to me.

I read these lines again on awaking this morning. Since then—

Can it only have been an illusion? . . . Or perhaps— The saints experienced those hours of failure and loss. But most certainly never this dull revolt, this spiteful silence of the spirit which almost brings to hate. . . .

One o'clock: the last lamp is out in the village. Wind and rain.

The same solitude, the same silence. And no hope this time of forcing or turning away the obstacle. Besides, there isn't any obstacle. Nothing. God! I breathe, I inhale the night, the night is entering into me by some inconceivable, unimaginable gap in my soul. I, myself, am the night.

Let me force myself to think of other agonies like mine. I can feel no compassion for these strangers. My solitude is complete and hateful. I can feel no pity for myself.

Supposing I were never to love again!

I lay at the foot of my bed, face downwards. Oh, no! I'm certainly not such a fool as to fancy that such methods do any good. I only wanted to make the true gesture of complete acceptance, self-abandonment. I was stretched at the edge of a gulf, a void, like a beggar, a drunkard, like a corpse. I waited there to be picked up. From the first second, even before my lips had touched the floor, this lie filled me with its shame. For I wasn't expecting anything.

What wouldn't I give to be able to suffer! Even pain holds aloof. Even the most usual, the most humble, the ordinary pain in my inside. I feel horribly well.

No fear of death, it is just as indifferent to me as life: that can't be put into words. I feel as though I had gone right back all the way I've come since God first drew me out of the void.

First I was no more than a spark, an atom of the glowing dust of divine charity. I am that again, and nothing more, lost in unfathomable night. But now the dust-spark has almost ceased to glow, it is nearly extinguished.

Awoke very late. Sleep must have come upon me suddenly, on the floor where I'd thrown myself down. It's already time to begin my mass. But before I go I must record this: *That whatsoever happens I will never mention this to anyone and especially not to M. le Curé de Torcy.*

This day is so limpid, the air so sweet, of miraculous lightness. . . . When I was a tiny boy, I remember how in the early morning I sometimes used to crouch down in a hedge, dripping with dew, and run back home wet to the skin, shivering, and full of happiness to get a good smack from my poor mother, and a big bowl of steaming hot milk.

All day I've kept recalling my childhood. I think of myself as of one dead.

(N.B.—The next few pages of the exercise-book in which this diary is written have been torn out. A few words still left in the margin have been very carefully erased.)

This morning Dr. Delbende was found lying at the edge of Bazancourt wood with his skull blown out, and his body already stiff. It had rolled down into a ditch thickly lined with hazel-trees. They think that his shotgun went off by accident when he tried to disentangle it from the branches.

I had meant to destroy this diary but on thinking it over have decided only to get rid of those pages which seemed to be useless; in any case I know them by heart, having repeated them so many times. It's like a voice always speaking to me, never silent day or night. I suppose this voice will cease when I do? Or else—

For several days I have been thinking a great deal about sin. In defining sin as a failure to obey God's law, I feel there is a risk of conveying too abstract an idea of it. People say such foolish things about sin, and as usual they never take the trouble to think. For centuries now doctors have been discussing disease. If they had been content to define it as a failure to obey the rules of health, they would long since have been in agreement. But they study it in the individual patient in the hope of curing him. And that is just what we priests are also attempting. So that really we aren't very impressed by sneers and smiles and jokes about sin.

And of course people always refuse to see beyond the individual fault. But after all the transgression itself is only the eruption. And the symptoms which most impress outsiders aren't always the gravest and most disquieting.

I believe, in fact I am certain, that many men never give out the whole of themselves, their deepest truth. They live on the surface, and yet, so rich is the soil of humanity that even this thin outer layer is able to yield a kind of meagre harvest which gives the illusion of real living. I've heard that during the last war timid little clerks would turn out to be real leaders; without knowing it, they had in them the passion to command. There is, to be sure, no resemblance there with what we mean when we use the beautiful word 'conversion'—*convertere* —but still it had sufficed that these poor creatures should experience the most primitive sort of heroism, heroism devoid of all purity. How many men will never have the least idea of what is meant by supernatural heroism, without which there can be no inner life! Yet by that very same inner life shall they be judged: after a little thought the thing becomes certain, quite obvious. Therefore? . . . Therefore when death has bereft them of all the artificial props with which society provides such people, they will find themselves as they really are, as they were without even knowing it—horrible undeveloped monsters, the stumps of men.

Fashioned thus, what can they say of sin? What do they know about it? The cancer which is eating into them is painless—like so many tumours. Probably at some period in their lives most of them felt only a vague discomfort, and it soon passed off. It is rare for a child not to have known any inner life, as Christianity understands it, however embryonic the form. One day or another all young lives are stirred by an urge which seems to compel; every pure young breast has depths which are raised to heroism. Not very urgently perhaps, but just strongly enough to show the little creature a glimpse, which sometimes half-consciously he accepts, of the huge risk that salvation entails, and gives to human life all its divinity. He has sensed something of good and evil, has seen them both in their pristine essence unalloyed by notions of social discipline and habit. But of course his reactions are those of a child, and of such a decisive solemn moment the grown-up man will keep no more than the memory of something rather childishly dramatic, something mischievously quaint, whose true meaning he never will realize, yet of which he may talk to the end of his days with a soft, rather too soft a smile, the almost lewd smile of old men. . . .

It is hard to measure the depths of puerility of those the word describes as 'serious men'! An inexplicable, truly supernatural puerility! Although I am only a young priest, I can't help smiling, sometimes. . . . And how kind, how indulgent they are to us! An Arras solicitor to whom I ministered on his death-bed, a man of considerable standing, a former senator, one of the richest men in the whole country, said to me once—apparently by way of apology for the touch of a quite benevolent scepticism with which he received my exhortations:

'Yes, yes, father, I quite understand. I used to feel just as you do yourself. I was very pious. Why, when I was a lad of eleven nothing on earth would have persuaded me to go to sleep without having said my three "Hail Marys"—and I even made myself say them all in one breath. Otherwise it might have been unlucky. That's how I felt about it.'

He supposed that was the point at which I had stuck, that we poor priests all stick at eleven years old. Finally, on the day before he died, I heard his confession. What could be said of it? Nothing much. A 'solicitor's life' could most times be expressed in very few words. . . .

The sin against hope—the deadliest sin and perhaps also the most cherished, the most indulged. It takes a long time to become aware of it, and the sadness which precedes and heralds its advent is so delicious! The richest of all the devil's elixirs, his ambrosia. Since the agony—

(The next page has been torn out.)

This morning—a surprising discovery. As a rule Mlle Louise leaves her prayer-book by her seat in church, on the small shelf placed there to hold them. It is a large book, and this morning I discovered it lying in the aisle; the many pictures of saints with which it is stuffed lay scattered. So I was obliged to turn over the leaves, though without much wanting to. Some writing on the back of the fly-leaf caught my eye—the name and address of mademoiselle—probably an old address—at Charleville in the Ardennes. The same writing as that of the anonymous letter. At least I think so.

What difference can that make now?

The great ones of this earth can dismiss all things unanswered, with a gesture, a glance, with even less. But God—

I have lost neither Faith, Hope nor Charity. . . . But in this life, what use to mortal man are eternal goods? What counts is the longing to possess them. I feel I have ceased to long for them.

I saw M. le Curé de Torcy at the funeral of his old friend. I can say this: that the thought of Dr. Delbende never leaves me. But even an agonizing thought is not, can never be, a prayer.

God sees and judges me.

I have decided to go on with this diary because one day I may find it useful to have kept a sincere, scrupulously exact account of what is happening to me in this time of trial. Who knows—useful to me or others? For though my heart has hardened within me (it seems I can no longer pity anyone, to pity has become as difficult as to pray: I realized this again to-night while I was sitting up with Adeline Soupault, although I was doing my best to help her) I still think with friendship of some future reader of this diary who probably will never exist. . . . A tenderness I am bound to censure since doubtless in the course of all this writing it is directed towards myself, and nobody else. I have 'turned author' or 'po-ate' as the Dean of Blangermont has it. . . . And yet— Let me set it down here, in all sincerity, that I have not grown slack in my work. Quite the contrary. The unbelievable improvement in my health is of great advantage to my job. And it is not quite accurate to say that I don't pray for Dr. Delbende. I do that, together with all my other duties. I've even knocked off wine during the last few days, but it left me dangerously weak.

A short talk with the Curé de Torcy. This wholly admirable priest is obviously intensely self-controlled. This strikes me instantly, and yet it would be very hard indeed to distinguish any outward sign; no gesture, no particular words, nothing betraying the least suggestion of will or effort. His face frankly displays his suffering, expressing it with a truly royal simplicity. At such moments even the very best people are apt to give themselves away with the kind of look which says to you more or less directly: 'You see how I'm sticking it out; don't praise me, it's my nature; thanks all the same.' But the Curé de Torcy looks straight at you, guilelessly. His eyes beg your compassion and sympathy. But with what nobility they beg! A king might beg in just that way. He had watched for two nights beside the body, and his *soutane*, as a rule so trim, so scrupulously neat, was rumpled in wide fan-shaped creases, and all stained. He had forgotten to shave, perhaps for the first time in his life.

But by this one sign you could see his mastery over himself: that supernatural strength which he gives out was in no way diminished. Though obviously tortured with grief (people are saying that Dr. Delbende committed suicide) he could still create around him a feeling of calm, of peace, of certainty. This morning I acted as his deacon. I seem to remember how usually at the consecration his finely shaped hands above the chalice would tremble slightly. To-day, not a tremor! They even had an authority, a majesty. It is truly impossible to describe the contrast with a face hollowed by insomnia, fatigue, and some agonizing vision—at which I can guess. . . .

He left at once, refusing to stay for the funeral lunch given by the doctor's niece—very much like Mme Pégriot in appearance, though even stouter. I went to the station with him, and since we had half an hour to wait for the train, we sat down together on a bench. He was very tired, and when I saw his face in full daylight it looked more haggard than ever. I had not yet noticed two wrinkles down the corners of his mouth, surprisingly sad and bitter lines. I think it was these which made me decide. I suddenly asked:

'Aren't you afraid the doctor may have—'

He cut me short, his imperious eyes seemed to nail the last words to my lips. It was very hard not to look away, but I know how he hates a shifty look. 'Flinching eyes' is what he calls it. Then his expression softened by degrees, he almost smiled.

I won't record all our conversation. Or was it really a conversation? Perhaps it didn't even last twenty minutes. . . . The little empty station-square with its double row of poplars looked even more deserted than usual. I remember a flight of wheeling pigeons, circling round and round as fast as they could, and so low that I could hear the beat of their wings.

I was right. He fears his old friend committed suicide. It seems the doctor had been letting depression get the better of him, having counted to the last moment on inheriting from a very old aunt who recently, in exchange for an annuity, placed her entire fortune in the hands of a certain well-known business man, agent to

His Grace the Bishop of S——. In his time the doctor had earned a great deal of money and had spent it lavishly in acts of rather eccentric generosity which were not always kept secret, so that people began to suspect him of wanting to go into politics. Then his younger colleagues encroached on his practice, but he never would consent to change his ways.

'You see, lad, he was never a man to make the best of a bad job. He was always telling me that it was unreasonable to fight what he was pleased to call human savagery and the general idiocy of life. He said that society could never be cured of its injustice, that whoever ended the one would end the other. He compared the illusions of social reformers to those of Pasteur's first disciples, who dreamed of an aseptic world. Really he considered himself an outlaw, no more than that—the survivor of a race long since extinct, even supposing it ever existed—still struggling on without hope or mercy against an invader who, in the course of centuries, had ended by becoming the lawful owner. "I only avenge myself," he'd say. He did not believe in a regular army—you understand? "When I happen to come across an injustice walking alone and unprotected, and I find it about my own weight, not too strong or too weak for me, I jump on its back and twist its neck." It came expensive though! Why, no later than last autumn, for instance, he paid all old Mother Gachevaume's debts, eleven thousand francs, because M. Duponsot who runs the flour mills, had an eye on her land and was meaning to bid for it. Obviously the death of his damned old aunt was the last straw. But after all—! Three or four hundred thousand francs! He'd have squandered that much in next to no time! Because the poor dear fellow

[114]

was becoming quite impossible in his old age! Why, he'd even got it into his head to keep—yes, keep!—that old soaker Rebattut, an ex-poacher as lazy as a skunk, who lives in a charcoal-seller's hut stuck on the edge of the Goubault estate. They say he's always running after little cow-girls, is never sober and didn't give two hoots for Dr. Delbende. Mind you, the doctor knew all about that. But he had his reasons. His own extra special reasons as usual!'

'What were they?'

'Well, he said this Rebattut was the best poacher he'd ever known, that you could no more keep him out of the woods than forbid him to eat and drink, and that if the police didn't leave him alone they'd only end by turning a harmless maniac into a dangerous brute. Poor old chap! He'd got all that mixed up in his brain with a lot more cranky notions, real obsessions they were! He used to say to me: "Giving men passions which they're not allowed to satisfy—that's a bit too thick for me. I'm not God, you know!" Of course he loathed the Marquis de Bolbec, and the marquis had sworn he'd make his gamekeepers goad Rebattut into doing something really serious for which he could be transported. Well, there you have it!'

I think I've already said in this diary that real sadness found no home with M. le Curé de Torcy. His soul is gay. At this very moment, now that I no longer observed his face—he was sitting with his head held very high and looking straight out—a certain note in his voice surprised me. Though grave, it never could be called a sad voice; it vibrates with imperceptible inner joy; so profound a joy that nothing in this world could shake it, like the vast, calm waters under storms.

He went on to tell me many more things, almost mad, unbelievable things. At fourteen Dr. Delbende had intended to be a missionary; he lost his faith in the course of medical studies. He was the favourite student of a certain very famous doctor—I forget the name—and all his friends prophesied a brilliant future for him. Everyone was amazed when he started a practice in this out-of-the-way place. At that time he said he hadn't the money to take his final degrees and in any case, he was in a bad state of health, due to overwork. But he was inconsolable at not being able to believe. He had some extraordinary ways. He would hurl questions at a crucifix hanging on his bedroom wall. Sometimes he would sob at its feet with his head in his hands, or he would even defy it, shaking his fist.

No doubt I could have listened more calmly to all this a few days previously. But just then I hadn't the courage. It was like a stream of molten lead being poured into an open wound. Never have I suffered like that, and I shall probably never suffer again, not even in death. All I could do was to sit there staring at the ground. If I had raised my eyes to the Curé de Torcy, I really think I should have cried out. Unluckily at such moments as these, it is harder to control your tongue than your eyes.

'If he really did kill himself, do you think—?'

The Curé de Torcy started, as though my question had raised him suddenly from a dream. Indeed, for the last five minutes his voice had sounded a little dreamy; I could feel that he was looking into my mind, and he must have guessed a good deal!

'If anyone else had asked me that!'

A long pause. The little square looked as bright, as

empty as ever; at regular intervals the heavy birds, wheeling monotonously, seemed to swoop upon us from a great height. I sat stupidly waiting till they were over us, with their whistling like the swish of a great scythe.

'God is the sole judge,' he said at last, calmly. 'And Maxence' (this was the first time I had heard him use his old friend's Christian name) 'was a just man. God judges the just. Do you think I ever bothered my head much about fools, or mere knaves? What 'ud be the use of saints then? They pay to redeem that sort of trash. They're strong enough, whereas—'

His hands were on his knees, his shoulders spread a broad shadow before him.

'We're at war, you see. We've got to keep facing the enemy. Face up to it, he said, you remember? That was his motto. Well in war, does it make all that difference if a third- or fourth-liner, some idiot with a cushy job at the base, happens to get cold feet? Or a putrid old civilian with nothing to do but read his paper, what does that matter at headquarters? But the picked front-liners! A chest is a chest when you get to the trenches. And one less counts! There are always saints. And by saints I mean those who have been given more than others. Rich men! I've always had a secret kind of a notion that if we could take a god's-eye view of human societies, we'd have the key to a good many things we can't understand. After all, God made man in His image: when man tried to build a social order to suit himself he's bound to make a clumsy copy of the other, the true society. . . . Our division into rich and poor must be based on some great law of the universe. In the eyes of the church the rich man is here to shield the poor, like his elder brother. Well, of course, he

[117]

often does it without even wanting to, by the sheer action of economic force, as they say. A millionaire goes smash and thousands are chucked out into the streets. So you can just imagine what happens in the invisible world when one of those rich men I've just been talking about, a steward of divine grace, turns tail! The solvency of the mediocre is nothing. Whereas the solvency of a saint! What a scandal if *he* should happen to fail! You've got to be crazy to refuse to see that the sole justification of inequality in the supernatural order is its risk. Our risk! Both yours and mine.'

Throughout all this he still remained bolt upright, and never moved. Anyone seeing him sitting there on that cold, sunny winter afternoon, would have taken him for some worthy country priest, gossiping of parish trivialities, boasting good-naturedly to a young, deferential colleague.

'Now remember what I am going to say to you: perhaps all the harm really came from his loathing of mediocre people: "You hate mediocrities," I kept telling him. He rarely denied it, because I say again, he was a just man. Mediocrities are a trap set by the devil. Mean-spirited people are far too complex for us; they're God's business, not ours; but in the meantime we should shelter mediocrity, take it under our wing. Poor devils, they need some keeping warm! "If you really sought Our Lord you'd end by finding Him," I used to say. He always answered: "I'm looking for God among the poor, where I've the best chance of ever finding Him." But the trouble was that his "poor" were chaps of his own sort. They weren't really the poor at all, they were rebels, masters! I said to him one day: "And suppose Jesus were really waiting for you in the guise of one of these worthy

people you despise so? Because apart from sin, He takes
on Himself and sanctifies all our wretchedness. A coward may be only some poor creature crushed down by
overwhelming social forces like a rat caught under a
beam; a miser may be miserably anxious, deeply convinced of his impotence and racked with fear of not
"making good." Some people who seem brutally heart-
less may suffer from a kind of "poverty-phobia"—one
often meets it—a terror as difficult to explain as the nervous fear of mice or spiders. "Do you ever look for Christ
among people of that kind?" I asked him. "And if you
don't, then what are you grousing about? You've missed
Christ, yourself." And perhaps, after all, he did miss
Him. . . .'

To-night (or rather just after sunset) I again heard
somebody move in the presbytery yard. I suppose they
were going to pull the bell when suddenly I opened the
little skylight above the window. The steps scurried
away. A child perhaps?
M. le Comte has just taken his leave. The pretext of his
visit a heavy shower. Water squelched from his high
boots at every step. The three or four rabbits he had
shot made a dripping mess of earthy blood and grey fur
at the bottom of his game-bag—horrible! He slung it
against the wall, and through the string netting, amid
rumpled fur, I caught sight of a still lustrous eye, a very
gentle eye which looked at me while he was talking.
He apologized for coming straight to the point, without any beating about the bush, and with soldierly frankness. It appears that all over the village Sulpice has got
the reputation of very loose, abominable behaviour. During his military service he 'only just missed a court-

martial,' to use M. le Comte's own words. A sly, vicious fellow, such is the verdict. Gossip, as usual, nothing definite, mere rumour and supposition. For instance, Sulpice was in service for a few months with a retired colonial judge of very doubtful reputation. I answered that we can't choose our masters. M. le Comte shrugged, with a quick glance in my direction, from head to foot, which said very plainly: 'Is he a fool, or does he pretend he is?'

I admit that my attitude must have come as rather a surprise. I suppose he expected protestations. I remained calm, though I daren't say indifferent. My own pain is enough for me. And I listened with the queer sensation that he wasn't talking to me at all—to the man I was and am no longer. What he said came too late. And M. le Comte himself was too tardy a visitor. This time his cordiality seemed affected, a little vulgar even. Nor do I care much for his eyes which shift all over the place, from one end of the room to the other with surprising quickness, till they come back to fasten themselves on me.

I had just finished supper, the earthen wine-jar was still on the table. He poured himself out a glass without ceremony and remarked: 'This is a very sour wine of yours. It isn't healthy, M. le Curé. You ought to keep your jug as clean as possible. Have it rinsed out with boiling water.'

Mitonnet came this evening as usual. He has rather a pain in his side: complains of not being able to get his breath, and coughs a good deal. Just as I was about to have a talk with him, disgust suddenly took possession of me, a cold shudder, and I left him there to get on with his work (he is doing a very neat job replacing some rotten boards in my floor). I went out to walk up and down the road. And of course when I came in again I still hadn't made any decision. He was working his plane on one of the boards and so could neither see nor hear me, and yet he suddenly turned round and our eyes met. In his I saw surprise and then tension, and then the lie. Not this or that particular lie, but the *will to lie*. The effect was that of clouding water, muddy. And then—I was still watching him, the whole thing only lasted a few seconds—the real look crept back into his eyes, under the scum. . . . It was indescribable. His lips had begun to quiver. He picked up his tools, wrapped them very carefully in a cloth and left me without saying a word.

I ought to have kept him and made inquiries. I couldn't do it. And I couldn't keep my eyes from the pitiful sight of him as he slouched off along the road. But by degrees he walked upright again and passing the Degas's house he even raised his cap in a very swaggering way. A few steps further and he would be humming one of his favourite, terribly sentimental ditties, the text of which, carefully copied out, he always keeps in his little note-book.

Went back exhausted to my room—an astonishing weariness. I don't in the least understand what can have happened. Though his outward manner is rather shy, Sulpice is quite brazen underneath. He has a persuasive tongue and knows it all too well. I'm amazed he shouldn't even have tried to excuse himself—an easy matter for him, as he must think little of my judgement and knowledge of life. And then, how can he have guessed? I don't think I spoke one word and I'm sure I didn't look angry or scornful. Will he come back?

As I lay down on the bed to try and get a little sleep,

something seemed to snap inside me, in my chest, and I began to tremble. I'm shaking still as I write these lines.

No, I have not lost my faith. The expression 'to lose one's faith,' as one might a purse or a ring of keys, has always seemed to me rather foolish. It must be one of those sayings of *bourgeois* piety, a legacy of those wretched priests of the eighteenth century who talked so much.

Faith is not a thing which one 'loses,' we merely cease to shape our lives by it. That is why old-fashioned confessors are not far wrong in showing a certain amount of scepticism when dealing with 'intellectual crises,' doubtless far more rare than people imagine. An educated man may come by degrees to tuck away his faith in some back corner of his brain, where he can find it again on reflection, by an effort of memory; yet even if he feels a tender regret for what no longer exists and might have been, the term 'faith' would nevertheless be inapplicable to such an abstraction, no more like real faith, to use a very well-worn simile, than the constellation of Cygnus is like a swan.

No, I have not lost my faith. The cruelty of this test, its devastation, like a thunderbolt, and so inexplicable, may have shattered my reason and my nerves, may have withered suddenly within me the joy of prayer—perhaps for ever, who can tell?—may have filled me to the very brim with a dark, more terrible resignation than the worst convulsions of despair in its cataclysmic fall; but my faith is still whole, for I can feel it. I cannot reach it now; I can find it neither in my poor mind, unable to link two ideas correctly, working only on half delirious images, nor in my sensibility, nor yet in my conscience. Sometimes I feel that my faith has withdrawn and still persists where certainly I should never have thought of seeking it, in my flesh, my wretched flesh, in my flesh and blood, my perishable flesh which yet was baptized. Let me try and put it as plainly, as innocently as possible. I have not lost faith because God has graciously kept me from impurity. No doubt most philosophers would smile at such a relation of thoughts! Obviously the very worst disorders could never so confuse a thinking man as to make him, for instance, doubt the validity of certain axioms in geometry. But with one exception: madness. After all, what do we know of madness? What do we really know of lust? What do we know of their hidden connections? Lust is a mysterious wound in the side of humanity; or rather at the very source of its life! To confound this lust in man with that desire which unites the sexes is like confusing a tumour with the very organ which it devours, a tumour whose very deformity horribly reproduces the shape. The world, helped by all the glamour of art, takes immense pains to hide away this shameful sore. It is as though with each new generation men feared a revolt of human dignity, a desperate revolt—the sheer refusal of still unsullied human beings. With what strange solicitude humanity keeps watch over its children, to soften in advance with enchanting images this degradation of first experience, an almost unavoidable mockery. And when, despite all this, the half-conscious plaint of flouted young human dignity, outraged by devils, is heard again, how quickly it can be smothered in laughter! What a cunning mixture of sentiment, pity, tenderness, irony surrounds adolescence, what knowing watchfulness! Young birds on their first flight are hardly so hovered around. And if the revulsion is too intense, if the precious child over whom angels still stand guard shudders with invincible disgust, what cajoling hands will offer him the basin of gold, chiselled by artists, jewelled by poets, while soft as the vast murmur of leaves and the splash of streams, the low-pitched orchestra of the world drowns the sound of his vomiting! But with me the world was not so tender. At twelve a little pauper knows a good deal. What use would it have been only to know? I had seen. Lust must be seen, not 'understood.' I had seen those hard and avid faces suddenly fixed in indescribable smiles. God! how is it we fail to realize that the mask of pleasure, stripped of all hypocrisy, is that of anguish? In my dreams, even now, I can still see their hungry faces; one night in ten I dream of them still. Such sad faces. As I squatted down, behind the bar—for I never stayed long in the dark outhouse where my aunt thought I was doing my homework—those faces surged above my head, and the dim light of a wretched lamp swaying by its copper chain, for ever jostled by some drunkard, set their shadows dancing over the ceiling. Little as I was, I could always distinguish one kind of drunkenness from another; from *the other*, the only kind which really scared me. The young servant—a wretched crippled girl with an ashen face—had only to come into the bar and those besotted eyes stared suddenly with such poignant fixity that even now I can't think calmly of it. Oh, of course—a child's imagination! The extraordinary vividness of such memories, the terrors they still awaken after so many years is sufficient in itself to render them suspect. . . . No doubt! But let worldlings see for themselves! I don't think we can ever learn much from ultra-sensitive, shifty faces, skilled in disguise, that hide themselves in lust, as beasts hide to die. And thousands of human beings, I'll agree, live disordered lives, prolonging to the very threshold of old age, sometimes even farther, the curiosity of their never-sated adolescence. What can we learn from such shallow creatures? Perhaps they are the playthings of demons, but not their prey.

It seems that God, in the mystery of His Own purpose, has not permitted them seriously to pledge their souls. Most probably they are children who failed to grow up, grubby yet not vicious urchins, victims of some wretched heredity displaying its mere harmless caricature, so that providence allows them still to profit by certain immunities of childhood. . . .

And besides— What are we to conclude? Because there are inoffensive maniacs, do no dangerous lunatics exist? Let moralists define, psychologists analyse and classify, poets sing their songs, painters play with their colours like a cat playing with its tail, and mountebanks make game of it all—what does it matter? Madness, I say again, is no better understood than lust, and society protects itself against both without really admitting them, with the same sly fear, the same secret shame, and using about the same methods. But if madness and lust are really one?

We priests are sneered at and always shall be—the accusation is such an easy one—as deeply envious, hypocritical haters of virility. Yet whosoever has experienced sin, with its parasitic growth, must know that lust is forever threatening to stifle virility as well as intelligence. Impotent to create, it can only contaminate in the germ the frail promise of humanity; it is probably at the very source, the primal cause of all human blemishes; and

[125]

when amid the windings of this huge jungle whose paths are unknown, we encounter Lust, just as she is, as she emerged forth from the hands of the Master of Prodigies, the cry from our hearts is not only terror but imprecation: 'You, you alone have set death loose upon the world!'

It is the fate of many priests, more zealous than wise, to presuppose a lack of candour: 'You don't believe because to believe, is inconvenient!' How many priests have I heard say that! Wouldn't it be more just to say: Purity is not imposed upon us as though it were a kind of punishment, it is one of those mysterious but obvious conditions of that supernatural knowledge of ourselves in the Divine, which we speak of as faith. Impurity does not destroy this knowledge, it slays our need of it. I no longer believe, because I have no wish to believe. You no longer wish to know yourself. This profound truth, your truth, has ceased to interest you. Insist as much as you please that dogmas, to which yesterday you assented, are still sole-present in your mind, that only reason rejects them. What does it matter? We can only really possess what we desire, since complete and absolute possession does not exist for a human being. You no longer want to possess yourself. You no longer desire your own joy. You can only love yourself through God. You no longer love yourself, and you will never love yourself again either in this world or hereafter— through all eternity.

(*The following lines, written on the margin of this page, heavily overscored, are still just legible.*)

[126]

I wrote this in a moment of overwhelming agony, agony of the heart and of all my senses. A mad rush of thoughts, words, images. In my soul nothing. God is silent. Silence.

I feel that the worst is still to come; the real temptation which I await is far beyond, advancing slowly upon me, heralded by delirious cries. And my miserable spirit is also crouching for it, silently. A fascination of body and soul. (The sharp withering horror of this misfortune. The spirit of prayer was not torn out of me, it fell away of itself as ripe fruit falls.) Horror came afterwards. It was only when I saw my empty hands that I realized the vessel had been broken.

I know this is no unusual trial. No doubt a doctor would say I was suffering simply from nervous strain, that it's very foolish to try and live on only a little bread and wine. But I don't feel tired, anything but. I feel much better! Yesterday I almost ate a meal—potatoes, butter. And I get through my work easily. Sometimes I only wish I had to struggle against myself! I think my courage would come back to me. Occasionally I feel the pain in my stomach. But now it comes all of a sudden. I don't wait from second to second as I used. . . .

I know, too, how much has been reported, for what it's worth, of the spiritual anguish of saints. Alas, it's a superficial resemblance! The saints can never have man aged to get used to their misfortune, but already I feel myself getting used to mine. And if ever I yield to the temptation of sharing my pain with anyone, no matter who, my last link with God will have been severed. I think eternal silence would begin for me.

Yesterday I went for a long walk down the road to Torcy. My solitude is now so deep, so truly inhuman, that I had a sudden impulse to go and pray at the grave of Dr. Delbende. Then I remembered his protégé, that Rebattut whom I had never seen. At the last minute my strength deserted me.

Mlle Chantal has been to see me. This evening I feel incapable of putting down anything whatsoever about so distressing a meeting. Fool that I am! I know nothing of my people. I never shall! I can't profit by my mistakes: they upset me too much, I must be one of those weak, miserable creatures, always so full of the best intentions, whose whole lives oscillate between ignorance and despair.

This morning, having said my mass, I rushed off to Torcy. The Curé has been ill at Lille, where he'd gone to stay with one of his nieces, and won't be back for at least a week or ten days. By that time—

It seems useless to write. Some secrets cannot be written—I *cannot*. And probably I should have no right.

My disappointment was so intense when I heard that M. le Curé had gone away, that I had to lean up against the wall to stop myself falling. His housekeeper watched me, more with curiosity than pity, a look I've encountered several times these last weeks in the eyes of very different people. Mme la Comtesse had just that look. So had Sulpice and others as well—as though I scared people in some way. . . .

Mme Martial, the washerwoman, was hanging up her washing in the yard, and as it took me some time to get my breath before starting back home, I couldn't help knowing that the two women were discussing me. One of them raised her voice a little and said, 'Poor lad,' in a way which made me all go hot. What do they know?

A terrible day for me. And the worst of it is I don't feel capable of any reasonable, measured appreciation of events whose deepest significance no doubt still eludes me. Oh, I've experienced many such hours of wilderness and distress; but I've always retained, in spite of myself, that inner peace wherein persons and events would be mirrored—a limpid pool reflecting each image. But now the spring itself is troubled.

Strange and shameful though it may be, although, through my own fault surely, I can now find such little comfort in prayer, I am yet able to recover some peace of mind sitting at this table before these white sheets of paper. If it could only have been a dream—a bad dream.

Owing to the funeral of Mme Ferrand, early mass was at six o'clock this morning. The choirboy didn't turn up; I thought I was alone in the church. At that hour, this time of the year, your gaze can barely travel further than the choir-steps; the rest is lost in shadow. Suddenly, very distinctly, I heard the faint click of a rosary being drawn along a wooden bench and down the aisle. Then nothing. When I gave the blessing I dared not look up.

She was waiting for me at the sacristy door; I knew it. Her thin face was even more contorted than the day before yesterday, and there was that fold of the lips, sneering and hard.

I said: 'You know I can't receive you here. Go home.' Her glance frightened me and I'd never thought myself a coward. Heavens, the hatred in her voice! And those eyes so proud and shameless. So one *can* hate without shame. . . .

'Mademoiselle,' I said, 'I'll do what I promised for you.'

'To-day?'

'To-day.'

'Because to-morrow, monsieur, it would be too late. She knows I went to the presbytery. She knows everything that goes on, the sly beast! I used not to be on my guard; her eyes grow upon one, they appear good and kind. Now I'd like to tear her eyes out, I would! Yes, and stamp on them like that!'

'How can you say that within a few steps of the Blessed Sacrament? Have you no fear of God?'

'I'll kill her,' she said. 'I'll kill her or I'll kill myself. You'll have to try and explain that away to your God, some day.'

She went on taking wildly without raising her voice; in fact, at times I could hardly hear. And I couldn't see her face well. She leaned towards me with one hand against the wall, the other holding a fox fur down her side, and her long shadow cast over the flagstones looked like a bow. Ah, those who believe confession draws us into dangerous contact with women are very mistaken. Why, the liars and the obsessed amongst them inspire mostly pity, and the shame of the truly sincere is catching. Now I could understand the secret power of women through history. The strange fatality of them. A man in a rage is like a lunatic. And the poor country girls I remember from my childhood, with their gesticulating, crying, and absurd emphasis made me laugh most times. I knew nothing of that quiet fury, which seems relentless, the whole female creature reaching out grandly for evil, and for her prey. And such freedom, such naturalness in wickedness, in hate, in shame was almost beautiful; a beauty not of this world nor of the next—older than that, older than sin itself perhaps—before the fall of the angels.

I have since endeavoured to thrust this thought away. An absurd and dangerous thought which seemed rather lovely at first when I was feeling vaguely for it.

The face of Mlle Chantal was very close to mine. Dawn was creeping slowly through the dirty windows of the sacristy, a winter dawn of great sadness. The silence between us had lasted but a few moments, the time of a *Salve Regina* (and, indeed, the words of the *Salve Regina* so fine, so pure, had unconsciously sprung to my lips).

She must have noticed I was praying. She stamped her foot with rage. I took her hand, an over-small, very supple hand which hardly stiffened in mine. Perhaps I was squeezing it harder than I knew. I said: 'First you must kneel.' She bent her knees slightly before the altar-rails, and with hands pressed against them, she looked at me with unbelievable insolence and despair. 'Say: "Dear God, I feel bound to offend you, now, but it is not I who wish to offend, but the devil in my heart." ' And she repeated after me, word for word, in the voice of a small child reciting. After all she was almost a little girl. Her long fur had slipped down to the ground and I was treading on it. Suddenly she jumped up, seemed to escape from me, and with her face turned towards the altar she muttered between her teeth: 'You can send me to Hell for all I care.' I pretended not to hear. What was the use?

'Mademoiselle,' I said, 'I am not going on with this talk here, in the middle of the church. There is only one place where I can hear you.' I drew her gently to the confessional. She knelt of her own accord.

'I don't wish to confess,' she said.

'I'm not asking you to. You need only remember that these wooden walls have known of so much shame that they are as though inured. You may be a young lady of gentle birth, but pride here is a sin like any other—a little more dirt on the muck-heap.'

'Enough of that,' she said. 'You know perfectly well I only want justice. And what do I care about dirt? Dirt is to be humiliated as I am. Since that horrible woman came into the house I've eaten more dirt than bread.'

'Those are words you've picked up in novels. You're only a child. Why can't you talk like a child?'

'A child! I stopped being a child long ago. I know all there is to be known, now. I know enough to last me the rest of my life.'

'Keep calm.'

'I am calm. I'm a lot calmer than you are! I heard them in the night. I was right under their window in the park. They don't even bother to draw the curtains now.' (She began to laugh horribly. As she would not remain on her knees, she had to stand bent double with her head pressed against the partition, and she was choking with rage, too.) 'At all costs they're going to find a way of turning me out. I know it. I've to go to England next Tuesday. Mother has a cousin living there. She considers it a very proper, very practical arrangement. Proper! I could die laughing! But *she* believes everything they tell her, anything, like a frog gobbling flies. Bah!'

'Your mother—' I began. But she answered me in words that were almost vile and that I dare not repeat. She said the unhappy woman had not known how to protect her joy, her life. That she was a fool and a coward.

'You've been listening at doors,' I interrupted. 'You've been peeping through keyholes. You've been trying your hand at spying. You, a lady, and so proud! I'm only a peasant's son. I spent two years of my youth in a foul pub where *you'd* never have set foot, but I wouldn't do what you have done were it to save my life.'

Suddenly she straightened herself and stood before the confessional with bent head, her face still as hard. I cried: 'On your knees,' and she obeyed me.

I had been reproaching myself, two days earlier, with taking over-seriously what was possibly mere obscure jealousy, unhealthy dreaming and fantasy. We have been so frequently forewarned against the malice of those whom our old moralistic treatises refer to so amusingly as *the weaker sex*. I could well imagine the shrug of M. le Curé de Torcy. But then I was alone at my table, mechanically thinking over words retained by memory, from which the true expression had fled for good. Whilst now I had before me a distorted face, whose disfigurement was not due to pain, but to a deep inner panic. I had seen features thus strained before, but only on the faces of the dying, and naturally I had thought the cause to be of common physical order. Doctors will tell you of the facial change which heralds the approach of death. But doctors are often wrong. What could I say, what could I do to help this wounded creature whose life seemed to be flowing away from some secret hurt? In spite of all I felt I had better remain silent a little longer, run the risk of it. I had found a little strength to pray. She was silent, too.

Just then a peculiar thing happened. I am not trying

to explain it. I shall put it down as it occurred. I am so tired, so overwrought that I may even have dreamt it. Well, as I was staring into the deep shadow where even in full daylight I can barely recognize anyone, the face of Mlle Chantal began to appear to me, by degrees. And this image remained under my gaze, in a wonderful fleeting way, and I kept quite still for fear the slightest movement would have made it disappear. Of course, I never thought of that then. It only occurred to me later. I am wondering if this vision had something to do with my prayer, *was* my prayer, in some way? My prayer was sad and so was the image. I could hardly bear such sadness and yet I was anxious to share it, to assume it in its entirety, to let it flood my soul, my heart, my bones, my whole being. The confused rumble of inner hostile voices which had troubled me for the last few weeks was silenced by it. The old silence had returned to me. The blessed quiet wherein the voice of God can be heard—God will speak. . . .

I came out of the confessional. She had risen before me. We found ourselves face to face again, but I could not recognize my vision. She was extremely—almost absurdly—pale. Her hands were trembling.

'I can't stand any more,' she said, in a childish voice. 'Why did you look at me like that? Can't you leave me alone?' Her eyes were dry and burning. I did not know how to reply. I led her slowly to the church door.

'If you loved your father you would not be in this terrible state of revolt. Do you call that love?'

'I don't love him any more,' she replied. 'I think I hate him. I hate them all!' Words hissed through her lips, and she gave a gasp at the end of each sentence—a gasp of disgust or weariness, I hardly know. 'I don't

[134]

want you to take me for a little fool,' she said now, with self-sufficient pride. 'Mother thinks I know "nothing of life" as she puts it. I tell you, I'd have to be blindfolded. Why our servants are a set of gossiping monkeys, and she thinks them perfect. "A most reliable lot." She chose them, of course. But I should have been sent away to a boarding-school. By the time I was ten, perhaps before—there wasn't much I didn't know. I was terribly upset and disgusted, of course, but I accepted it all as one makes up one's mind to illness and death, and many other horrible things one must be resigned to. There was my father, you see. He was everything to me: a master, a king, a god—and a friend, a very great friend. He always used to talk to me when I was little. He treated me almost like an equal. I wore a locket next to my heart, with his picture and a lock of his hair. Mother never understood him. She—'

'Don't speak of your mother. You don't love her. And anyhow—'

"Go on, say what you've got to say. I hate her. I've always hated—'

'Hold your tongue. No doubt invisible spirits of evil lurk in all homes, even Christian homes. The most vicious of them has been growing in your heart for a long time, now. And you didn't know—'

'All the better,' she said. 'Let it grow to be horrible and hideous. I've no more respect for my father, now. I've lost faith in him. And I don't care about anything else. He has deceived me. One can deceive a daughter just as well as a wife. It's not the same. It's worse. But I'll have my revenge. I'll run away to Paris, I'll disgrace myself, and I'll write and say: "That's what you've made me!" Then he'll suffer what I've suffered.'

[135]

I thought for a while. It seemed I could read other words on her lips as she was speaking—words to which she gave no voice, yet they burnt their way, one by one, into my brain. So that I called out, almost in spite of myself: 'You won't do that. I know you're not tempted that way.'

She began to shake so violently that she had to lean with both hands against the wall, for support. And another strange thing happened which again I can only recount without attempting to explain. It may have been a shot in the dark, yet I knew I was right:

'Give me that letter—that letter in your bag—at once.'

She made no attempt to resist. She just sighed deeply and held out the envelope with a shrug.

'*You* must be the devil,' she said.

We left quietly, but I had difficulty in standing straight, the pain in my stomach, which I had nearly forgotten, was returning, more biting than I had ever known it. An expression of dear old Dr. Delbende came back to my mind: 'skewer-pain.' That was it all right. I remember the badger M. le Comte once nailed to the ground under my eyes with a boar-spear, and which lay agonizing in a ditch, pierced through and through, forsaken even by the dogs.

At all events Mlle Chantal was not troubling about me. She walked between the graves, head high in the air. I hardly dared look at her; I had her letter in my hand, and she cast her eyes over it at times, sideways, with a strange look. It was hard to keep up with her. I was in fear of crying out at each step, and so bit violently into my lips. Finally, I decided such a struggle against pain must have its roots in great pride, so I simply asked her to wait a minute as I couldn't go on.

I think it was the first time I really looked into the face of a woman. Not that I usually avoid them, and sometimes I have found them attractive, but without being as scrupulous as some of my colleagues, I know too well the malice surrounding me not to observe the indispensable reserve of a priest. Now I was carried away by curiosity. I am not ashamed of it. I think it must have been the curiosity of a soldier who will take a chance outside the trench to see the enemy face to face at last, or possibly— I remember when I was seven or eight going with my grandmother to see an old cousin who had just died. I was left alone in the room, and in just the same way I lifted up the shroud to take one look at that face.

Some faces are open and unsullied, purity shines through them. Doubtless the face under my eyes had once been thus. And now it had become in some way closed, impenetrable. Purity was there no longer, but neither anger, disdain nor shame had yet been able to efface the mysterious hallmark. They were only so many grimaces. An unusual, almost alarming nobility of expression bore witness to the power of evil, of sin, that sin which was not her own—God, are we really such wretched creatures that a proud soul in revolt must needs turn against itself?

'You are helpless,' I told her. (We were standing at the very end of the churchyard near the little door which leads into Casimir's orchard, that derelict corner where the grass is so tall that it hides the graves, graves forgotten there for the last century.) 'Another priest might have refused to hear you out. I have listened: so be it. But I shall not accept your challenge. God accepts no challenge.'

'Give me back that letter,' she said, 'and you needn't bother any more. I can fight my own battles.'

'Your own battles? Against whom, against what? Evil is stronger than you, my girl. Are you so proud as to think yourself out of reach?'

'I can get out of the mud, anyhow.'

'You yourself are no more than mud, my child.'

'Words! Does your God forbid one to love one's father now?'

'Don't use that word, "love," ' I said to her. 'You've lost the right, and doubtless the power. Love! All over the world there are millions imploring God for it, ready to die a thousand deaths if one drop of water could touch their parched lips, one drop of that water which was granted to the woman of Samaria—and yet they must beg for it in vain. Why, I who tell you this—'

I checked myself in time. But she must have understood, because she seemed overwhelmed. Although I was speaking in an undertone—or perhaps because of that —sheer effort to control myself must have given my voice a peculiar emphasis. I felt my words shaking in my breast. No doubt this girl thought I was crazy. Her eyes kept avoiding mine, and the little shadow in the hollow of each cheek seemed to be spreading. 'Yes,' I went on, 'keep such excuses for others. I am nothing more than a poor priest, very unworthy and very wretched, but I know what sin is. And you don't. All sins are alike. There is only one sin. I'm not speaking to you in riddles. Such truths are within reach of the humblest Christian if only he be willing to receive them from us. The world of sin confronts the world of grace like the reflected picture of a landscape in the blackness of very still, deep waters. There is not only a communion of saints; there is also a communion of sinners. In their hatred of one another, their contempt, sinners unite, embrace, intermingle, become as one; one day in the eyes of Eternal God they will be no more than a mass of perpetual slime over which the vast tide of divine love, that sea of living, roaring flame which gave birth to all things, passes vainly. Who are you to condemn another's sin? He who condemns sin becomes part of it, espouses it. You hate this woman and feel yourself so far removed from her, when *your* hate and *her* sin are as two branches of the same tree. Who cares for your quarrels? Mere empty gestures, meaningless cries—spent breath. Come what may, death will soon have struck you both to silence, to rigid quiet. Who cares, if from now on you are linked together in evil, trapped all three in the same snare of vice, the same bond of evil flesh, companions—yes, companions for all eternity.'

I must be giving a very poor account of my actual words, since nothing remains clearly in my memory but the changing expressions on the face where I seemed to be reading them.

'That's enough!' she said in a muffled voice. But her eyes did not ask for mercy. I have never seen, and probably shall never see, a face so hard. And yet instinctively I felt this was her great and final struggle against God, that evil was leaving her. Could this tortured face really be the one I had seen looking so childlike only a few weeks previously? I couldn't have told her age now; and perhaps she had no age. Pride is ageless. Pain is ageless, too.

There was a long silence; then she left me, suddenly, without a word. . . . What have I done?

5

CAME BACK VERY LATE from Aubin where I had some sick calls after dinner. Useless to try and get any sleep. How could I have let her go like that? I did not even ask what she expected of me.

The letter is still in my pocket, but I've only just looked at the envelope: it's addressed to M. le Comte.

My 'skewer' pain in the pit of the stomach still continues. I can feel it even in my back. Incessant queasiness. I am glad not to be able to think. This fierce distraction of pain is stronger than anguish. I am reminded of the skittish horses which as a little boy I used to go and watch being shod at Cardinet's forge. As soon as the rope, flecked with blood and foam, had been twisted round the poor beasts' muzzles they were still, their ears set back, their long legs trembling. 'That's done for you, you big stiff,' the smith would say with a huge laugh.

'It's done for me,' too.

The pain has suddenly stopped. It had been so unceasing, so monotonous, that helped by fatigue I had very nearly fallen asleep. When it left me I jumped out of bed, my head throbbing, but my mind horribly clear, with the impression—the certainty, of having heard someone call my name.

My lamp was still burning on the table.

I looked all round the garden but in vain. I *knew* that I should not find anyone. All that still seems like a dream, yet every detail stands out vividly, lit by a kind of mental clarity, a frozen light, too intense for even the smallest shadow in which I might seek some rest, some safety. . . . It is thus that after death a man must see himself. . . . Ah, yes! What have I done!

For weeks I had not prayed, had not been able to pray. Unable? Who knows? That supreme grace has got to be earned like any other, and I no doubt had ceased to merit it. And so at last God had withdrawn Himself from me—of this at any rate I am sure. From that instant I was as nothing, and yet I kept it to myself! Worse still: I gloried in my secrecy. I thought of it as fine, heroic. I *did* try to see the Curé de Torcy. But I should have gone to my superior, the Dean of Blangermont, and confessed. I ought to have said: 'I am no longer fit to guide a parish. I have neither prudence, nor judgement, nor common sense, nor real humility. God has punished me. Send me back to my seminary, I am a danger to souls.'

That man would have understood. And who, after reading this miserable journal, every line of which reveals my weakness, my wretched weakness, who would not understand? Is this the showing of a leader, the head of a parish, a guardian of souls? For I ought to be master of my parish, yet I give myself away to them for what I am—a pitiful beggar, going from door to door with outstretched hand, not even daring to knock. Oh, yes— I've worked hard enough! I've done my best, and what's the use? My best is nothing. A leader is not judged by his mere intentions: once he has assumed responsibility, he must answer for his results. By concealing the state of my health, was I really doing no more than obey the impulse—a crazy, heroic impulse—to do my duty? And had I any right to take the risk? A leader's risk is the risk of all.

I ought never to have received Mlle Chantal the day before yesterday. Her first visit to the presbytery was hardly conventional. And at least I ought to have interrupted her sooner, but as usual I followed my own impulse. I refused to see anything else but the girl before me, tottering as though on the brink of a double gulf of hate and despair. O agonized face! Such a face can never have lied, such anguish. . . . And yet other agonies have not managed to rouse such pity in me. Why should this pain have seemed such an intolerable challenge? My memories of unhappy childhood are still too vivid, I feel. I too experienced once this terrified shrinking from all the sorrow and shame of life. . . . God! Such revelations of impurity would prove the most ordinary of tests, if only they did not show us ourselves. That hideous voice, never yet heard, wakes in us its long murmuring echo.

And what then? I ought simply to have acted with all the more prudence and discretion. Yet instead I hit out right and left at the risk—while I struck the ravening beast—of wounding its defenceless innocent prey. No priest worthy of the name sees only the concrete instance. I feel that as usual I refused to notice ordinary everyday necessity, the conventions of social and family life, the compromises, no doubt most lawful, which these engender. An anarchist, a poet, a dreamer! The Dean of Blangermont was quite right.

Have just spent a long time at my window in spite of the cold. The moonlight spreads a kind of luminous down over the valley, so light that every stirring in the air trawls it out into long misty trails hovering up obliquely into the sky, which seem to float at a dizzy height. Yet so near in reality. . . . So near that I can see some tatters of it drifting over the tips of the poplars. O will-o'-the-wisps!

In reality we know nothing of the world, we are not in the world.

On my left a large and sombre moon haloed round with light which by contrast had the sheen of a basalt rock, a mineral density. That is the highest point of the park, a plantation of elms, and towards the summit of the hill, tall pines which hurricanes from the west each year mutilate. The Château is on the other slope, it turns its back on the village, on us all.

No, no matter how hard I try, I can't recall one word of that conversation, not one actual phrase. . . . As though my attempt to produce a summary of it in this diary had finally wiped it out. My memory is a blank. Yet one thing strikes me. Whereas I usually find it impossible to string ten words together without stumbling, I seem to remember a flood of speech. Perhaps for the first time I voiced, without hesitation, without beating about the bush, and also, I fear, without any scruples, my own very vivid sensation of evil. But it is more than sensation, almost a vision, nothing abstract about it. Briefly it was my own image of evil, of the power of evil, since as a rule I try to push the thought away from me. It hurts too much, it forces me to realize the meaning of certain inexplicable deaths, of certain suicides. . . . Many souls, yes, many more than we dare imagine, souls apparently quite indifferent to any religion, any morality even, must at last, on one day out of all their days, have come to suspect—an instant will do it—something of this satanic possession and longed to escape it, no matter how. Solidarity in evil, there is the horror of it! Since crimes, no matter how atrocious, no more reveal the nature of evil than the greatest works of saints the splendour of God. In the Higher Seminary when we begin our study of certain books published in the last century by some Freemason journalist—Leo Taxil, I think—under the lying title: *The Secret Books of Confessors*, what strikes us first is the very limited choice of wrong which men have at their disposal, I won't say for offending, but outraging God, for miserably plagiarizing true evil. . . . Satan is too hard a master. He would never command as did the Other with divine simplicity: 'Do likewise.' The devil will have no victims resemble him. He permits only a rough caricature, impotent, abject, which has to serve as food for eternal irony, the mordant irony of the depths.

The world of evil is so far beyond our understanding! Nor can I really succeed in picturing hell as a world, a universe. It is nothing, never will be anything but a half-formed shape, the hideous shape of an abortion, a stunted thing on the very verge of all existence. I think of sullied, translucent patches on the sea. Does the Monster care that there should be one criminal more or less? Immediately he sucks down the crime into himself, makes it one with his own horrible substance, digests without once rousing from his terrifying eternal lethargy. Yet historians, moralists, even philosophers refuse to see anything but the criminal, they re-create evil in the image and likeness of humanity. They form no idea of essential evil, that vast yearning for the void, for emptiness; since if ever our species is to perish it will die of boredom, of stale disgust. Humanity will have been slowly eaten up as a beam by invisible fungi, which transform in a few weeks a block of oakwood into spongy matter which our fingers have no difficulty in breaking. And the moralist will dissertate on passions, the statesman redouble his police, the educationalist draw up new courses of study—treasures will be squandered wholesale for the useless moulding of a dough which contains no leaven.

(As for instance the world wars of to-day which would seem to show such prodigious human activity, are in fact indictments of the growing apathy of humanity. In the end, at certain stated periods, they will lead huge flocks of resigned sheep to be slaughtered.)

We are told that the earth is still quite young, after thousands of centuries, still as it were in the pristine stages of its planetary evolution. Evil too is only at its beginning.

God, I presumed upon my strength. You cast me off into despair as we fling a scarce-born animal into the water, tiny and blind.

This night feels as though it would never end. Outside the air is so calm, so pure, that every fifteen minutes I distinctly hear the clear chimes of the church at Morienval, three kilometres away. . . . Any self-controlled man would doubtless only smile at my agony, but can we ever control presentiments?

How could I let her go? Why didn't I call her back? The letter was there on my table. I had taken it out of my pocket unconsciously, with a sheaf of papers. Strange, incomprehensible detail: *I no longer thought of it.* But I need a firm effort of will, of attention, to find again deep down within me, something of that irresistible impulse which made me say those words I still seem to hear: 'Give me that letter!' Can I really have said them? I wonder. It may always be that mademoiselle, beguiled by remorse and by her fear, fancied herself unable to hide her secret. She may have handed over her letter spontaneously. My imagination had done the rest. . . .

I have just thrown her letter into the fire. I watched it burning. Through the envelope, eaten into by flames, a corner of the paper became visible, charred up in an instant. For a second, white on black, the writing traced itself, and I thought I distinctly saw the words: 'To God. . . .'

My stomach pains have come back, fierce, intolerable. It needs an effort not to lie and roll about the floor, moaning like a sick beast. Only God can know what I am suffering. But does He know?

(*N.B.—These last words, written in the margin, have been scratched out.*)

I called this morning at the Château on the first pretext that came along—the arrangements to be made for the service which Mme la Comtesse has celebrated every six months in memory of the dead members of her family. I felt so strung up that I stopped for a long while at the park gates, watching the old gardener Clovis chopping up dead wood just as usual. His calm was good for me.

The butler left me waiting a few minutes and suddenly, with a start of terror, I remembered how last month madame had already settled her account with me. What should I say to her? Through the half-open door I could see a table laid for breakfast which probably they had only just finished. I set myself to count the cups, their number confused itself in my mind. Mme la Comtesse, standing in the drawing-room doorway had been watching me—for the last minute—shortsightedly. I think she shrugged, but without malice: 'Always the same, poor lad! We shall never alter him,' or something like it, she must have meant.

We went into a little room which leads out of the lounge. She pointed to a chair I could not see, and at last she herself pushed it towards me. My cowardice filled me with shame. 'I've come,' I said, 'to talk about your daughter, madame.'

A brief silence. Certainly of all the beings over whom God's providence day and night benignly watches, I felt the most miserable, the most forsaken.

'I'm listening,' she said. 'Don't mind what you say to me. I fancy I know much more than you do about my poor little girl.'

I began again: 'Madame, only God can read our hearts. We make mistakes, the most clear-sighted of us.'

'And do you' (she feigned to be intent on probing the fire), 'do you consider yourself clear-sighted?'

She may have been trying to hurt me. But at that instant I was incapable of taking any kind of offence. Usually my dominant feeling is that of the powerlessness of us all, poor feeble creatures that we are—our invincible blindness. And now the feeling was stronger than ever in me. It was like a vice round my heart.

'Madame,' I said, 'no matter how high our birth or riches may have placed us, still we are all the servants of someone else. But I am everybody's servant. And "servant" is even too big a word for a wretched little priest. Really I should say: "a thing to be used by everyone," or even less, if God so wills it.'

'Can one be less than a thing?'

'There are useless things, things people throw away because they can find no use for them. And if, for instance, I should ever be considered by my superiors as incapable even of discharging the modest duties with which they entrusted me, I should be such a thing.'

'If that's what you really think of yourself, I consider you highly imprudent to take it upon you—'

'Madame, I take nothing upon me. That poker there is only an instrument in your hands. Had God endowed it with just enough consciousness to put itself into your hands whensoever you needed it, that would be more or less what I am for all of you—what I wish to be.'

She smiled, though certainly her face was expressive of something quite different from gaiety, or ironic smiling. But I was amazed at my own calm. Perhaps it contrasted so entirely with the humility of my spoken words that this intrigued her and made her uncomfortable. Several times she sighed, eyeing me furtively.

'What do you want to tell me about my daughter?'

'I saw her yesterday in church.'

'In church? I should never have thought it. Children who rebel against their parents have no business in church.'

'A church is for everyone, madame.'

She looked at me again, this time straight in the face.

[148]

Her eyes still seemed to smile, whereas all the lower half of her face showed surprise, distrust, indefinable obstinacy.

'You're the dupe of a little intriguing girl.'

'Don't drive her to despair,' I said. 'God does not allow it.'

For a moment I took refuge within myself. The logs in the fireplace were crackling. Outside the open window, through net curtains, the broad green sweep of turf ended in a dark wall of pines, under brooding sky. A sky like a stagnant pool. The words I had just said astounded me. They were so far removed from what I had been thinking fifteen minutes earlier. I also knew them to be irreparable, that now I should have to speak on to the very end. Nor did the woman there before me in the least resemble what I had imagined her.

'Monsieur le Curé,' she said, 'I've no doubt your intentions are of the best. Since you admit your own inexperience, I won't trouble about that. Besides there are certain situations of which no man—whether he's experienced or not—can ever know anything. It needs a woman to see them as they are. Men only believe in appearances. And there are disorders which—'

'All disorder comes of the same father, the father of lies.'

'There are different degrees—'

'No doubt,' I said, 'but we know there's only one kind of order, that which comes from charity.'

She burst out laughing, a cruel laugh, full of hate: 'I certainly never expected—' she began. But I think she read surprise and pity in my face, for she checked herself instantly. 'What do you know? What's she been

[149]

telling you? Girls of her age are always unhappy, mis-understood. And they always find some simpleton to believe them—'

I looked straight at her. How can I have been so bold as to speak as I did?

'You don't love your daughter, madame.'

'How dare you—'

'Madame, God is my witness that I came here to-day in the hope of being of service to you all. And I'm not clever enough to have thought out anything beforehand. You yourself put those words into my mouth, and I'm very sorry they offend you.'

'I suppose you think you can read my heart.'

'Yes, madame, I think I can,' I answered. I was afraid she would lose her temper, begin to abuse me. Her grey eyes, usually so mild, seemed to darken. But in the end she bowed her head, and with the poker began drawing circles in the ashes.

'Do you realize,' she said at last softly, 'that your superiors would take a very severe view of this intrusion?'

'My superiors may refuse to support me, if they feel they must; they have every right.'

'I know what you are. You're a very well-meaning young priest, quite without vanity or ambition, and you certainly have no love of intrigue. But somebody has been influencing you. This tone of yours, this bumptious arrogance. . . . Really I wonder if I'm awake. Come now, say what's on your mind. You think I'm a bad, heart-less mother?'

'I don't presume to judge you—'

'Well, then what—'

'Neither can I allow myself to judge your daughter.

But I know what it is to suffer. I've suffered myself—'

'At your age?'

'Age makes no difference. And I know that suffering speaks in its own words, words that can't be taken literally. It blasphemes everything: family, country, the social order, and even God—'

'And you approve of that?'

'No, but I try to understand it. A priest can't shrink from sores any more than a doctor. He must be able to look at pus and wounds and gangrene. All the wounds of the soul give out pus, madame.' Suddenly her face looked pale and she made a movement as if to rise. 'That's why I haven't remembered what mademoiselle said to me. In any case I had no right. A priest pays attention only to suffering, provided that suffering is real. What do the words which express it matter, even if they're so many lies?'

'Yes—lies and truth on the same level, a nice moral way of looking at things.'

'I'm not a professor of moral theology,' I said.

Obviously she was losing patience and I expected to be told to go. I knew that she longed to send me packing, but each time her eyes encountered my sorry face— which I could see in the glass, the green reflection from the lawn making it look even more livid, more absurd— she raised her chin almost imperceptibly, seemed to re-discover the strength, the will to convince me, to have the last word.

'My daughter is simply jealous of her governess. I suppose she told you all kinds of terrible things?'

'I think she's chiefly jealous of her father's affection. . . .'

'Jealous of her father? And what about me then?'

'She *ought* to be comforted, reassured—'

'I suppose I should go down on my knees and beg her pardon?'

'At least you shouldn't let her go away from you, from here, with her heart full of despair—'

'All the same, she's going—'

'You can compel her. God will be judge.'

I rose, and so did she in the same instant. I could read a kind of terror in her eyes. She seemed both to dread that I should leave her, and at the same time to struggle against the impulse to let me know her pitiful secret. She could not keep it. It escaped at last, just as her daughter's had.

'You don't know what my suffering has been. You know nothing whatever about life. As a child of five my daughter was just what she is to-day. "I want everything, this instant!" That's been her motto. Oh, you priests! What strange notions you have of family life. One has only to hear you' (she laughed) 'at a funeral: "respected father," "united family," "the best of mothers," "comforting sight," "the social unit," "our dear France"—and so on and so forth. The strange thing isn't that you should talk like that, but the way you really imagine we take you seriously. You revel in it. The family, father—'

She broke off so sharply that literally she seemed to swallow her words. Could this really be the same quiet lady whose face framed in black lace had looked so mild on my first visit to the Château, as she sat pensively, almost lost in the far depths of her big armchair? . . . Even her voice was hard to recognize, it had become strident, dragging out the ends of the words. I think she knew it, and suffered agonies at not being able to curb herself. I did not know what to make of such weakness in a woman so self-controlled as a rule. For my daring can be explained: probably I had lost my nerve, gone blindly on burning my boats as shy people often do, to make quite certain of doing my duty. But she? It would have been so easy for her to disconcert me! Probably she need only have smiled in a certain way.

God, if it were my own chaotic thoughts, my rebellious heart? Is the agony I endure contagious? For some time now I have had the impression that my mere presence will draw sin out, summon it up to the surface, into the eyes, the lips, the voice. . . . As though the enemy scorned to hide himself from such a puny adversary, as though he came to defy me openly, laugh in my face.

We remained standing side by side. I remember how rain lashed on the window, how Clovis having finished his job, wiped his hands on his blue apron. From the other side of the hall came the sound of glasses chinked together, of dishes being cleared away. It was all calm, peaceful, ordinary.

She began again: 'A nice sort of victim: she's more like a savage little animal! That's what she is!' She eyed me furtively. I had no answer, I held my tongue. This silence seemed to stir her rage. 'I wonder why I'm telling you the secrets of my life. Never mind—I certainly won't lie to you. It's true that I longed to bear a son. I had one, he only lived eighteen months. His sister hated him already. Yes, hated him, child as she was! As for his father—'

She had to catch her breath before continuing. Her eyes were staring; her hands hanging at her sides, made a clutching movement as though seeking some invisible support. She seemed to be slipping on an incline.

[153]

'On his last day they went out for a walk together. When they came back my boy was dead. They became inseparable. And how clever she was! Oh, of course that surprises you. You imagine that a girl has to grow up before she can become a woman. You priests are often so very simple. When a kitten plays with a ball of wool I don't know if she really thinks about mice—but she behaves exactly as though she did. They say a man needs comforting. Quite so—but only one kind of comfort, the kind his nature demands, the kind he was born for. What does the truth matter? Haven't we mothers all given our sons a taste for lies, lies which from the cradle upwards lull them, reassure them, send them to sleep: lies as soft and warm as a breast! Well, I was very soon to realize how that little girl was the real mistress of the house, and I was expected to look on, to be "self-sacrificing," a mere servant. I who lived on memories of my son, who was always seeing him again, his little chair, his clothes, a broken toy—the pain of it! And you see, I'm not the sort of woman who can stoop to dishonourable rivalry. Besides, there wasn't any remedy. Domestic unhappiness at its worst has something in it rather ridiculous. I just went on living. And I've had to live between two people who exactly suited one another, although they were entirely different, whose incessant anxiety for my welfare—always in league with one another—got on my nerves. Oh, blame me if you like, I tell you it broke my heart, it poisoned me a thousand times; I'd much rather have had them hate me. Anyway, I didn't give in. I bore it in silence. In those days I was still young and much admired. When you know you're attractive, that whenever you choose you can love and be loved, it isn't difficult to be virtuous,

at least not for women like me. Mere pride is enough
to keep us straight. And I've never failed in a single
duty. Sometimes I've even found happiness. My husband's a very ordinary man. That's easy to see. However could Chantal, who at times is almost savagely clear-
sighted, have failed to notice? But she never realized—
not till the day when— Don't forget that all my married
life he's been unfaithful, time and again—so grossly,
stupidly, like a schoolboy, that really I wasn't even hurt.
It's Chantal who's been deceived. . . . Far more than I
ever have!'

She was silent again. I think I touched her arm mechanically. I could not have felt more pity, or more surprise.

'Madame, I understand,' I said. 'And I don't want you
ever to regret having told such an insignificant person,
things which only the priest has a right to know.'

Her eyes met mine in a wild glance: 'You've got to
hear it all now.' Her voice was shrill. 'It's what you've
asked for.'

'I asked for nothing.'

'Why did you come here then? And besides you've a
trick of drawing one out. You're a sly little priest! . . .
Well, let's get it over! What did Chantal say to you?
Try and tell me the truth.' She rapped the floor impa-
tiently with her foot, as her daughter had. She was standing with her elbow resting on the mantelpiece; her hand
closed round an ancient fan lying there with other orna-
ments, and I watched the tortoise-shell handle slowly
cracking between her fingers. 'She loathes the governess.
It's the same with every stranger who comes to the
house.' I still kept silent. 'Well, answer me, please. I suppose she told you that her father—no good denying it,

[155]

I can see the truth in your face. And you believed her!
A wretched little beast, who dares—' She could not finish
this. I think either my look, or silence, or the strange
current I gave forth—such deep sadness—always impeded
her before she could manage to raise her tone, so that
each time she had to begin again in a voice only a shade
harsher than her normal one, though it shook with anger.
I think this impotence which at first only irritated, made
her uneasy in the end. As her grip slackened the broken
fan slipped out of her hand, and she swept the bits im-
patiently under the clock. 'I lost my temper,' she began,
but her voice was far too sweet to be natural. She reminded me of a clumsy workman trying his tools one
after the other without finding what he needs, and fling-
ing them over his shoulder in a rage. 'Surely it's your
turn to say something now. Why have you come here,
what do you want?'

'Mlle Chantal told me she would be going away very
soon.'

'Very soon indeed, I can assure you. And it's all been
settled for some time, now. She's been lying to you.
What right have you to object to—' She broke off again,
forcing a laugh.

'No right whatsoever, I only wanted to know what
you intend, and if your decision is really final.'

'It is, most decidedly. Really I can't see how a girl of
that age can consider a few months stay in England,
with friends of ours, as a terrible ordeal which she can't
face.'

'That's why I thought we might come to some understanding in the hope of persuading mademoiselle to give
way to you, listen to you. . . .'

'Listen to me? She'd die first.'

'I certainly fear she may be driven to extremes.'
' "To extremes." How well you put it! I suppose you're suggesting she's going to kill herself. Why, it's the last thing she'd ever think of! She's terrified of a sore throat; she's horribly afraid of death. In that alone she takes after her father.'

'Madame, those are the very ones that kill themselves.'

'Really, you know—'

'Void fascinates those who daren't look into it. They throw themselves in, for fear of falling.'

'Who taught you that? You must have seen it somewhere in a book. It can't be simply your own experience. Are you so afraid of having to die?'

'Yes, madame. But please allow me to answer plainly. Death is a very narrow difficult passage—certainly not constructed for the proud.' Then I lost control: 'I fear my own death less than yours,' I told her. It is true that just then I saw her dead, or fancied I saw her. And no doubt as it rose in my eyes, the picture must have passed before hers, for she stifled a cry—a sort of fierce moaning. Then she went over to the window.

'My husband is entitled to keep on anyone he likes—in his own house. And the governess has no means of her own. We can't just turn her out into the street to satisfy the spite of a shameless little girl.' Once more she found herself unable to continue at the same pitch, and her voice faltered. 'It's quite conceivable my husband may have been too—too attentive, too familiar. Men of his age like to be sentimental—or like to persuade themselves they are.' Again she paused. 'After all, what business is it of mine? Do you mean to suggest that now, after years of grotesque humiliations—behind my back he's run after anything, any servant, the most impossible little drabs—that now, when I'm only an old woman, resigned to being one, I'm to start "seeing" things, making scenes, running risks? And for what? Is my daughter's pride of more consequence than mine? Can't she go through what I've had to go through?'

She had made this horrible statement without raising her voice. There she stood in the wide tall window-niche, one arm loose at her side, the other straight above her head, its hand crumpling the net curtain; she flung me these words as she might have spat out burning venom. Through dripping panes I could see the park, noble and calm, its lawns majestically curved, its grave old trees. . . . Surely I should only have pitied this woman. But though, as a rule, I find it easy to accept and partake in the shame of another's sin, the contrast of the graceful house with its loathsome secrets made me indignant. For indeed the folly of human beings seemed as nothing beside their stubborn malice, the sly help which under the eye of God Himself they will give to all the powers of evil, of confusion and death. When you think how ignorance, misery and disease eat into thousands of innocent lives—and then, when Providence miraculously spares some haven in which peace might flourish, human lusts must needs creep into it, and once ensconced, howl bestially, night and day!

'Madame,' I said to her, 'be careful!'

'Careful of whom, of what? You, I suppose. But there's no need to be dramatic. I've never told what you've just heard to anyone.'

'Not even your confessor?'

'It has nothing to do with my confessor. These are feelings which I can't control. But I've never let them influence my conduct. This is a Christian household, father.'

'Christian!' I cried. The word was like a bullet in my chest. It scorched. 'You may bid Christ welcome, but what do you do to Him when He comes? He was also welcomed by Caiaphas.'

'Caiaphas? Are you mad? I don't reproach my daughter for not understanding me, or my husband either. Some kinds of misunderstanding can never be bridged. One just gets used to them.'

'Yes, madame, one gets used to not loving. Satan has profaned everything, even the resignation of saints.'

'You reason like all the working classes. Every family has its secrets. What good would it do us to wash our dirty linen in public? I might have been unfaithful to my husband, considering the way he behaved. But there's nothing in *my* past to be ashamed of.'

'Blessed would be the sins that left any shame in you. God grant you may despise yourself.'

'What a strange moral code—'

'I'm not saying it's the moral code of worldlings. What does family prestige matter to God, or dignity or culture, if it's all no more than a silk shroud on a rotting corpse?'

'I suppose you'd much prefer a scandal?'

'Do you really think the poor are deaf and blind? Unluckily they're far too sharp sighted. Madame, the most stupidly blind of all people are the satisfied rich. You can hide vice away in your houses, but poor men smell it out from afar. We're told so much about pagan vices. But at least pagan slaves had only to submit like animals, and once a year their pagan masters smiled at the Saturnalia. Whereas you abuse the word of God which teaches the poor to obey in their hearts. You fancy you can steal by cunning what you ought to take on your bended knees, as a gift from on High. There's no greater danger in the world than rich men's hypocrisy.'

'Rich! I could give you the names of a dozen farmers who are far better off than we are. My dear Abbé, we're quite modest little people.'

'They think of you as their masters, their overlords. Power is built on nothing except the illusions of poor men—'

'Rubbish! As though "poor men" even cared about our family secrets.'

'Madame,' I said, 'in reality we're only one family, the great family of humanity, of whom our Lord Jesus is head. And you rich might have been His favourite children. Think of the Old Testament in which this world's goods are often the outward sign of heavenly favour. Ask yourself, madame! Wasn't it rather a rare privilege to be born exempt from the temporal servitude, which makes the lives of those who have nothing, a monotonous hunt for daily bread, an exhausting struggle with hunger and thirst, the insatiable belly demanding its pittance? Your houses should be houses of prayer, of peace. Have you never been moved by poor men's fidelity, the image of you they form in their simple minds? Why should you always speak of their *envy*, without understanding that what they ask of you is not so much your worldly goods, as something very hard to define, which they themselves can put no name to; yet at times it consoles their loneliness; a dream of splendour, of magnificence, a tawdry dream, a poor man's dream—and yet God blesses it!'

She moved towards me as if to send me about my business. I could feel that my last words had given her time to regain control. I was sorry I'd said them. I read them now with misgiving. Not that I take them back—oh, no. But they are human words—and nothing more. They express the most cruel disappointment, the deepest I ever knew as a child. And certainly others beside myself, millions of my kind and class, will feel the same. It is part of the poor man's inheritance, an essential element in his poverty, doubtless it *is* poverty itself. God ordains that beggars should beg for greatness, as for all else, when greatness shines out of them, and they don't know it.

I took up my hat from a chair. As soon as she saw me about to leave, my hand on the door-knob, she gave a strange sudden start that unhinged me.

'You're a queer sort of priest!' Her voice shook with impatience, exasperation. 'I've never met another like you. Well, at least let's part friends.'

'How could I not be your friend, madame? I'm your priest, your pastor.'

'Words! What exactly do you know about me?'

'Only what you've told me.'

'You won't succeed if you're just trying to worry me. I've too much common sense.' I said no more. 'At least,' she began to tap her foot, 'I suppose we're to be judged by our actions. How have I sinned? It's true my daughter and I are strangers. But so far we haven't let anyone see it. And now in this crisis I'm obeying my husband. If he should be wrong—oh, of course he thinks his daughter will come back to him!' Something in her expression changed. She bit her lips, too late.

'And do *you* think so, madame?'

God! She jerked back her head, and I saw—saw in a flash—her admission rise in spite of herself from the deep of her implacable soul. Caught in the act of lying, eyes said 'yes,' while 'no' came from between parted lips, as from the invincible depths of her.

I think she was amazed by her own 'no,' but she did not try to take it back. Of all hate domestic hate is the most dangerous, it assuages itself by perpetual conflict, it is like those open abscesses without fever which slowly poison.

'Madame, you turn your child out of doors and know that it will be for ever.'

'That depends on her.'

'I mean to oppose you.'

'You don't know her. She's too proud to stay here on sufferance. She wouldn't stand it.'

My patience suddenly gave out. 'God will break you,' I shouted. She uttered a kind of moaning cry. But not a cry of defeat imploring mercy—a sigh rather, the deep sigh of a creature gathering up strength for defiance.

'Break me! God's broken me already. What more can He do? He's taken my son. I no longer fear Him.'

'God took him from you for a time, and your hard heart—'

'Silence!'

'Your hard heart may keep you from him for all eternity.'

'You're blaspheming. God doesn't revenge Himself.'

'Revenge Himself? No. That's a human saying. It only has meaning for you.'

'Is my son to hate me, then? The son I bore, and nursed at my breast!'

'You won't hate, you'll cease to know one another.'

'Hold your tongue!'

'No, madame, too many priests have held their tongues,

and I wish it had only been from pity. But we're cowards. We let you talk, once we've established a principle. And what have you laymen made of hell? A kind of penal servitude for eternity, on the lines of your convict prisons on earth, to which you condemn in advance all the wretched felons your police have hunted from the beginning—"enemies of society," as you call them. You're kind enough to include the blasphemers and the profane. What proud or reasonable man could stomach such a notion of God's justice? And when you find that notion inconvenient, it's easy enough for you to put it on one side. Hell is judged by the standards of the world, and hell is not of this world, it is of the other world, and still less of this Christian society. An eternal expiation—! The miracle is that we on earth were ever able to think of such a thing, when scarcely has our sin gone out of us, and one look, a sign, a dumb appeal suffices for grace and pardon to swoop down, as an eagle from topmost skies. It's because the lowest of human beings, even though he no longer thinks he can love, still has in him the power of loving. Our very hate is resplendent, and the least tormented of the fiends would warm himself in what we call our despair, as in a morning of glittering sunshine. Hell is not to love any more, madame. Not to love any more! That sounds quite ordinary to you. To a human being still alive, it means to love less or love elsewhere. To understand is still a way of loving. But suppose this faculty which seems so inseparably ours, of our very essence, should disappear! Oh, prodigy! To stop loving, to stop understanding—and yet to live. The error common to us all is to invest these damned with something still inherently alive, something of our own inherent mobility, whereas in truth time and movement have ceased for them; they are fixed for ever. Alas, if God's own hand were to lead us to one of these unhappy *things*, even if once it had been the dearest of our friends, what could we say to it? Truly, if one of us, if a living man, the vilest, most contemptible of the living, were cast into those burning depths, I should still be ready to share his suffering, I would claim him from his executioner. . . . To share his suffering! The sorrow, the unutterable loss of those charred stones which once were men, is that they have nothing more to be shared.'

I think the above is more or less what I said to her, and on paper my words may look quite impressive. But I know that as I spoke them they came so clumsily, so haltingly, as to seem ridiculous. I could scarcely manage to frame the last few of them intelligibly. I was exhausted. Anyone seeing me there, as I stood with my back against the wall, twisting my hat between my fingers, and faced with this imperious lady, would have taken me for a culprit (and doubtless I was really that) whose excuses are not believed. She watched me with extraordinary attention.

'There's no sin which could ever justify—' She sounded hoarse. I seemed to hear her through the kind of thick mist which deadens sound. As I listened sadness overwhelmed me, indefinable sadness against which I felt quite powerless. That may have been the worst temptation in my whole life. But then God helped me. Suddenly I could feel a tear on my cheek, a single tear, as we see them on the faces of the dying, at the furthest limit of their griefs. She watched this tear fall.

'Did you hear what I said? Did you understand me? I was saying that no sin could ever justify—'

'No, I hadn't heard,' I admitted.

Her eyes never left mine. 'You must rest a bit. Why you're not fit to walk a yard. I'm stronger than you. Come now! This is hardly what we're taught, you know. It's all moonshine, poetry, nothing more! I don't believe you're really unkind. I'm certain when you think it over, you'll be hot with shame at this wretched blackmail. Nothing, either in this world or the next, can separate us from what we've loved more than ourselves, more than life, more than getting into heaven.'

'Madame,' I answered, 'even in this world, the slightest thing, a mere stroke, can make us cease to know the people whom we've loved best of all.'

'Death isn't like madness—'

'No, indeed. We know even less about it.'

'Love is stronger than death—that stands written in your books.'

'But it isn't we who invented love. Love has its own order, its own laws.'

'God is love's master.'

'No, not its master. God is love itself. . . . If you want to love don't place yourself beyond love's reach.'

She rested both hands on my arm, her face was almost touching mine: 'This is absurd. You talk to me as though I were a criminal. So all my husband's unfaithfulness goes for nothing—and my daughter's coldness, her rebellion, all that goes for nothing, nothing, nothing!'

'Madame, I speak to you as a priest, and according to the light which God has given me. You'd be wrong to think me a callow idealist. I know quite well there are many other homes like this—or still more unhappy. But an evil which spares one may kill another, and I think God has allowed me to see the perils which threatens you, and you alone.'

'Why not say at once that it's all my doing?'

'Oh, madame, nobody can see in advance what one bad thought may have as its consequence. Evil thoughts are like good ones: thousands may be scattered by the wind, or overgrown or dried up by the sun. Only one takes root. The seeds of good and evil are everywhere. Our great misfortune is that human justice always intervenes too late. We only repress or brand the act, without ever being able to go back further than the culprit. But hidden sins poison the air which others breathe, and without such corruption at the source, many a wretched man, tainted unconsciously, would never have become a criminal.'

'That's all rubbish—sheer rubbish, morbid dreaming!' (Her face was livid.) 'We couldn't go on living if we thought of such things.'

'No, madame, I don't think we could. I don't suppose if God had given us the clear knowledge of how closely we are bound to one another both in good and evil, that we could go on living, as you say.'

No doubt the above suggests all this had been thought out beforehand, that my words were part of a general plan. I swear they were not. I was defending myself and that was all.

She answered after a long pause: 'Would you deign to show me my hidden sin? The worm in the fruit?'

'You must resign yourself to—to God. Open your heart to Him.'

I dared not speak more plainly of her dead child, and the word 'resign' seemed to astonish her.

'Resign myself? To what?' Then suddenly she understood.

I sometimes meet a 'hardened' sinner. Usually they defend themselves against God by a mere species of blind instinct. It is even pitiful to watch an old man pleading for his vice, with the silly fierce sulkiness of a child. But now I saw rebellion, authentic rebellion, flash out upon a human face. Neither the eyes, fixed and dim, expressed it, nor the mouth, nor even the head itself which far from being proudly raised, drooped over her shoulder, appeared to sag as under an invisible load. Oh, not all the rhetoric of blasphemy has anything to approach such dire simplicity! It was as though a sudden flaming up of will had left her body inert, impassive, utterly void from this great expenditure of being.

'Resign myself?' Her gentle voice froze. 'What do you mean? Don't you think me resigned enough? If I hadn't been resigned! It makes me ashamed.' (Her tone was as soft as ever and yet her words had a strange intonation, a queer, metallic ring in them.) 'I tell you I've often envied weaker women who haven't the strength to toil up these hills. But we're such a tough lot! I should have killed my wretched body, so that it shouldn't forget. Not all of us can manage to kill ourselves—'

'That's not the resignation I mean, as you well know,' I said to her.

'Well then—what? I go to mass, I make my Easter. I might have given up going to church altogether—I did think of it at one time. But I considered that sort of thing beneath me.'

'Madame, no blasphemy you could utter would be as bad as what you've just said! Your words have all the callousness of hell in them.' She stared at the wall and did not answer. 'How dare you treat God in such a way? You close your heart against Him and you—'

[167]

'At least I've lived in peace—and I might have died in it—'

'That's no longer possible.'

She reared like a viper: 'I've ceased to bother about God. When you've forced me to admit that I hate Him, will you be any better off, you idiot?'

'You no longer hate Him. Hate is indifference and contempt. Now at last you're face to face with Him.'

She still stared into space and would not reply. At that moment I was seized with unnameable fear. All I had said, all she had answered, this whole endless dialogue became meaningless. Would any sensible man have viewed it otherwise? I had let myself be tricked by a girl enraged with jealousy and pride, and that was all. I had imagined I saw suicide in her eyes, as distinct in them, as clearly written, as a word scribbled on a wall. It had been no more than the kind of thoughtless impulse whose very violence makes it suspect. And this woman, standing as though to be judged by me, had doubtless lived for many years in that horrible quietness of the desolate, which of all forms of despair is the most atrocious, the most incurable, the least human. But such suffering is precisely of the kind which priests should only approach in fear and trembling. I had tried to liven this frozen heart in an instant, bring light into the innermost recess of a conscience which perhaps God's mercy intended still to leave in the pitiful dark. What was I to say? Or do? I felt like a man who has scrambled to the summit of a peak without once stopping to draw breath; he stands in amazement, his head reels, he opens his eyes and looks below him, unable to climb further or go back. It was then that—no, there are no words for it!—that while I struggled with all my might against doubt and

terror, a spirit of prayer came back to my heart. Let me
put it quite clearly: from the very start of this strange
interview I never once had ceased to 'pray' in the sense
which shallow Christians give to the word. A wretched
creature into which air is being pumped may look exactly
as though it were breathing. That is nothing. Then air
suddenly whistles through the lungs, inflates each separate delicate tissue already shrivelled, the arteries throb
to the first violent influx of new blood—the whole being
is like a ship creaking under swollen sails.

She had sunk into a chair, her head rested between her
hands. The torn lace of her mantilla trailed from her
shoulders; with a gentle movement she slipped it off and
dropped it quietly at her feet. I watched each gesture
closely, yet I had a strange feeling that we were neither
of us there, in this arid little drawing-room, that the room
was empty.

I watched her draw out a medallion worn round her
neck on a plain silver chain; and then, as quietly as ever,
with a gentleness more devastating than any violence, she
pressed open the cover with her finger-nail. The glass
tinkled down on to the carpet, but she paid no heed. A
lock of yellow hair curled round her fingers, like a band
of gold.

'Will you swear to me—' she began. But instantly she
read in my eyes that I understood and would swear to
nothing.

'My daughter,' I said (the word came from me spontaneously), 'God is not to be bargained with. We must
give ourselves up to Him unconditionally. Give Him
everything. He will give you back even more—I am
neither a prophet nor a sage, and He alone has ever returned from the place to which we all are going.' She

did not protest. She only bent a little nearer to earth, and I saw her shoulders twitching with every word. 'But at least I can assure you of this: there are not two separate kingdoms, one for the living, and one for the dead. There is only God's kingdom and, living or dead, we are all therein.' I said this, I could have said something else. Words seemed so trivial at that moment. I felt as though a mysterious hand had struck a breach in who knows what invisible rampart, so that peace flowed in from every side, majestically finding its level, peace unknown to the earth, the soft peace of the dead, like deep water.

'It seems quite plain to me,' she said in a voice miraculously different, yet very calm. 'Do you know what I was thinking just now, a moment ago? Perhaps I oughtn't to tell you what I was thinking. Well, I said to myself: Suppose that in this world or the next, somewhere was a place where God doesn't exist: though I had to die a thousand deaths there, to die stoically, every second— well, if it existed, I'd take my boy to that place' (she dared not call her dead child by his name) 'and I'd say to God: "Now, stamp us out! Now do your worst!" I suppose that sounds horrible to you?'

'No, madame.'

'No? How do you mean?'

'Because I too, madame, sometimes I—' I could find no more words. I could see Dr. Delbende there before me: his old, tired, inflexible eyes were set on mine, eyes I feared to read. And I heard, or thought I heard, the groaning of so many men, their dry sobs, their sighs, the rattle of their grief, grief of our wretched humanity pressed to earth, its fearsome murmurings.

'Listen,' she said gently, 'how can one possibly—? Even children, even good little children whose hearts are true. . . . Have you ever seen a child die?'

'No, madame.'

'He was so good all the time he was dying. He folded his little hands, he looked so serious and—and I tried to make him drink just before it happened—and a drop of milk was left on his mouth.' She was trembling now. I seemed to be standing there alone between God and this tortured human being. It was like a huge throbbing in my breast, but our Lord gave me strength to face her.

'Madame,' I said, 'if our God were a pagan god or the god of intellectuals—and for me it comes to much the same—He might fly to His remotest heaven and our grief would force Him down to earth again. But you know that our God came to be among us. Shake your fist at Him, spit in His face, scourge Him, and finally crucify Him: what does it matter? *My daughter, it's already been done to Him.*' She dared not look at the medallion, which she still held. But how little I realized what she would do.

'Repeat what you said just now about hell. Hell is—not to love any more.'

'Yes, madame.'

'Well, say it again!'

'Hell is not to love any more. As long as we remain in this life we can still deceive ourselves, think that we love by our own will, that we love independently of God. But we're like madmen stretching our hands to clasp the moon reflected in water. I'm sorry: I express it so clumsily!'

An odd smile came into her face, but the taut look was

[171]

in no way broken—a deathly smile. She had closed her
fingers on the medallion, with her other hand she was
pressing this clenched fist against her breast.

'What is it you want me to say?'

'Say: "Thy Kingdom come." '

' "Thy Kingdom come." '

' "Thy will be done on earth." '

' "Thy will be done—" ' She sprang to her feet, her
clenched hand still over her breast.

'Listen! You must often have said it! Now you must
say it with all your heart.'

'I've never said the "Our Father" since—since— But
you know that! *You* know things before you're told
them.' She shrugged her shoulders, and now she was
angry. Then she did something I didn't understand till
later. Her forehead was wet and shining. 'I *can't*,' she
was muttering, 'I seem to be losing him twice over.'

'The kingdom that you have prayed will come, is
yours too, and his,' I said to her.

'All right then: Thy kingdom come.' She looked up
at me and I met her eyes. So we remained for a few seconds, and then she said: 'It's to you I surrender.'

'To me!'

'Yes, to you. I've sinned against God. I must have
hated Him. Yes, I know now that I should have died
with this hate still in my heart, but I won't surrender—
except to you.'

'I'm too stupid and insignificant. It's as though you
were to put a gold coin in a pierced hand.'

'An hour ago my life seemed so perfectly arranged,
everything in its proper place. And you've left nothing
standing—nothing at all.'

'Give it to God, just as it is!'

'I'll either give Him all or nothing. My people are made that way.'

'Give everything.'

'Oh, you don't understand! You think you've managed to make me docile. The dregs of my pride would still be enough to send you to hell.'

'Give your pride with all the rest! Give everything!'

Then I saw her eyes shining strangely, but it was too late to stop her. She flung her medallion straight into the midst of the glowing logs. I scrambled down on to my knees and plunged my arm into the fire. I could not feel any burning. For one second I fancied my fingers had closed round a wisp of pale gold hair, but it slipped away from them, fell into the heart of the fire. Behind me there arose a terrible silence, and I did not dare turn round. The cloth of my sleeve was charred right up to the elbow.

'What madness,' I stammered, 'how could you dare?'

She had retreated to the wall against which she leaned, and pressed her hands. 'I'm sorry.' Her voice was humble.

'Do you take God for an executioner? God wants us to be merciful with ourselves. And besides, our sorrows are not our own. He takes them on Himself, into His heart. We have no right to seek them there, mock them, outrage them. Do you understand?'

'What's done is done. I can't help it now.'

'My daughter, you must be at peace,' I said. And then I blessed her.

My fingers were beginning to bleed a little, the skin had blistered. She tore up a handkerchief and bandaged them. We exchanged no words. The peace I had invoked for her had descended also upon me; and it was so ordinary, so simple, that no outsider could ever have shaken

[173]

it. For indeed we had returned so quietly to everyday life, that not the most attentive onlooker could have gauged the mystery of this secret, which already was no longer ours.

She has asked me to hear her confession to-morrow. I have made her promise to tell nobody of what passed between us, and on my side I have vowed absolute silence. 'No matter what may happen,' I said; and my heart sank with these last words, and again sadness overcame me, 'God's will be done.'

I left the Château at mid-day, and had to start at once for Dombasle. On my way back I stopped on the fringe of the wood from which one has a view of wide flat country, long scarcely visible slopes which trail slowly downwards to the sea. I had bought some bread and butter in the village and I ate it hungrily. The kind of torpor had come over me which I feel after every decisive moment, every real trial in my life: a not unpleasant dullness of thought bringing with it a strange sensation of lightness, of joy. What sort of joy? I can find no word. A shapeless joy. That which had to be, has been and is no longer—no more than that. I got back home very late and met old Clovis on the road. He gave me a small packet from Mme la Comtesse. I could not make up my mind to open it, and yet I knew what was inside. It was the little empty medallion, strung at the end of its broken chain. There was also a letter. Here it is. A curious letter:

'MONSIEUR LE CURÉ, I don't suppose you can imagine my state of mind when you left me, since all such questions of psychology probably mean nothing at all to you.

What can I say to you? I have lived in the most horrible solitude, alone with the desperate memory of a child. And it seems to me that another child has brought me to life again. I hope you won't be annoyed with me for regarding you as a child. Because you are! May God keep you one for ever!

'I wonder what you've done to me. How did you manage it? Or rather, I no longer ask myself. All's well. I didn't think one could ever possibly be resigned. And really this isn't resignation! There is no resignation in me, and there I wasn't wrong in my presentiment. I'm not resigned, I'm *happy*. I don't want anything.

'Don't expect me to-morrow. I shall go and confess to Father—as usual. I shall try to do it with as much sincerity as I can, but also as discreetly as I can. Isn't that right? All these things are so simple. Once I've said: "I've wilfully sinned against hope, every day for eleven years," I shall have told him all there is to tell. Hope! I'd held it dead in my arms, on a windy, desolate, horrible evening in March! I'd felt the last breath of hope on my cheeks, on a spot which I know. Yet *now* I hope again! This hope is really all my very own, nobody else's: no more what philosophers call "hope" than the word "love" is like being loved. This hope is the flesh of my flesh. I can't express it. I should have to speak as a little child.

'I wanted you to know all this to-night. I had to tell you. And don't let's mention it ever again. Never again. How peaceful that sounds! Never. I'm saying it under my breath as I write—and it seems to express miraculously, ineffably, the peace you've given me.'

I slipped this letter into my *Imitation*, an old book which belonged to mother, with the scent of her lavender still clinging to it, the lavender she kept in a sachet among her linen, in the old-fashioned way. She seldom read it, because the print is so small and on such thin pages that her poor fingers, rough from the wash-tub, could never manage to turn them easily.

'Never. Never again.' Why is it? Why are those words so full of peace?

I'm sleepy. To finish saying my office, I had to keep walking up and down, my eyes wouldn't stay open. Am I happy or not? I don't know.

Half-past six. Madame la Comtesse died last night.

I spent the first hours of this horrible day in a state very like rebellion. To rebel is not to understand, and I can't understand! We can usually bear trials that at first sight seem beyond our strength—which of us knows his own strength? But I felt ridiculous in my grief, unable to do anything useful, a nuisance to everyone. This shameful distress was so acute that I could not stop myself from grimacing. In window-panes, in mirrors, I saw a face which seemed disfigured less by sorrow than by fear, with the pitiful twitch that implores mercy, that looks like a hideous smile. God!

While I ran hopelessly to and fro, everyone else was displaying the greatest efficiency, and in the end they left me alone. M. le Comte seemed not even to notice me; Mlle Chantal pretended not to know I was there.

It happened at about two this morning. Mme la Comtesse slipped out of bed, and in falling broke an alarm-clock on the table, though, of course, they only found her dead body a long time afterwards. Her left arm had already begun to stiffen and was slightly bent. For several months she had been suffering from vague pains which the doctor considered of no importance; angina pectoris, no doubt.

I arrived at the Château out of breath and dripping with sweat. I don't quite know what I was hoping for. It needed a great and absurd effort to cross the threshold of her room; my teeth were chattering. Am I really so cowardly? Upon her face was a square of muslin, and I scarcely recognized her features, though I could see her lips very distinctly, where they touched the material. I longed so hard for her to smile, the enigmatic smile of the dead which goes so well with their marvellous quiet. But she wasn't smiling. Her mouth, drawn down at the right corner, had a twist of indifference, of disdain, of derision even. My hand, when I raised it to bless her, felt like lead.

By a strange coincidence two nuns had come yesterday evening to make a collection at the Château, and since this was the last stage of their rounds, M. le Comte had been intending to take them back to the station to-day in his car. So they had slept there. I found them sitting in her room, looking so small in habits too large for them, their coarse little shoes caked with mud. I'm afraid my manner disconcerted them. They kept watching me round the corner of their eyes, first one then the other, so that I couldn't concentrate. I felt like a lump of ice except for the hollow place in my chest which burned like fire. I thought I should faint. With God's help at last I managed to pray. Now I regret nothing, though I've searched my conscience through and through. What should I regret? And yet there's this: mightn't I have watched during the night, mightn't I for just a few hours longer have kept intact the memory of that talk, which would be our last? And our first also.

[177]

The first and the last! 'Am I happy or not,' I wrote. . . .
Fool that I was! I know that never before have I experienced, or shall again, hours of such fullness, so sweet, so filled with a look, a presence, a human life—sitting last night with my elbows on the table, holding between my hands the book to which I had entrusted her letter, as to a rare friend. And this which I was to lose so soon I buried of my own free will in sleep—black, dreamless sleep.

It's all over now. Already the living picture has begun to fade, and I know that my memory will keep nothing save the image of a dead woman upon whom God has set His hand. What could I expect to retain in mind of such strange happenings, through which I tapped my way like a blind man? Our Lord had need of a witness, and I was chosen, doubtless for lack of anyone better, as one calls in a passer-by. I should be crazy indeed to imagine that I had a part, a real part in it. Already it is too much that God should have given me the grace to be present when a soul became reconciled to hope again —those solemn nuptials!

At about two I had to leave the Château, and my catechism-class lasted much longer than I expected, since we're well into our quarterly exam. I should have liked to watch the night beside her body, but the nuns are still there, and His Reverence, Canon la Motte-Beuvron, an uncle of M. le Comte, has decided to watch with them. I dared not insist! And besides, M. le Comte is still very frigid in his manner towards me, almost hostile, I cannot think why.

The canon, whom I also seem quite unmistakably to exasperate, took me aside for a few minutes to ask me whether Mme la Comtesse had said anything at all about her health in the course of our interview yesterday. I could see quite well that this was a hint to me to speak. Ought I to have told him anything? I think not. I should have had to tell all. And this secret, which was never altogether mine, is mine no longer: or rather it has now been taken from me, for ever. How can I know what use might be made of it by ignorance, jealousy, perhaps even hatred? Now that this horrible rivalry has no more meaning, can I risk reviving even its memory? And not only its memory, since I fear that it might still live on for a long while. Such feelings are of the kind from which death does not always draw the sting. And what I heard, if I repeated it, might seem to justify past rancour. Mademoiselle is young, and I know by experience how lasting, sometimes ineffaceable, are youthful impressions. . . . So I only told the canon that Mme la Comtesse had expressed the wish to restore harmony in her household.

'Really?' he answered me dryly. 'Are you her confessor, then?'

'No.' I'm bound to admit that I was rather annoyed by his tone. 'I think she was ready for death,' I added. He eyed me in a rather queer way.

I went back for the last time to look at her. The nuns were saying the last decade of the rosary. Flowers and wreaths were piled up along the wall, brought by friends and relations who all day long have never stopped coming to the Château, and whose almost cheerful voices fill the house. Each minute brought a flare of headlights, a car would come flashing past the window, I heard the gravel crunch on the drive, the chauffeurs shouting to one another, the sound of motor-horns. None of all this interrupted the monotonous purr of the two good nuns; they might have been spinning.

The candle-light showed me her face through the gauze better than daylight. These few hours had appeased and softened it, and the larger rings round her closed eyelids gave her eyes a kind of pensiveness. Certainly it was still a proud face. But now it seemed to have turned away from an enemy faced and braved for so long, to sink gradually into infinite meditation, too deep to share. How far it was from us, and beyond our power! Suddenly I saw her poor thin hands crossed on her breast, very slim, very delicate, far more truly dead than her face. I even saw a little mark, a scratch which I had noticed yesterday, as she pressed the medallion to her heart. The thin strip of lint was still attached to it. I don't know why that broke my heart. The memory of her struggle before my eyes, that fight for eternal life from which she emerged exhausted, victorious, became painfully vivid, shattering. . . . How could I have known that such a day would have no to-morrow, that she and I had faced each other on the very verge of the visible world, over the gulf of All Light? Why could we not have crossed together? 'Be at peace,' I told her. And she had knelt to receive this peace. May she keep it for ever. It will be I that gave it her. Oh, miracle—thus to be able to give what we ourselves do not possess, sweet miracle of our empty hands! Hope which was shrivelling in my heart flowered again in hers; the spirit of prayer which I thought lost in me for ever was given back to her by God and—who can tell—perhaps in *my* name! Lord, I am stripped bare of all things, as you alone can strip us bare, whose fearful care nothing escapes, nor your terrible love! I lifted the muslin from her face, and stroked her high, pure forehead, full of silence. And poor as I am, an insignificant little priest, looking upon this woman only yesterday so far my superior in age, birth, fortune, intellect, I still knew—yes, knew—what fatherhood means.

My way out of the Château led through the gallery. The doors of the drawing-room and dining-room were wide open. People were crowding round the table, munching sandwiches before starting back home. Such is the custom in the neighbourhood. Some would be caught now and again unawares, by a member of the family, their cheeks swollen with food, and they would hastily struggle to look doleful and sympathetic. The old ladies—dare I write it?—had an especially famished look: it was hideous. Mlle Chantal turned her back as I passed, and I heard a kind of buzz. I think they were talking about me.

I have just been to look out of the window. Over at the Château the procession of cars continues still, like the dull sounds of a far-off party. . . . She's to be buried on Saturday.

6

First thing this morning I went round to the Château. M. le Comte sent word that he much regretted he couldn't see me, and that Canon la Motte-Beuvron would be at the presbytery round about two o'clock to discuss arrangements for the funeral. What can be happening?

The two nuns thought I looked so poorly that they were determined to ask the butler to bring a glass of port for me, which I was very glad of. This butler—a nephew of old Clovis, who is usually a very civil lad and anxious to please—was quite stiff when I spoke kindly to him. (Of course, servants in these great houses always dislike familiarity, usually of a rather tactless kind, from people of my sort.) But he was waiting at table last night, and may have overheard something. What?

Only half an hour in which to have lunch, change my cassock (it is beginning to rain again) and tidy up the house a little. It's been in an awful mess for the last few days, and I don't want to shock the canon who seems already so set against me. So I suppose I could find something better to do than sit here writing all this. Yet more than ever I need this diary. It is only during these snatched moments that I am aware of some effort to see clearly into myself. Nowadays thought comes so slowly, my memory is very bad—I mean for recent happening, not others!—my imagination so sluggish, that I must tire myself out with work in order to shake off some vague, uneasy, daydream which, alas, prayer alone cannot always dispel. As soon as I stop, I feel myself sinking into a coma which blurs into misty, pathless landscapes, in which I completely lose my bearings, the perspective of the last few days. If I keep to it strictly, morning and evening, my diary breaks up this wilderness, and sometimes I slip the last few pages into my pocket, to read them again on my long dull tramps from one end of the parish to another, when I am tempted to give way to this strange mesmerism.

Does this mean my diary is taking up too much of my life? I cannot tell. Only God can tell.

The canon has just left. Not at all the kind of priest I was expecting. Why wouldn't he be more honest and straight-forward with me? No doubt he wanted to, but these men of the world are so reined-in and anxious to avoid showing their feelings.

We began by making arrangements for the funeral, which M. le Comte wants properly done, but not extravagantly, according to the wishes often expressed by his wife. Then we both sat in silence for some time, and I began to feel very uneasy. The canon gazed up at the ceiling, mechanically opening and shutting his heavy gold watch.

'I ought to tell you,' he observed at last, 'that my nephew, Omer' (M. le Comte's name is Omer, which I didn't know) 'wishes to see you privately this evening.'

I told him I had arranged with the sacristan to help me get out the curtains for the funeral at four o'clock, and I would go straight on to the Château.

'Nonsense, my dear child, you can see him here. You go on as if you were their private chaplain! In fact I advise you to be very guarded in what you say to him. Don't be drawn into discussing any of your duties as a priest.'

'How do you mean?'

He thought a moment before answering.

'You did see my niece Chantal here, didn't you?'

'Mlle Chantal came to see me, canon.'

'She's a dangerous and difficult girl. No doubt she got round you.'

'I was very hard on her. I think I got the better of her, really.'

'She hates you.'

'I don't believe it. She fancies she hates me, canon, which isn't the same thing.'

'Do you think you can influence her?'

'Certainly not for the moment. But perhaps she'll never forget how once a poor soul like myself held out against her, and that there is no way of deceiving God.'

'Hers was a very different version.'

'She can please herself. Mademoiselle is too proud not to be ashamed sooner or later of telling lies, and she'll be ashamed of this one. To be ashamed is what she needs.'

'But you?'

'I? Why, look at my face,' I said. 'Surely if our Lord created it for anything, He made it to be slapped, and it hasn't been slapped yet.'

At that instant he happened to notice the kitchen door, which was half open, and saw the table still with its square of oil-cloth, and bread and apples (somebody brought me a windfall yesterday) and the half-empty bottle of wine.

'You don't take much care of yourself.'

'I can't digest easily,' I said. 'Very few things agree with me—just bread, fruit and wine.'

'From the look of you, I'm afraid wine will do you more harm than good. We aren't always well when we feel we are.'

I tried to explain that this was a seasoned Bordeaux I had got from the gamekeeper. He smiled. 'Father,' he began again, as though addressing an equal, almost with deference, 'we probably haven't one idea in common as to how a parish ought to be run, but you are master here, you have the right to speak, only you must be understood. I have obeyed too often in my time not to know real authority, no matter where I find it. Be discreet in the use of yours. Your power over some souls must be great. I am an old priest. I know how the seminaries mould boys down to the same ordinary level, till often there's unfortunately nothing to choose between them. But they couldn't do anything with you. And the secret of your strength lies in the fact that you are unaware, or daren't realize, how different you are from the others.'

'You can't really mean this,' I said. A vague uneasiness had possessed me; I shivered as my nerves turned cold, facing that indefinable stare.

'Father, it isn't a question of knowing the extent of one's power; what matters is how to use it. What's the good of power that's never used, or only half used? You put forth the whole of yours in major issues as in minor ones, no doubt unknowingly. Which explains many things.'

While he was saying all this he took a sheet of paper from my desk, pulled out the pen and ink and passed them to me.

'I don't need to be told what passed between you and —and the deceased,' he said. 'But I want to cut short all silly and possibly dangerous gossip. My nephew is moving heaven and earth, and His Grace is so simple that he takes him for a person of real importance. Write me a short account of your conversation the day before yesterday with the countess. I don't in the least suggest that you should disclose anything which may have been entrusted to your honour as a priest—that goes without saying—or merely to your plain discretion. Besides I promise that whatever you may write will not leave my pocket except for the benefit of His Grace. But I don't like all this talking. . . .' As I did not answer, he stared at me again, longer, with eyes deliberately extinguished —with dead eyes. There was no movement in his face. 'You don't trust me,' he went on with a quiet conviction that was unanswerable. I said I couldn't see how such a conversation could be reported at all, there had been no witness, and consequently Mme la Comtesse was the only person who could have authorized its disclosure. 'You don't know the bureaucratic mind,' he shrugged. 'If I deliver your report it will be gratefully accepted, filed, and no one will think any more about it. Otherwise you'll only get mixed up in all sorts of verbal explanations that will lead nowhere, since you'll never be able to speak their language. Even if you tell them that two and two make four, they'll still class you as hysterical, a kind of lunatic.' I said nothing. He laid his hand on my shoulder. 'Well, that's that. I'd like to see you again tomorrow, if you don't mind. Frankly I came here to-day to prepare you for my nephew's visit. But what's the use? You're not the sort who can talk without saying anything, and unfortunately that's what's wanted now.'

'But what have I done?' I exclaimed. 'What have they got against me?'

'Being what you are, there is no help for it. You see, my dear child, these people don't hate you for being simple, they're on their guard against it, that's all. Your simplicity is a kind of flame which scorches them. You go through the world with that lowly smile of yours as though you begged their pardon for being alive, while all the time you carry a torch which you seem to mistake for a crozier. Nine times out of ten they'll tear it from you, and stamp it out. Your chance is merely the tenth, you see? To tell the truth I hadn't a very high opinion of my late niece. Those Treville-Sommerange girls have always been rather a queer lot, and I believe the devil himself would have his work cut out to fetch a sigh from their lips or a tear from their eyes. Well, see my nephew, and say just what you want to him. But remember he's a fool. And don't be impressed by his name, title and the other twaddle which I fear your generosity has made too much of. There's no longer any aristocracy, my friend, get that into your head. I knew two or three real aristocrats when I was young. They were absurd creatures, but always intensely individual. They remind me of those tiny eight-inch oak trees, which the Japanese cultivate in flower-pots. The flower-pots are our customs and conventions. No family can hold out against the slow sapping process of greed, when the law is the same for everyone, and public opinion the standard. The aristocrats of to-day are only shamefaced *bourgeois*.'

I saw him out and even walked a little way with him. I think he was still expecting me to be frank, in some way to take him into my confidence, but I preferred to say nothing. I could not rid myself of certain unpleasant impressions, which in any case could not have escaped those strange eyes that returned to me every now and again, with inquisitive calm. How could I tell him that I hadn't the least idea of M. le Comte's grievance, and that we had been talking at cross-purposes without the canon's realizing it?

No use going to the church now, it is so late, the sacristan will have done all that's necessary.

M. le Comte's visit has left me still in the dark. I had cleared the table, tidied everything, but *of course* went and left the cupboard-door open. And *he* must needs look straight at the bottle of wine, just as the canon did. It's a kind of challenge. When I think of my daily fare, which would not satisfy many a pauper, I find somewhat irritating this general amazement at my drinking anything besides water. I stood up and deliberately shut the cupboard-door.

M. le Comte was most frigid, yet polite. I don't think he knew his uncle had been to see me, and I had to go into the details of the funeral all over again. He knows more than I do about the prices, haggles over the cost of candles, and even inked in the exact spot on my plan, where he wants the coffin to be. Yet he looked exhausted and really sad, even his voice seemed different, less unpleasantly nasal. And in his quiet black suit and heavy boots, he reminded me of some well-to-do peasant. This old man in his Sunday-best, I thought. Is this, then, the husband, the father? . . . How glibly we talk about 'family-life,' as we do also of 'my country.' We ought to say many prayers for families. Families frighten me. May God be merciful with them.

Yet I am sure the canon was right. M. le Comte, for all his efforts to hide it, became gradually more on edge. At last I thought he was going to speak out, but then a dreadful thing happened. Rummaging in my desk to find a printed form we needed, I had scattered papers all over the place. As I was hurriedly sorting them, I fancied I heard him catch his breath behind me; I waited and waited for him to say something, intentionally taking my time. At last the sensation became so acute that I swung round and nearly bumped into him. He was standing right behind me, looking very uncomfortable and holding out a folded sheet of paper that had slipped under the table. It was her letter. I nearly gave a cry, and as I took it from him he must have known I was trembling, for our fingers touched. Somehow I think he was afraid. After a few trivial remarks we parted formally. I am to go to the Château to-morrow morning.

I have watched all night: day is beginning. My window has been open, and I am shivering. I can hardly hold this pen, but I seem to be breathing more freely, to be calmer. Though I got no sleep, this cold which goes right through me does just as well. An hour or two ago when I was praying, squatting on my heels with my cheek against the wooden table, I suddenly felt such a hollow emptiness, I thought I was going to die. It made me happy.

Fortunately there was a little wine left in the bottle. I drank it, very hot and sugared. Obviously a man of my age can hardly expect to keep up his strength on a few glasses of wine, vegetables, and an occasional rasher of bacon. I am making a serious mistake in repeatedly putting off going to see the Lille specialist.

I don't think I'm a coward, but it's so hard to struggle against a sort of torpor which isn't indifference, nor is it resignation: almost in spite of myself I seek in it a remedy for all my pain. It is very easy to surrender to God's will when it is proved to you day after day that you can do no good. But in the end one would thankfully accept, as divine favours, set-backs and humiliations which are simply the inevitable results of our folly. This diary is of immense help in forcing me to see my own share of responsibility in so much bitter disappointment. And now again, I've only to set pen to paper to awaken in me the knowledge of my deep inexplicable incompetence, superhuman clumsiness.

(Who, a quarter of an hour ago, would have thought I could ever have written that! It's quite wise. Yet there it is.)

Went round to the Château yesterday morning as I had promised. It was Mlle Chantal who opened the door to me. Which put me on my guard. I hoped she would receive me in the lounge, but instead she almost pushed me into the small drawing-room where the blinds were drawn. The broken fan was still on the mantelpiece, behind the clock. I think she caught me looking at it. Her face was harder than ever. She was about to sit down in the armchair where two days earlier— Just then I thought there was a gleam in her eyes, and I said: 'Mademoiselle, I haven't much time, and I would rather stand.'

She flushed, her lips twitched angrily.

'Why?'

'Because I have no business to be here—nor have you.'

She said a horrible thing then, so out of keeping with her youth that I can only think a devil prompted her. She said: 'I'm not afraid of dead people.' I turned my back on her. She darted to the door, barring my way with outspread arms. 'Do you want me to pretend? I *would* pray if I could. I've even tried to. How can I pray with *this* inside me . . . ? And she touched her breast.

'What?'

'Call it what you like, I call it joy. Of course you'll say I'm a monster?'

'There are no monsters.'

'If the next world's all they make out, mother'll understand now. She never loved me. She loathed me ever since my brother died. You want the truth, don't you?'

'My opinion wouldn't matter to you. . . .'

'You know it does, but you won't deign to admit it. You're just as proud as me, really.'

'You talk as a child,' I said. 'And you blaspheme as a child, too.' I moved towards the door, but she caught hold of the handle.

'The governess is packing up. She goes on Thursday. You see, what I want, I get.'

'What use is that? It won't help you. If you stay as you are, you'll aways find something to hate. And were you able to understand, I would even tell you—'

'What?'

'Well—it's your own self you hate, just you.'

She thought. 'Oh, stuff!' She said at last, 'I *shall* hate myself if I don't get everything I want. I mean to be happy, or—it's their fault, anyway. Keeping me cooped up in this rotten hole. I'll bet some girls would find out how to let off steam even here. It does you good. But I can't bear "scenes." I think they're foul. I'd rather put up with anything, and make no fuss. It's great fun I can tell you, when you're seeing red, to sit quiet as a mouse over your sewing, with your eyes demurely lowered, biting your tongue: great fun! Mother was like that, you know. We would sit for hours, stitching away side by side, caught up in our dreams and frustrations—and father blissfully unaware! At such times, there's an odd feeling of something huge growing inside you, and the whole of your life wouldn't be long enough to let it all out. . . . Of course you'll think I'm just a hypocrite, and lying.'

'What I think of you is known to God alone.'

'That's just what makes me so wild. Nobody knows what you really think. But I'm going to *make* you see me as I really am. Is it true that there are people who see one's soul? How do they do it?'

'Aren't you ashamed of talking such nonsense? Do you suppose I haven't realized by now that you have wronged me—I don't know how—and that you're itching to shout it in my face.'

'Oh, I see. You're going to start talking about "forgiving" now, and play at being a little martyr.'

'Get that out of your head,' I said. 'The Master I serve is a powerful one, and as a priest I can only absolve in His name. Charity isn't what we suppose, and if you'll only think over all you have learnt, you'll have to agree with me. There's a time for mercy and a time for justice, and the only final grief is one day to stand impenitent under Merciful Eyes.'

'All right, I shan't tell you anything.'

She moved away from the door to let me pass. As I

went out there was a last picture of her, back against the wall, arms hanging loose, her head low on her breast.

M. le Comte did not come in until a quarter of an hour later. He was fresh in from the fields with muddy boots and a pipe in his mouth. He was looking quite happy. I thought he smelled slightly of drink. He seemed surprised to see me.

'My daughter will have given you the papers—details of my mother-in-law's funeral at which your predecessor officiated. I want this one to be much the same.'

'Unfortunately prices have risen since then.'

'Talk it over with my daughter.'

'But mademoiselle gave me no papers.'

'How's that? Haven't you seen her?'

'Yes, I've just been talking to her.'

'Well, I'm—! Call mademoiselle,' he said to the parlour-maid. Mademoiselle was still in the small drawing-room. I should think she was just behind the door, for she appeared at once. M. le Comte's expression altered so rapidly, I was amazed. He looked extremely uneasy. She eyed him sadly with a smile, as one does a wayward child. She even nodded across to me. Uncanny poise in one so young!

'M. le Curé and I were talking of other things,' she said sweetly. 'I think you should give him a free hand, all this red-tape and haggling is absurd. And, by the way, you must sign that cheque for Mlle Ferrnand. Remember she's leaving to-night.'

'What d'you mean, to-night? Won't she be at the funeral? Won't everyone think it very odd?'

'Everyone? I don't suppose anyone is likely to miss her. Anyhow, she wants to go.'

Obviously I was making M. le Comte feel uncomfortable, he was red to the ears. But his daughter's voice was still perfectly poised, so calm, that he found it impossible not to take her tone.

'Six months wages,' he muttered, 'I call that extravagance, ridiculous. . . .'

'But that's what you and mother decided when you were considering giving her notice. Besides three thousand francs will only just be enough for her cruise, poor old thing—the fare's two thousand five hundred.'

'What cruise? I thought she was going to her aunt's at Lille for a rest.'

'Oh, no! She's been yearning for a Mediterranean cruise for the last ten years. Why shouldn't she have a good time for once? Life here wasn't much fun for her anyway.'

M. le Comte decided to be cross.

'All right, all right, keep that sort of remark to yourself. Well, what are you waiting for now?'

'The cheque. Your cheque-book's in the desk in the drawing-room.'

'Go to blazes!'

'Just as you please, father. I was only hoping to get you out of going over it all with mademoiselle—she's terribly upset.'

Now, for the first time he looked his daughter full in the face. She met his eyes with surprised innocence, and though I feel convinced she was playing a vile part, yet there was something in her attitude, a precocious, bitter, still childish dignity, that moved me.

Certainly she was judging her father, and this judgment was final, no doubt implacable, yet with sadness in it. And it was not scorn which put this elderly man at her mercy—it was this same sadness. For he had nothing in him, alas, to harmonize with such pain: he did not understand it.

'All right, I'll make out the cheque,' he said. 'Come back in ten minutes.' She smiled her thanks. He turned to me rather stiffly: 'She's a very delicate, sensitive child, she has to be humoured. The governess didn't humour her sufficiently. Her poor mother was able to keep the peace between them, but now—' He walked ahead of me into the dining-room, but didn't offer me a chair. 'M. le Curé,' he went on, 'I'll be frank with you. I respect the clergy, my people have always been on excellent terms with your predecessors, but those were terms of mutual deference, respect, and very occasionally friendship. I won't have a priest meddling in my family affairs.'

'Sometimes we get involved without wishing it,' I said.

'You've been the cause—the unwilling, or at least un-conscious cause—of—er—a great misfortune. I want this talk you have just had with my daughter to be the last. Everyone, even your superiors, would agree that a priest as young as you are, couldn't expect to be the spiritual adviser of a girl of that age. Chantal is already far too impressionable. Of course I've nothing against religion. But the first duty of the church is to preserve the family and society, to condemn indulgence, to stand for order and moderation in all things.'

'How should I be the cause of your misfortune?' I asked.

'My uncle La Motte-Beuvron will enlighten you on that point. It is enough, now, for you to know that I disapprove of your indiscretions, and that your character' —he paused a moment—'your character *as well as your— habits,* is in my opinion a real danger to this parish. Good morning.'

He turned his back. I did not venture to go upstairs. I feel we should only approach the dead when we ourselves are calm. I was too unhinged by what had been said to me, and could find no meaning for it. My character, if you like, but why habits? What habits?

I walked back home along the lane, for some unknown reason called Paradise Lane: a muddy pathway between hedges. Then I had to rush straight to the church, where the sacristan had been waiting for a long time. My altar furnishings are in a terrible condition, and there is no doubt I should have avoided a lot of trouble by going over them carefully at an earlier date.

The sacristan is a rather surly old man, but his peevish and almost uncivil manner masks a capricious, fantastic mind. More often than one thinks, peasants possess this odd, almost feminine quality which we imagine to be the sole privilege of the 'idle rich.' God knows how many of them are not so much as aware of this hidden fragility—creatures walled-in for generations by their own silence, deep beyond their means of breaking it, and even beyond all urge towards release, for workaday toil is so innocently linked in their thought with the slow unfolding of dreams. Until a day when— Oh, my isolated poor!

After beating the dust out of the hangings we sat down for a rest in the sacristy on the long *prie-dieu*. I saw him bending forward into the shadow, his huge hands patiently clasped around gaunt knees, and his sparse grey hair gleaming with perspiration, plastered to his brow.

'What does the parish think of me?' I asked suddenly. As I had never discussed anything important with him before, such a question could well have seemed ridiculous; I hardly expected an answer. And he certainly made me wait for it.

'They be sayin' you don't eat nothin',' he growled at last in a hollow voice, 'an' that you go spinnin' yarns at your catechism class enough to turn them little girls' 'eads.'

'And what do *you* say, Arsène?'

There was an even longer pause this time, so I turned away and went on with what I was doing.

'I don't think you be old enough—'

I tried to laugh, though I wasn't feeling like it: 'That'll come with time, Arsène.'

But he went on patiently, stubbornly thinking it out, without attending to me.

'A priest's like a lawyer—'e's there if you be needin' 'im. 'E don't need to go meddlin' with folk.'

'But look here, Arsène, a lawyer works for himself. I work for our Lord. People don't often come to God all on their own.'

He had picked up his stick and was propping his chin with it. He might have been asleep.

'To God'—he went on at last—'to God, you sez. I be seventy-three year old and I ain't never seen it 'appen yet. Everybody's born one way an' dies the same way. All our folk be church folk. Me granfer was a bell-ringer at Lyons, me poor old ma was in service with M. le Curé de Wilman, an' there b'ain't one o' ours passed on without the sacrament. It be in our blood, no gettin' away from it.'

'You'll meet them all again in heaven,' I said.

This time he thought for ages. I was watching him round the corner of my eye, whilst still at my work, having given up all hope of his speaking again, when he pronounced this final oracle, in a frayed and unforgettable voice—a voice which seemed to issue from the dust of the ages:

'When you be dead, everythin' be dead.'

I pretended not to understand. I didn't feel able to reply, and anyhow what was the use?

Such blasphemy he couldn't really have meant; he was merely expressing his failure to imagine that eternal life, of which his limited experience denied him proof. But the simple wisdom of his kind yet assured him of its reality, and he believed blindly, without expression—a legitimate, though grumbling—heir to those countless baptized forebears of his. . . . Nevertheless, his words froze me, and suddenly I had lost heart. I said I felt ill and left him, walking home alone in the wind and rain.

Now that I have got this down I am staring bewildered at the open window, and the night outside, at the mess on my table, at all the myriad odd signs in which, as in weird hieroglyphics, I alone can read the agony of the last few hours. Is my mind clearer? Or has the very knife of my uneasiness which led me to associate various incidents, unimportant in themselves, become blunted with weariness, sleeplessness and disgust? I can't tell. It all seems grotesque now. Why didn't I demand of M. le Comte the explanation which Canon la Motte-Beuvron himself considered necessary? In the first place because I suspect some vile trick of Mlle Chantal's, which I dread discovering. And then, so long as Mme la Comtesse still lies under her own roof, let them hold their tongues! Later, maybe— But there won't be any later. My position in the parish has now become so precarious that

M. le Comte's request to His Grace will certainly be successful.

Nevertheless, as I read these pages, and though I can find no real fault with them, they appear very futile. No reasoning yet has ever created real grief—grief of the spirit. Or conquered it, once it has come into us, God knows through what gap in our being. . . . Such grief did not enter, it was within us. More and more firmly am I convinced that what we call sadness, anguish, despair, as though to persuade ourselves that these are only states of the Spirit, are the Spirit itself. I believe that ever since his fall, man's condition is such that neither around him nor within him can he perceive anything, except in the form of agony.

I have shut the window and lit the fire. One of my sub-parishes is so distant that I have a dispensation from fasting on days when I go there to say mass. So far I have not availed myself of it. I am going to warm a bowl of wine and sugar for myself to-day.

Have read the Countess' letter again. I seem to see her and hear her voice—'I don't want anything.' Her long ordeal was over, fulfilled. Mine is just beginning. Is it the same? Maybe God has wished to bind to *my* shoulders the burden from which He has released His weary servant. Whence came that joy shot through with fear, that menacing sweetness, at the very moment I blessed her? The woman to whom I had given absolution, whom death was to win a few hours later on the threshold of her tranquil room so peaceful in its security (I remember how the next day they had found her watch still hanging on the wall where she had placed it the night before), already belonged to the unseen world. Unknowingly I had seen, mirrored on her brow, the final peace of the Dead.

Surely that must be paid for.

(N.B.—Several pages here have been torn out, in haste apparently. A few words in the margins are illegible, having been erased so violently that in many places the pen has pierced the paper.

One page remains intact with these few lines:)

Resolved though I am not to destroy this diary, I felt bound to take out these pages, written in what really amounted to delirium. And I wish to bear witness against myself that this trial—the greatest disappointment of my wretched life, for I can imagine none worse—found me at first unresigned and without courage, and I was tempted to . . .

(The sentence is unfinished, a few lines are missing at the top of the following page.)

. . . 'which will have to be severed, at all costs.' 'What d'you mean, at all costs?' I said. 'I don't understand. All these subtleties are beyond me. I'm only a wretched little priest who asks simply to pass unnoticed. If I *do* make mistakes they can't be so big, if I *do* make a fool of myself, people should laugh. And besides, couldn't they give me time to see my way? But there it is, we're short of priests. And whose fault is that? Picked troops, as they're called, go off to the monasteries, and it's mere peasants like me that are left for the parishes. And you know perfectly well I'm not even a peasant. Real peasants look down on our sort, lackeys, servants who get sent anywhere as their masters choose, when we're not rogues, poachers, useless rabble, not fit to mix with decent folk. Oh, I'm not saying I'm a fool. Better if I were. Neither saint nor hero, nor even—'

'Shut up,' said the Curé de Torcy. 'Don't be so childish.' The wind was keen, and suddenly I saw his dear face quite blue with the cold. 'Get in here, I'm frozen.' It was the little hut where Clovis stacks his firewood. 'I can't go home with you now, what 'ud they think? Besides, M. Bigre of the garage is driving me back to Torcy. You see really I should've stayed a few days longer in Lille. This weather's no good to me.'

'So you came for my sake?' I asked. At first he shrugged his shoulders, angrily.

'What about the funeral? Anyway, that's none of your business, my dear boy—I do as I like. Come and see me to-morrow.'

'Neither to-morrow, nor the next day, nor this week, in all probability, unless—'

'Don't talk about "unless" to me. Come or don't come. You work things out too much. You get your adverbs all muddled. Life ought to be as clearly constructed as a French sentence. Each one of us serves God in his own way, in his own language. . . . But you—your very appearance, your manner, that cloak, for instance!'

'Cloak? My aunt gave it me.'

'You look like a romantic German poet. As for your face!' His expression was one I had never known in him, one of hate almost. I think at first he forced himself to speak severely, but now his hardest words came of their own accord, and perhaps he disliked not being able to stop them.

'I can't help my face,' I said.

'Yes, you can. In the first place you feed yourself

ridiculously. I ought to give you a good talking to about
that. I wonder if it's ever dawned on you how—' He
broke off. 'No, that can wait,' he went on in a softer
tone. 'We can't discuss it here in this shed. Anyway,
your meals are just idiotic, and then you wonder why
you get a pain. . . . If I went on like that I'd have pains
in the belly too. And as for your soul, my boy, I fear it's
much the same. You don't pray enough. You suffer so
much you *can't* pray, if you want my opinion. We
should eat in proportion to the work we do, and pray
according to the measure of our troubles.'

'It's because I can't pray!' I cried out. And then I
wished I hadn't said it, for his eyes went hard.

'If you can't pray—at least *say* your prayers! Look!
I've done some struggling in my time, too. The devil
used to make me loathe prayers so, once, that I'd sweat
all over my rosary getting through it. Try to realize
that!'

'Oh, I *realize*—' I said, so readily that he looked
me closely up and down, but without malice—almost
kindly. . . .

'Listen,' he said, 'I don't think I've been wrong about
you. Will you try and answer this? Mind you, I only
give you my test for what it's worth—it's simply a notion of mine, a way of taking my bearings, and naturally
it's landed me in the soup many a time. I've thought a
lot about the question of vocation. We're all called to
the priesthood, I agree, but not always in the same way.
So to get things straight I start off by taking each one
of us back where he belongs in Holy Writ. It makes us
a couple o' thousand years younger, but what of it?
Time doesn't worry our Lord, He sees right the way
through. I tell myself that long before we were born—

from a "human" point of view—Jesus met us somewhere, in Bethlehem, or perhaps Nazareth, or along the road to Galilee—anywhere. And one day among all the other days, His eyes happened to rest upon you and me and so we were called, each in his own particular way, according to the time, place and circumstance. This isn't theology, I'm preaching. . . . It's simply my own imagination, what I think, what I dream. It amounts to this: If the un-forgetting soul in us, which remembers eternally, could yank its wretched body back across the centuries, up this huge slope of two thousand years, we should be taken back to that very spot where— Now, what's wrong? What on earth's the matter?' I hadn't realized there were tears on my face, I wasn't even thinking of it. 'What are you blubbering for?' The truth is that *my* place for all time has been Mount Olivet yes, in that instant—strangely in that very instant, when He set His hand on Peter's shoulder asking him the useless question, almost naïve yet so tender, so deeply courteous: *Why sleep ye?* It was a very ordinary, natural reaction of which till then I had been unaware. And suddenly— 'What's up now?' The Curé de Torcy snapped again, irritably. 'You're not even listening to me, you're dreaming. Lad, if you want to pray, you mustn't dream. Prayers seep out of you in dreams. Nothing worse for the soul than losing blood like that.'

I opened my mouth. I meant to answer, but couldn't. Never mind. Isn't it enough that Our Lord this day should have granted me, through the lips of my old teacher, the revelation that I am never to be torn from that eternal place chosen for me—that I remain the prisoner of His Agony in the Garden. Who would dare take such an honour upon himself?

I dried my eyes and wiped my nose, so awkwardly that the Curé smiled.

'I didn't know you were such a baby, sonny, you're almost played out.' (But as he spoke he was watching me so closely again that I had great difficulty in not telling him. I saw his eyes going round the edge of my secret. Yes, he's a judge of souls—a master!) At last he shrugged, as though giving it up. 'Well, that'll do for now. We can't stick in this shed all day. After all, perhaps Almighty God intends to keep you in sorrow. But I always think these worries, however much they may try us at the time, shouldn't warp our wisdom when the saving of a soul is at stake. I've been hearing all sorts of disturbing things about you. Still, I know how spiteful people can be. But you did behave like an ass with the poor dear Countess—you were showing off!'

'I don't know what you mean.'

'Did you ever read *The Hostage*, by Paul Claudel?' I said I hadn't the slightest idea of whom or what he was talking. 'So much the better. It's all about a holy young woman who listens to a priest like you. She goes back on her word, marries an old rip, and frets herself silly—the whole idea being to save the Pope from going to prison. As though, ever since the days of St. Peter, that wouldn't be a more suitable place for a Pope, than a palace daubed all over by those Renaissance painters—the rascals—who had their trollops pose as Our Lady! Mind you, Claudel's a genius in his way, I'm not denying it, but writers are all the same: when they get on to holy things they wallow in the sublime—they lay it on thick. Sanctity has nothing to do with being sublime, and if I'd had that heroine in my confessional I'd have made her change that silly bird's name to a proper Christian name for a start:

she was called "Swan," of all things! And then I'd have told her to stick to her word, because once you've broken it, even His Holiness the Pope can't mend it for you.'

'But where do I come in?'

'All that medallion business!'

'What medallion?' I couldn't understand.

'You were *seen*, you ass, you were *heard*. Don't worry, there's no miracle about it.'

'Who saw us?'

'Her daughter. But surely La Motte-Beuvron's told you—don't look so blank!'

'No.'

'What d'you mean, no? Well, I've put my foot in it properly. Suppose I'd better go on now.' I remained silent and had become cooler. If Mlle Chantal had turned things round, she had done it skilfully, and I might be caught up in a network of half-truths from which I could not hope to cut clear, without the risk myself of betraying the dead. M. le Curé looked amazed at my silence.

'I wonder what you mean by resignation. . . . Forcing a mother to throw the last memory of her dead child into the fire—why, it's like some Jewish tale—there's quite an Old Testament smack about it. And what right had you to speak of eternal separation? You can't blackmail souls, my lad.'

'You put it that way,' I said, 'I could put it differently. But what's the use? The essentials are true.'

'And is that all you can say?'

'Yes.'

I thought he was about to be very angry; but he had turned pale, almost livid, and I knew then how much he loved me.

'Don't let's hang around here any longer,' he muttered, 'and mind you don't see that girl again—she's a fiend!'

'I shall not refuse her, I shall refuse no one so long as I am a priest of this parish.'

'She says her mother fought against you to the last, that you left her in a terrible state, distracted. Is that true?'

'No.'

'Well how *did* you leave her?'

'I left her with God—in peace.'

'Ah.' (He gave a deep sigh.) 'But suppose she died confronted with your pitiless demands?'

'She died in peace.'

'How do you know?' I wasn't even tempted to speak of the letter. If the words didn't sound ridiculous, I would say that now I was silence itself. Silence and night. 'Anyway, she's dead. What are people to think? Scenes like that don't help anyone with a bad heart.'

I held my tongue, and on this we parted.

I walked slowly home. I wasn't unhappy. I even felt delivered of a great burden. That talk with M. le Curé de Torcy was as a dress-rehearsal for many others with my superiors, and almost with joy I found I had nothing to say. For two days, without being really aware of it, I had dreaded being accused of something I had never done. Then I should have been bound to speak. Instead I was free. Free to let them judge my actions from all their different points of view. It was also a great relief to think that Mlle Chantal may have been honestly mistaken regarding the nature of a conversation which probably she had only half heard. I expect she was in the garden, under the unusually high window.

Back in the presbytery I was quite surprised to find

I was hungry. My store of apples is not yet exhausted—
I bake them with fresh butter. I've plenty of eggs, too.
My wine's certainly not as good as it was, but warmed
up with sugar it's not too bad. Feeling so chilly I filled
my small saucepan this time. It holds enough for a large
glass, no more, I swear. Just as I was finishing my meal,
in came M. le Curé de Torcy. I could scarcely move for
sheer surprise. When at last I stumbled to my feet I must
have looked quite wild. In getting up I knocked over the
bottle with my left hand and sent it crashing. Black,
muddy wine trickled over the tiles.

'My poor child,' he said. And he kept repeating in a
gentle voice: 'So that's it? . . . That's how it is. . . .' For
the moment I didn't understand, I could understand
nothing, except that this strange peace within me was
once again the prelude to trouble. 'That's not even wine
—it's foul stuff. You're just poisoning yourself, you fool!'

'It's all I've got.'

'You should've asked me for some.'

'I swear that—'

'You hold your tongue.' He kicked the broken bottle
into a corner, as though it was something filthy. I waited
for him to finish, I couldn't speak. 'My poor lad, how
can you expect to look fit with that juice inside you?
It's a wonder you're even alive!' He faced me, both
hands deep in the pockets of his cassock, and a certain
bracing of his shoulders warned me that he was going to
say it all now, that he wasn't going to spare me. 'I was
too late for M. Bigre's car. Glad I was, now! Sit down.'

'No,' I said. And I felt my voice weakening inside me,
as it always does when some secret instinct tells me the
time has come, that I've got to square up to things. Which
doesn't always mean to oppose. I even believe I could

have confessed anything then, to have been left in peace, alone with God. But nothing in the world could have stopped my standing up.

'Look,' he went on, 'I'm not mad with you. And don't imagine I'm calling you a drunkard. Friend Delbende put his finger on the spot from the word go. Most of us country-folk have the drink in our blood. Your lot may have taken to it no more than the rest, maybe less, but they'd poor stuff to eat, or didn't eat at all. And lacking better, they swilled themselves with that kind of brew—fit to kill a horse. So you see, this thirst was bound to get you in the end, and all said and done it isn't even yours. And mind you it lasts, it goes on for centuries—poor people's thirst! It's a certain legacy! Five wealthy generations can't always slake it: it's in the bones, in the marrow. No good saying none of this ever dawned on you —I know it didn't. And even if you say you take about as much a day as an old maid, that makes no difference. You're pickled in it, poor lad! And slowly you've drifted into the way of getting from wine—and what wine!—the strength and pluck you'll find in a piece of good honest steak—thick steak. The worst that can happen to us mortals is to die, and you were in a fair way to killing yourself. And it 'ud be no consolation thinking you put yourself under the sod with a dose that wouldn't even keep an Anjou vine-dresser in normal health and joy! And mind, you weren't offending Our Lord. But now I've warned you, sonny, you would offend Him next time.'

He paused. Unconsciously I was looking at him as I had looked at Mitonnet, or mademoiselle, or— Yes, the same sadness flooded me. But this is a man of strength and peace, a true servant of God—a man. He too was squaring up to it. As across a wide, invisible road, from afar, we seemed to be saying good-bye.

'And now,' he ended, rather more hoarse than usual, 'don't go getting ideas into your head. I've told you straight what I think. And you're a jolly decent little priest, anyway! I don't want to say anything against the poor departed lady, but on the other hand—'

'Please don't,' I interrupted.

'Very well.' I wanted to leave him, as I had in the gardener's hut an hour ago. But now he was my guest, so I had to wait. And then—thanks be to God—my old teacher didn't fail me after all; once again he gave me of his best. His troubled eyes were suddenly themselves again, his voice was the voice I knew: robust, fearless and strangely gay.

'Go on with your work,' he said. 'Keep at the little daily things that need doing, till the rest comes. Concentrate. Think of a lad at his homework, trying so hard and his tongue sticking out. That's how Our Lord would have us be when He gives us up to our own strength. Little things—they don't look much, yet they bring peace. Like wild flowers which seem to have no scent, till you get a field full of 'em. And he who prays for little things—is innocent. There's an angel in every little thing. Do you pray to angels?'

'Why—yes—of course.'

'We don't pray often enough to the angels. Theologians are always a bit scared of them because of old eastern heresies—just a nervous complex. The world is full of angels. And what of Our Lady? Do you pray to Our Lady?'

'Why, naturally!'

'We all say that—but do you pray to her as you should,

as befits her? She is Our Mother—the mother of all flesh, a new Eve. But she is also our daughter. The ancient world of sorrow, the world before the access of grace, cradled her to its heavy heart for many centuries, dimly awaiting a *virgo genetrix*. For centuries and centuries those ancient hands, so full of sin, cherished the wondrous girl-child whose name even was unknown. A little girl, the queen of the Angels! And she's *still* a little girl, remember! The Middle Ages understood that well enough. They understood everything. But you can't stop fools from reconstructing "the drama of the Incarnation," as they call it! People who seem to think it adds to the dignity of a simple magistrate to dress him up like Punch, and plaster gold braid over a station-master's sleeve, are too nervous to tell unbelievers that the one and only drama, the drama of dramas—since there is no other—was played without scenery, was never really staged. Think of it! The Word was made Flesh and not one of the journalists of those days even knew it was happening! When surely their experience should have taught them that true greatness, even human greatness, genius and courage, love, too—that "love" of theirs—it's the devil to recognize 'em! So that ninety-nine times out of a hundred they have to take bouquets of rhetoric to the graves. The dead alone receive their homage. The blessedness of God! The simplicity of God, that terrible simplicity which damned the pride of the angels. Yes, the devil must have taken one look at it, and the huge flaming torch at the peak of creation was plunged down into the night. The Jews were certainly pretty dense, or they'd have known that God-become-man, achieving man-made perfection might well pass unnoticed—you had to keep your eyes skinned. That triumphant entry into Jerusalem, for instance—so lovely! Our Lord deigned to taste of human triumph, as of other things, as of death. He rejected none of our joys, He only rejected sin. His death! What a good job of it He made, not one thing lacking! But His triumph is one for children, don't you think? There's a painting of Epinal with the baby donkey and its mother, the palms, and country folk clapping their hands. A charming, slightly ironical parody of royal splendour. Our Lord seems to smile. Our Lord often smiles. He says to us: "Don't take all these things too seriously, though there *are* permissible triumphs: as when Joan of Arc shall ride again into Orleans under flowers and banners, in fine cloth-of-gold—I don't want her to think she's doing wrong. As you're so keen on it, My poor babes, I have sanctified your triumph, I have blessed it, as I blessed the wine from your vineyards." And it's just the same with miracles. He performs no more than necessary. Miracles are the pictures—the pretty pictures in the book. But remember this, lad, Our Lady knew neither triumph nor miracle. Her Son preserved her from the least tip-touch of the savage wing of human glory. No one has ever lived, suffered, died in such simplicity, in such deep ignorance of her own dignity, a dignity crowning her above angels. For she was *born* without sin—in what amazing isolation! A pool so clear, so pure, that even her own image—created only for the sacred joy of the Father—was not to be reflected. The Virgin was Innocence. Think what we must seem to her, we humans. Of course she hates sin, but after all she has never known it, that experience which the holiest saints have never lacked, St. Francis of Assisi himself, seraphic though he may be. The eyes of Our Lady are the only real child-eyes that have ever been raised to our shame and sorrow.

[211]

Yes, lad, to pray to her as you should, you must feel those eyes of hers upon you: they are not indulgent—for there is no indulgence without something of bitter experience—they are eyes of gentle pity, wondering sadness, and with something more in them, never yet known or expressed, something which makes her younger than sin, younger than the race from which she sprang, and though a mother, by grace, Mother of all grace, our little youngest sister.'

'Thank you,' I said. I could think of nothing else to say. And I spoke so coldly, too. 'I would like you to bless me,' I went on, in the same voice. Actually, for ten minutes I had been fighting with pain, my horrible pain that had never been so urgent before. God, the ache itself would be bearable! But now this dreadful sickness takes the heart right out of me. We were in the doorway.

'You're in trouble,' he said. '*You* must bless me.' And he took my hand and raised it quickly to his brow. Then he was gone. There was certainly a strong wind blowing, but for the first time I saw he hadn't straightened his tall figure: he walked bowed.

After he had gone I sat for a while in my kitchen; I didn't want to think too much. If what has happened, I thought, seems of such importance to me now, it's because I believe myself to be innocent. Certainly there are many priests who can be unwise, and that's all I'm accused of. It's very likely that emotion *did* hasten the death of Mme la Comtesse, and M. le Curé de Torcy is only mistaken therefore with regard to the real nature of our conversation. Extraordinary though it may appear, this idea has brought me relief. Shall I, who am always deeply conscious of my failings, hesitate to class myself with all the other mediocre priests? Perhaps my first successes at school were so sweet to the unhappy little boy I then was, that the memory of them has lingered in spite of everything. I can't quite stomach the idea that after being a 'brilliant' scholar—too brilliant!— I must now sit on a back bench with the duffers. I tell myself, too, that M. le Curé's last reproach wasn't as unjust as it first seemed. Not that I've an uneasy conscience about it: the way I feed, which he finds so preposterous, isn't of my own choosing. My inside will stand no other, and that's that. Anyway, his mistake will have shocked nobody. Dr. Delbende must have prepared the ground, and the silly incident of the broken bottle merely confirmed a preconceived opinion.

Finally I smiled at my fears. No doubt Mme Pégriot, Mitonnet, M. le Comte, and one or two others, are well aware that I take my wine. What of it? It would be ridiculous to accuse me—as though of a crime—of what is at most mere greediness, and shared by many of my colleagues. And God knows I'm not called greedy.

(I haven't touched this diary for the last two days; I've been loath to continue with it. But on second thoughts I fear this is no valid scruple, but rather a sense of shame. So I shall try and go on till the end. . . .)

After the Curé de Torcy had gone I went out. I had to inquire about a parishioner, M. Duclos, who was ill. I found him dying. Yet the doctor had said it was only a mild attack of pneumonia; but he's a big man and his heart gave out suddenly. His wife was crouching by the hearth, calmly getting herself a cup of coffee. She was quite indifferent. She merely said: 'Mebbe you're right—

'e's goin'.' A few minutes later she lifted up the sheet and remarked again: ' 'E's losin' 'is 'old. This be the finish.' When I got back with the Holy Oils, he was dead.

I'd been hurrying. And I shouldn't have drunk her large cup of black coffee and gin. Gin makes me sick. Dr. Delbende's idea must be right. My nausea is so like that of repletion, a horrible repletion. The smell is enough. My tongue seems to swell like a sponge in my mouth.

I should have gone home. At home, alone in my room, experience has slowly taught me many dodges which some might laugh at, yet they have helped me to tackle my pain, to ease it. Anyone in constant pain will soon realize how it has to be got round, how cunning will get the better of it. Each pain has its particular personality and method, but they are all stupidly spiteful, and a defence which has worked once can be repeated again and again. At all events, though I knew this was no trifling attack, I made the mistake of trying to hold out against it. Which God allowed. But I was the loser.

It was soon dark. To make matters worse I had to pay some more calls on the outskirts of Galbat, where the roads are very bad. It wasn't raining, but the clay soil stuck to my soles—it never dries till August. At each cottage they made room for me round the stove piled with huge lumps of Bruays coal. My head was throbbing, and as I could hardly hear what they said, my replies were rather haphazard—I must have appeared very strange! Still, I stuck it out; a round of the backwaters of Galbat is always exhausting, as the houses lie so far apart dotted over the meadows, and I wanted to get it all over in one evening. Every now and then I stole a glance at my notebook, crossing out names as I went on—the list seemed endless. When it was all over I felt so ill I couldn't face the main road again, so I followed the edge of the wood. This way led me very close to the Dumouchels' whom I wanted to see. For the last two weeks Seraphita hadn't turned up to catechism, and I had decided to speak to her father. I trudged on quite confidently at first. My pain seemed less violent, I mostly felt giddy and sick. I clearly remember getting beyond the bend of Auchy wood. A little further on I must have fainted for the first time. I thought I was still struggling on, yet I felt the icy clay against my cheek. At last I got up. I even hunted for my rosary amongst the brambles. My poor head was played out. Visions of the Virgin Child, as M. le Curé had described her, kept on appearing to me, and however hard I tried to regain complete consciousness, my prayers merged into dreams which at times I realized were absurd. Impossible to say how long I had been walking thus. Happy or otherwise, these ghosts were no good to the terrible pain, doubling me. This alone, I believe, kept me from sinking into madness, it was the one anchorage in this tide of vain fantasies. Here as I write they still pursue me, but fill me with no remorse, thank heaven, since my mind would not accept them, refused such boldness. . . . How powerful are the words of a man of God! Not that I ever believed in a vision in the accepted sense: I can swear that I did not, since the memory of wretchedness, of indignity clings to me still. Yet the picture shaping itself in me was not of those that can be welcomed or repelled at will. Dare I even write it down?

(Ten lines crossed out here.)

. . . the sublime being whose tiny hands hushed the thunder, hands full of graces—I watched her hands. I kept seeing them and not seeing them, and as the pain surged up in me and I felt myself reeling again, I caught one of those hands in mine. It was a child's hand—a child of the poor—rough already from the wash-tub. And then—how can I express it?—I didn't want it to be a dream, yet I remember closing my eyes. I feared, in opening them, to look upon the face before which all must kneel. Yet I saw it. And it was the face of a child, too—or a very young girl—only without the spark of youth. It seemed the very face of grief, but a grief I had never known, which I could in no way share. It was so near to my heart, the wretched heart of a man, and yet out of my reach. . . . There is no human sorrow lacking bitterness, but this sweet sorrow lacked even strife—it was only surrender. It made me think of a vast soft night. It was infinite. Sorrow, after all, springs from experience of human wrong, and such knowledge is never pure: this sorrow was innocent. I understood then some sayings of M. le Curé which had seemed obscure at the time. In some miraculous way God must have veiled that virgin sorrow, for blind and callous though they are, men would surely have known their beloved daughter: the last-born of their ancient race, celestial hostage round which demons howl. They would have all risen together and made for her a rampart of their mortal flesh.

I must have wandered on for some time, but I had strayed off the path and was stumbling through thick sodden grass which squelched with each step. When I realized my mistake, I was under a hedge which seemed too thick and high for me to climb over. So I walked on, following it. Water was dripping from branches down my neck and on to my arms. The pain was slowly going, but I kept coughing up something warm which seemed to taste of tears. Even to reach for my handkerchief felt quite impossible. But I hadn't lost consciousness, I was simply a prey to my suffering, or rather to the menace of it—for the certainty of its return was a greater agony than the pain itself—and I kept at its heels, as a dog at the heels of his master. I was telling myself I would fall any minute, and be found half dead in the grass—*another* scandal! I fancy I called out. Suddenly my arm was no longer holding on to the hedge, and the ground seemed to slide from under my feet. Without realizing it I had reached the lane, and now my forehead and knees hit the stones. The next minute I thought I had got myself up and was walking on. Then I knew it was only a dream. The night was suddenly darker and nearer. I thought I had fallen again, but now it was headlong into Nothing. And the void closed over me.

Memory came back as I opened my eyes. It seemed the sun was rising. But it was only the reflection of a lantern on the hedge opposite. There was another light to the left amongst the trees, and I immediately recognized the Dumouchels' cottage by its absurd veranda. My cassock was soaked and sticking to my back; I was alone.

The lantern had been placed very near to my head— it was one of those paraffin, stable lanterns that give out more smoke than light. A big fly was buzzing round it. I tried to get up, and failed, though I felt some strength returning, and my pain was gone. At last I was able to sit up. From the other side of the hedge came heavy breathing and lowing of cattle. I realized that even were I able to stand, it was too late to get away, and I must needs be patient and face the curiosity of whoever found me, when he came back for his lantern. And I thought that the very last place I'd have chosen to be picked up was almost at the Dumouchels' doorstep. I got to my knees, and suddenly we were face to face. Standing, she was no higher than me. Her little pinched face was not a whit less sly than usual, but what struck me first was a look of gentle importance, rather solemn, almost comic. It was Seraphita, and I smiled. Perhaps she thought I was laughing at her. Her grey eyes lit with that wicked gleam I knew—the 'grown-up' look which had often made me lower my own. Then I saw she was carrying a bowl of water with a dirty bit of rag floating in it. She put it between her knees.

'I went an' filled it at the pond,' she said. 'Safer. There's a crowd of 'em up home 'cause of my cousin Victor gettin' married. I came out to get the cattle in.'

'Mind you don't get into trouble!'

'Trouble? I never get into no trouble. Once my dad was raisin' his hand against me and I sez: "If you touch me I'll take Rusty where the bad grass is, an' she'll swell up an' die." Rusty's our best cow.'

'You shouldn't have said that; it's wrong.'

'I'll tell you what's wrong,' she answered back, malice wriggling her shoulders—'it's bein' in a state like what you're in.' I felt nervous as she eyed me inquisitively. 'Bit o' luck I found you. One o' me clogs rolled into the path as I was chasin' the cows, so I climbed down here, an' I thought you was dead.'

'I'm better. I'm getting up.'

"Don't go walkin' home in *that* state!'

'What state?'

'You bin' sick. You've got your face smeared all over

like you'd been eatin' blackberries.' I tried to take the
bowl, but nearly dropped it. 'You're shakin' too much,'
she said. 'You let me, I'm used to it, I can tell you. Lor',
it was a lot wors'n this when our Narcisse was wedded.
What's that you're sayin'?'

My teeth were chattering. At last she understood that
I wanted her to come to the presbytery to-morrow, and
then I'd explain everything.

'Not likely. I bin tellin' tales about you—awful things!
Y'ought to give me a hidin'. I'm jealous, see, jealous as a
cat—a horrid jealous beast. An' you be careful o' the
others too! They're a slimy lot.'

She was wiping my forehead and cheeks as she talked.
The coolness of the water freshened me, and I stood up,
but I was still shuddering. Then that went too. My little
Samaritan lifted the lantern up to my chin, the better to
judge the job she'd made of me, no doubt.

'I'll come with you to the end o' the lane if you like.
Mind the holes. Out o' the grazin', an' you'll be all right.'

She walked ahead of me, then as the lane widened
came to my side, and a few steps further on slipped her
hand into mine like a good little girl. Neither of us spoke.
Cows mooed dismally. A long way back was the sound
of a door banging.

'I got to go,' she said. But she faced me squarely, tip-
toed on her little legs. 'Mind you go to bed when you
get in, nothin' better. But you've no one to get you a
nice hot cup o' coffee! A man an' no woman is a pretty
mess, I reckon.' I couldn't look away from her face. It
was all so embittered, almost withered, except her brow,
still pure. I would never have thought it could be so pure.
'Don't take no notice o' what I said,' she went on. ' 'Course
I know you didn't do it on purpose. Someone's been

poppin' ash in your glass—they think it's funny, a kind o' joke. Only thanks to me, see—they won't notice nothin', they'll be caught out proper. . . .'

'Where ye got ter, ye little bitch?' It was her father's voice. She leaped silently over the hedge, like a cat, her clogs in one hand and the lantern in the other.

'Sh! Get off with you! I was dreamin' o' you only last night. An' you looked so sad, just like what you do now, an' I woke up cryin'.'

When I got in I had to wash my *soutane*. The cloth was stiff and the water turned red.

I knew I had vomited a lot of blood.

7

WHEN I WENT TO BED I had almost made up my mind to catch the first train to Lille in the morning. My surprise was so great—fear of death came later—that if old Dr. Delbende had been alive, I would probably have run all the way to Desvres, in the middle of the night. But the unexpected happened, as always. I slept soundly and woke up at cockcrow feeling perfectly well. I was even seized with uncontrollable laughter as I took a close-up view of my sorry countenance, whilst scraping away with my razor: no scythe could ever get the better of my beard—a real tramp's or carter's stubble. After all, the blood on my cassock may come from nose-bleeding. Why should such an obvious explanation not have been the first to occur to me? Yet the haemorrhage must have happened during the short time I lay unconscious, and I seem to recollect a horrible sickness before I fainted. All the same I'll go to Lille for a consultation this week without fail.

After mass I went to see my colleague d'Haucolte to ask him to take my place during my absence. I don't know him very well, but he is about my age, and inspires me with confidence. In spite of all my efforts to sponge it down, the front of my *soutane* is a dreadful sight. I told him a bottle of red ink in my cupboard had upset over me, and he kindly lent me an old cassock of his. What can he have thought of me? I could read nothing in his face.

M. le Curé de Torcy was moved yesterday to a nursing-home in Amiens. He has had a heart-attack, apparently nothing very serious, but he needs care and a nurse to look after him. He left a note for me, scribbled in pencil, just before they moved him into the ambulance:

'Little muddler, mind and pray to the good God and come and see me at Amiens next week.'

Just as I was coming out of the church I found myself face to face with Mlle Louise. I had thought her miles from here. Apparently she had walked all the way from Arches, her shoes were caked with mud, her face looked dirty and very tired; through the holes of one woollen glove, her fingers appeared. She who used always to be so neat, so careful! It worried me terribly. And yet I knew from the first word that hers was not a sorrow that can be told. She said she had received no wages for the last six months, that M. le Comte's solicitor made her an unsatisfactory offer which she could not accept, that she daren't leave Arches and is living there at the hotel.

'Monsieur must be feeling dreadfully lonely; he's weak and selfish, quite a slave to his habits, his daughter will soon have him under her thumb.'

I could see she was still hoping for something, I dare not say what. She was forcing herself to speak as 'correctly' as ever, and at moments her voice reminds me of Mme la Comtesse, from whom she has also caught the trick of drooping lids over short-sighted eyes. Chosen humility can be truly regal, but vanity run to seed is not a pretty sight. . . .

'Even madame,' she said, 'never let herself forget that I'm a lady. Besides my great-uncle, Colonel Heudebert, married one of the Noisels—the Noisels are connections of theirs. God sends me this cross—'

I couldn't help interrupting: 'You shouldn't invoke the name of God so lightly.'

'Oh, it's easy enough for you to condemn me and look down on me—you don't know what loneliness is.'

'No one ever does know,' I replied. 'No one ever discovers the depths of his own loneliness.'

'Still you've got plenty to do, the time soon goes.'

I couldn't help smiling: 'You ought to go away now,' I told her. 'Leave this part of the world. I promise to get you whatever is owing, and I'll send it on to any address you like.'

'Thanks to mademoiselle, I suppose? Poor child, I don't think any ill of her. I forgive her. She's a wild creature, but kind at heart. If only we could have it all out frankly, somehow I think—' She had stripped off one glove and was screwing it nervously into the palm of her hand. Certainly I felt very sorry for her—and slightly disgusted.

'Mademoiselle,' I said. 'For want of a better reason, your pride alone should not allow you to make such overtures, which in any case would be quite useless. And the wonder of it is that you should hope to involve me in them.'

'Pride? Can you expect me to leave this part where I've lived so happily, always been treated with such respect, almost as the equal of my employers, to go wan-

dering about like a beggar? Do you call that pride? Only
yesterday some of the people in the market who would
once have bowed down to the ground when I passed
them, pretended not to see me.'

'Pretend not to see them either. Have some pride.'

'Pride, always pride! What *is* pride, anyway? I never
knew that pride was one of the theological virtues. I'm
even surprised at your using such a word.'

'Excuse me,' I said, 'if you wish to speak to the priest,
he will ask you for a confession of your sins, to have the
right to give you absolution.'

'I don't want anything like that.'

'In that case let me talk to you in a way that you can
understand.'

'In a human way?'

'Why not? It's a fine thing to rise above pride, but
you must have pride in order to do so. I have no right
to speak freely of honour in the worldly sense, it is no
subject of conversation for a poor priest like myself, but
I sometimes feel we're apt to belittle honour. We're all
of us liable to lie down in the mud; it seems a cool, soft
couch when hearts are jaded. And shame, you know, is
a sleep like any other, a heavy sleep, a dreamless intoxica-
tion. . . . If a last shred of pride can stiffen the back of
some wretched creature, why quibble about it?'

'So you think I'm like that.'

'Yes,' I said to her. 'And if I venture to humiliate you,
it is only so as to spare you another far worse humiliation, which would degrade you for ever in your own
eyes. Give up this idea of going to see Mlle Chantal, you
would debase yourself to no purpose, you would be
crushed, trampled on—'

I paused. I could see she was forcing herself into a

state of rebellion and fury. I searched my mind for words of comfort, but those which I found would merely have intensified her self-pity, I feared. They would have released the ignoble tears. Never before had I so completely realized my powerlessness in face of certain kinds of suffering which I cannot share, strive as I may.

'Yes, I see how it is,' she said. 'You don't hesitate between Chantal and me. I'm no match for her. She has broken my spirit.'

This reminded me of something I had said during my last meeting with Mme la Comtesse: 'God will break you,' I had said. At such a moment this memory hurt me.

'There's nothing in you to break,' I cried. At the time I was sorry to have said it, but not now; it came from my heart.

'It's you she's made a fool of,' said mademoiselle, her face twitching unpleasantly. She did not raise her voice, merely spoke more and more rapidly; nor can I remember all she said, it poured like an endless stream through her chapped lips.

'She loathes you. She's loathed you from the first. She's got a devilish way of seeing through everything. And she's sly! Nothing escapes her. She's no sooner poked her nose out of doors than the children run after her and she stuffs them with sweets, so of course they worship her. She worms things out of them concerning you, they tell all kinds of tales about the way you behave in your catechism class, and she imitates your walk and mimics your voice. . . . It's obvious she's obsessed with you! And if she gets anyone on her mind, like that, they suffer for it, I can tell you! She'll track them down, she'll end by killing them, she's merciless, you wait and see. Why only the day before yesterday—'

I felt as though she had struck me full in the chest. I cried out: 'Hold your tongue!'

'But you've *got* to know what she's like.'

'I *know* already,' I said. 'You can't understand her.'

She lifted her miserable face up to mine. It was livid, almost grey, and the wind had dried her tears, leaving glistening streaks, smudged away in the hollows of the cheek-bones.

'I had a talk to Famechon, the head-gardener; he waits at table when François is out: Chantal has told her father the whole story and they were both tickled to death by it. She found a little book on the ground near Dumouchel's house. It had your name written in it. So then she thought she'd pump Seraphita, and of course that kid blabbed it all out, as usual. . . .'

I was staring stupidly, tongue-tied. Even now, when vengeance must have been sweet, fury could not change those wretched eyes, they retained the tame resignation of a domestic beast, only her face was a shade less sallow.

'It appears that the child found you snoring there, in the lane.'

I turned my back on her. She ran behind me, and when I saw her hand on my sleeve I could not control a stiffening of disgust; it needed an effort to take it in mine and remove it gently.

'Leave me,' I said. 'I shall pray for you.' At last I was sorry for her. 'I promise you it shall all be cleared up. I shall see M. le Comte on your behalf.'

She left me hastily, her head low, a little on one side, like a wounded animal.

Canon la Motte-Beuvron has left Ambricourt. I have not seen him again.

To-day I caught sight of Seraphita. She was sitting at the top of a hillock minding her cow. I went towards her, not too close. She ran away.

My nervousness has lately become a real obsession. It is hard to conquer that childish unreasonable terror, which makes me turn with a jump whenever I feel the eyes of a passer-by. My heart comes into my mouth, and I can't breathe freely again until I've heard his 'good morning' in answer to mine. When at last it comes I've ceased to hope for it.

And yet people are no longer so inquisitive. They've 'summed me up,' what more do they need? They have now quite a normal, reassuring, plausible explanation of my behaviour, and can turn their thoughts to more serious things. I 'tipple' everyone knows that—'a secret drinker.' Surely that ought to be enough for them. But unluckily there still remains the uncomfortable fact that I look 'like death.' I can't do anything about it, and it is by no means the look of a toper. They won't forgive me for it.

I was very uneasy about the catechism class on Thursday. Not that I was expecting to be 'ragged,' as they say in the *lycées* (little peasants don't 'rag'), but I feared whisperings and smiles. Yet nothing happened.

Seraphita came late, out of breath and crimson in the face. She seemed to be limping. At the end of the lesson as I was giving the blessing, I saw her slip out behind the others, and before I had come to the 'amen' I already heard the impatient scurrying of her clogs, clicking over the flagstones.

When the church was empty I found under the pulpit the large blue and white handkerchief, too big for her overall pocket, which she often forgets. I was sure she would never dare go home without this precious possession, since Mme Dumouchel is known to be much attached to her belongings.

And back she came. She darted noiselessly to her seat, for now she had taken off her clogs. She was limping more than ever, but when I called to her from the back of the church, she walked almost normally.

'Here's your hanky—don't forget it again.'

She was very pale. I had rarely seen her thus, for she generally flushes up at the least emotion. Fiercely she snatched away the handkerchief without a 'thank you.' Then she stood still with her bad leg curled up under her. 'Run along,' I said gently. She went one step towards the door, then came straight up to me squaring her small shoulders magnificently.

'Mlle Chantal *made* me—at first' (she stood on tip-toe the better to be able to look me straight in the face), 'an' then—an' then—'

'Then you went on because you wanted to. Well, little girls are terrible chatterboxes.'

'I'm not a chatterbox. I'm bad.'

'Sure?'

'Sure as God can see me.' (With her grubby ink-stained thumb she made the sign of the cross on her forehead and lips.) 'I keep thinkin' o' things you say to the others—nice things, f'rinstance you called Zelida: "little girl"—"little girl," that great fat one-eyed bitch! No one but you 'ud even have *thought* o'such a thing!'

'You're jealous.'

She half closed her eyes with a deep sigh, as though to see far into the hidden places of her mind.

'It isn't that you're anythin' to look at,' she muttered

between her teeth, with inconceivable gravity. 'It's just 'cause you're sad. You're sad even when you smile. I think if I only knew why you was sad—I shouldn't be wicked no more.'

'I'm sad,' I told her, 'because God isn't loved enough.'

She shook her head. The dirty blue ribbon with which her skimpy hair is gathered up on the top of her head, had come untied and fluttered absurdly round her chin. Obviously what I had said seemed obscure, very obscure to her. . . . But she was not long in answering:

'I'm sad, too,' she said. 'I like bein' sad. It makes up for your sins, in a way, I sez to meself—'

'Are you such a terrible sinner?'

'Well—' she threw me a quick reproachful glance of secret understanding, 'you know how it is. It's not that I get much fun out o' the boys. They're not worth much. Silly lot, they are. Proper mad dogs—'

'Aren't you ashamed?'

'I'm ashamed all right. Isabelle an' Noemie an' me, we often met 'em up on the sandpit, at the top o' the big Malicorne hill. First we play at slidin' down. . . . 'Course, I'm the worst of any. But when they're gone, I pretend to be dead.'

'Pretend to be dead.'

'Sure. I make a hole in the sand and lie down there flat on my back, with my hands folded and my eyes shut. If I wriggle the tiniest bit the sand gets down my neck an' in my ears an' mouth, even. I wish it wasn't a game an' I *was* dead. After talkin' to Mlle Chantal I lay there for hours. When I got in my dad gave me a lickin'. I cried, too. I don't, hardly ever—'

'You don't cry?'

'No. I think it's horrid, beastly. . . . When you cry,

[229]

all your sadness comes pourin' out, as though your heart was meltin' like butter—nasty! That's to say—' She blinked her eyes again—'one 'ud have to find another—a better way o' cryin', somehow—I suppose you think that's silly?'

'No,' I said. I hesitated; the least clumsiness, I could feel, might frighten off this fierce little creature for ever. 'One day you'll see that prayer is just that way of crying, the only tears that aren't soft.'

The word 'prayer' made her frown and she tilted up her face like a cat, turned her back and left me, limping more than ever.

'Why are you limping?'

She stood quite still, her whole body poised for flight, only her head turned back to look at me. She squared her shoulders again, and I came gently up to her; she was tugging her grey woollen skirt frantically down over her knee. Through a large tear in her stocking, I noticed her leg was purple.

'That's why you're limping,' I said. 'Whatever is it?' She jumped away, but I caught her hand, on the wing, as it were. She was struggling and disclosed, just above the calf, a thick string so tightly fastened that the flesh was cut in two great dark rolls.

She bounded off hopping on one leg between the benches. I caught her only two steps from the door. Her grave face silenced me at first.

'It's to punish me for havin' talked to Mlle Chantal. I promised I'd keep the string on all day.'

'You cut that off,' I said. I gave her my penknife and she obeyed without a word. But the sudden rush of blood must have hurt her terribly, for her face twisted up in a fierce grimace. If I had not held her, she would certainly have fallen. 'Promise not to do it again.' She nodded, still very gravely, and went, holding on to the wall with her hand. May God watch over her.

Last night I must have had a haemorrhage, nothing much, no doubt, yet not to be mistaken for nose-bleeding. It is foolish to keep on putting off my journey to Lille, so I have written to the doctor suggesting the 15th. In ten days. . . .
I have kept my promise to Mlle Louise. It cost me a great effort to go to the Château. Fortunately I met M. le Comte going up the drive. He seemed in no way surprised at my request, as though he had been waiting for it. And I went about it far more tactfully than I had hoped.

The doctor's reply came by return. He agrees to the date suggested. And I can be home the following morning. I am drinking strong black coffee instead of wine. It suits me, but keeps me awake at night, which would not be so bad, quite pleasant even, were it not for these rather worrying palpitations. The release of dawn is always a sweet relief: like some heavenly favour, like a smile. . . . Blessed be the mornings.
My strength is returning, with a sort of appetite. And the weather is fine, cold and dry. The fields are covered with white hoar-frost. The village has quite a different look, all the autumn heaviness has gone; as though the clarity of the air were drawing off this heaviness by degrees, and when the sun begins to set, I feel as though it hung in air, hovering over the earth, flying away, escap-

ing me. It is I who feel heavy, clamped to the soil by some great weight. Sometimes the illusion is such that I gaze down with a strange terror, with unaccountable repulsion, at my clumping boots. What are they doing here, in this light? I seem to watch them sinking in. . . .

Of course I am 'praying better.' But I no longer recognize my prayer. Once it had an obstinate, imploring quality, and even when, for instance, my whole mind was riveted on a passage in the breviary, deep in myself I still could feel my soul in touch with God, sometimes imploring, then insistent, imperious even—yes, I would have liked to snatch His graces from Him, to storm His tenderness. Now it is hard really to desire anything. My prayer, like the village, has no more weight to it, flies away. . . . Is that a good or a bad thing? I don't know.

Another slight haemorrhage. Mere spitting of blood, really. Fear of Death passed over me. The *thought* of death often enters my mind and sometimes I feel afraid. But to be afraid is not to *fear*. It only lasted a second. I don't know to what I can compare this flash of terror. Like the lash of a whip through the heart, perhaps— Passion before Death!

My lungs must be in a very bad state, I feel sure of it. Yet Dr. Delbende sounded me very carefully. Consumption cannot have made great strides in a few weeks. And one can soon get the better of that illness by determination and will to live. I possess both.

I paid my last 'domiciliary' visits to-day, as M. le Curé de Torcy used ironically to call them. If I did not so loathe the well-worn phrases of my colleagues, I would say they turned out most 'consoling.' And yet I had kept for the last those which seemed least likely to turn out favourably. Why have people and things suddenly become so easy to deal with? Or do I imagine it? Have I become unconscious of these petty vexations? Or has my insignificance, now generally recognized, in some way disarmed suspicion and antagonism? All this seems like a dream.

(Fear of death. It has come again, less violently, I think. But how strange is this shudder of my whole being round some unknown point in the chest. . . .)

I have just had a strange meeting. Oh, nothing really so very surprising! In my present state the slightest incident seems distorted, like a landscape seen through a mist. But I think I have met a friend: friendship came as a revelation. Such a confession would surprise many of my former school-fellows, who consider me extremely loyal to certain youthful affinities. My memory for dates, the precision with which I recall the days on which my friends were ordained, is well known, it is even a joke. But those are no more than affinities. I realize now that friendship can break out between two people, with that sudden violence which generally is only attributed to the revelation of love.

I was walking towards Mezargues when I heard, a long way behind me, the purr of a motor, a buzzing growing louder and softer by turns according to the whim of the breeze or the twist of the road. For some days now this noise is familiar, and no one even bothers to look round. They merely say, 'That's M. Olivier's motor-bike.' It's a remarkable German make, like a small glittering engine. M. Olivier's real name is Treville-Sommerange, he is a nephew of Mme la Comtesse. The old folk who remember him as a boy are always gossiping about him. He had to be sent away to join the army at eighteen, because he was so difficult to deal with.

I paused on the top of the hill to get my breath. The noise of the motor could not be heard for the next few seconds, no doubt owing to the great bend of Dillonne, then it blared forth again. It was like a cry—savagely imperious, menacing, desperate. Almost immediately the crest in front of me became as though crowned with sprouting flames—the sun was beating down hard on the polished steel—and the machine was already plunging down the hill with a powerful roar, to rise again with such speed that it seemed like a bound. I jumped out of its way with the sensation that my heart had come loose from my ribs. For one instant I did not realize the noise had ceased. I only heard the sharp screech of brakes, the skidding of wheels over the ground. And the silence was tremendous, more so than the noise.

M. Olivier was standing before me in a grey sweater reaching up to his ears, and bare-headed. I had never seen him so close. He has a quiet, thoughtful face and eyes so pale, it would be hard to state their exact colour. He smiled at me.

'Like to have a ride, father?' he asked, in a voice both soft and determined—heavens! a voice I knew at once, that of Mme la Comtesse. (I am not good at 'reading faces,' as they say, but I remember voices, never forget them, treasure them. . . . A blind man, who has nothing else to distract him, must learn so much from voices.)

'Why not, monsieur?' I said.

We eyed each other in silence. I saw surprise in his look, some irony, too. Beside this machine of blazing light, my cassock was like a sad black shadow. By what miracle can I have felt so young at that moment, as young—ah, yes, as young—as that glorious morning? In a flash I saw the sadness of my adolescence—not in the way drowning men are supposed to review their past life, before sinking, for this was no series of pictures passing almost instantaneously before my eyes—nothing like that. It was as though someone, some being (dead or alive, God knows!) were standing before me. But I was not sure of recognizing this creature, I could not be sure because—how strange it sounds—I saw him for the first time, I had never seen him before. My youth had passed me by, as many strangers pass so closely who might have become brothers, yet disappear for ever. I was never young because I never dared be young. Around me, no doubt, life went on and my companions knew and tasted that wondrous bitter spring, whilst I tried not to think of it and drugged myself with work. Many of them were very fond of me, no doubt. But the best of my friends must have shrunk in spite of themselves from the mark my earliest childhood had left on me: a little boy's knowledge of poverty and the shame of it. I should have opened my heart to them, but that which I most wished to tell was just what at all costs I wanted to hide —God, it all seems simple enough now! I was never young because no one wanted to be young with me.

Yes, things have become simple all of a sudden. The memory of it will never leave me. The clear sky, the tawny mist, pierced by golden shafts, the hills still white with frost, and that dazzling machine panting softly in the sun. . . . I realized that youth is blessed—that it is a risk worth running, a risk that is also blessed. And by a presentiment which I cannot explain, I also understood, I *know* that God did not wish me to die without knowing something of that risk—just enough, maybe, for my sacrifice to be complete when the time came.

For one poor short minute I was to taste that glory.

To talk thus of such an ordinary meeting must appear very foolish, I feel. What do I care? Not to be ridiculous in joy one must have learnt it from the very first, before the word could be shaped on the lips. I could never achieve, not for one second, that confidence and grace. Joy! A kind of pride, a gaiety, an absurd hope, entirely carnal, the carnal form of hope, I think, is what they call joy. Anyway, I felt young, really young, with this companion who was as young as I. We were young together.

'Where are you going, father?'

'To Mezargues.'

'Ever had a lift on one of these?'

I burst out laughing. I was thinking how twenty years earlier I would have fainted with pleasure just to run my hand, as I was doing now, down the long tank, all shuddering with the slow beats of the engine. Though I can never remember as a child ever having so much as dared to long for one of those toys that dazzle little poor children, a mechanical toy, a toy that *works*. Yet that dream must surely have remained intact in my heart. And slowly it crept up from the past, suddenly to burst forth in my sickly chest, where the hand of death had already touched me, perhaps. . . . The dream was all there, like a sun.

'I must say,' he said, 'you can pride yourself on taking me aback. Aren't you afraid?'

'No. Why should I be afraid?'

'No reason.'

'Look here,' I said.' From here to Mezargues I shouldn't

think we'll run into anyone. I don't want them to laugh at you.'

'It is I who am a fool,' he said, after a short silence.

I climbed somewhat clumsily on to a small rather uncomfortable seat, and the next minute the long slope we were facing flashed behind us, whilst the roar of the engine rose continuously higher and higher till it gave out one note only, wonderfully pure. It was like the song of light, it was light itself, and I felt I was watching, with my own eyes, the huge curve of that stupendous ascent. The country side did not come towards us, it opened out on all sides, and just beyond the wild skid of the road, seemed to turn majestically on itself, like a door opening on to another world.

I was quite unable to measure the space we covered, or the time. I only knew we were travelling quickly, very quickly, quicker and quicker. The wind we created was not, as at first, an obstacle against which I leaned with all my weight; it had become a whirling passage, a void between two rushing sections of air. I felt them flowing at my right, at my left, like two liquid walls, and when I tried to reach out an arm it was pressed to my side by some irresistible force. Thus we came to the sharp curve of Mezargues. The 'man at the wheel' turned round for a second. Perched on my seat I was a head above him, he had to look up at me. 'Look out,' he cried. His eyes were laughing in his tense face, the wind made his long fair hair stand up on end. The bank seemed to rush at us, then flew past in a reckless sidelong flight. The huge horizon reeled twice, and already we were plunging down the Gesvre hill. My companion called out something, I don't know what, I answered with a laugh, I felt happy, released, so far from everything.

Finally I realized that my attitude surprised him rather; he had probably expected to frighten me. Mezargues was behind us now. I hadn't the heart to protest. After all, I thought, it takes at least an hour on foot, so I still gain time.

We returned more quietly to the presbytery. The sky had clouded over and there was a sharp little wind blowing. I felt I was awakening from a dream.

By good luck the road was empty, we saw only old Madeleine gathering bundles of firewood. She didn't turn round. I thought M. Olivier was going on to the Château, but he asked me, with a warm smile, if he could come in for a while. I didn't know what to say. I would have given anything to be able to offer him a drink and something to eat, for a peasant of my sort will never get it out of his head that a soldier is always hungry and thirsty. Of course I didn't dare suggest any of my wine, which is now but a muddy brew, hardly presentable. But we lit a great log fire and he filled his pipe.

'Pity I'm going to-morrow. . . . We might have had another go. . . .'

'Once is enough for me,' I said. 'Folk won't exactly relish the sight of their parish priest flying over the roads at the speed of an express train. Besides I might kill myself.'

'You afraid of that?'

'No. At least, not exactly. . . . But what would monseigneur say?'

'I like you very much,' he said. 'We should have been friends.'

'I, your friend?'

'Sure. And it's not because I don't know enough about you. They're always talking you over at the Château.'

'Unfavourably?'

'Somewhat. My cousin's a regular bitch. A real Sommerange, she is.'

'What do you mean?'

'Well, I'm a Sommerange, too. Greedy, hard, never content, with a quite unmanageable quality which must be the devil's share in us; it fills us with deep enmity for ourselves, and our virtues in consequence are so like our vices that God Himself will have a job to separate the bad boys from the saints in the family—supposing there are any. The only characteristic we have in common is to loathe sentimentality like the plague. We hate sharing our pleasures with others, but at least we have the decency not to burden them with our troubles. It's a valuable quality when death comes, and I'm bound to say we're rather good at dying. There! Now you know as much as I do. All that put together makes quite a tolerable soldier. Unfortunately the profession isn't open to women as yet, and the result is that our women—Confound them! My poor aunt found a motto for them: All or nothing! One day I was saying to her that such a motto didn't mean much unless it could assume the form of a bet. And a wager of that kind could only be laid seriously on the point of death, don't you agree? But none of ours has ever come back to tell us if that bet was ever taken, and by whom.'

'I am sure you believe in God.'

'Our people,' he answered, 'never question the matter. We all believe in God, all, even the worst of us—the worst believe in Him most, perhaps. I think we must be too proud to sin without taking risks; we have always one witness to face: God.'

Such words should have torn my heart, for it was easy

to take them as blasphemous, and yet they in no way disturbed me.

'It's not a bad idea to face up to God,' I said. 'It compels a man to pledge the whole of himself—the whole of his hope, all the hope he is capable of, only sometimes God turns away His face. . . .'

He was watching me with his pale eyes.

'My uncle says you're a dirty little tyke of a priest, and he even makes out that you—' Blood rushed to my face. 'I shouldn't think you give two hoots for his opinion, he's a prize idiot. As for my cousin—'

'Please don't,' I said. I felt my eyes filling with tears, and could do so little to control this sudden weakness, that I began to shiver, for fear of yielding to it in spite of myself, and crept into the chimney corner to crouch among the cinders.

'It's the first time I've ever seen my cousin express a feeling with such— As a rule, she'll put a brazen-faced denial on all indiscreet suggestions, even the most frivolous kind.'

'Tell me what you think of me. . . .'

'Oh, *you?* If it wasn't for that black sheath, you'd be like any one of us. I saw that at first glance.'

I didn't understand (I don't understand even now). 'You don't mean that—?'

'Yes, I *do* mean that. But perhaps you don't realize that I serve in a foreign regiment.'

'A foreign regiment?'

'The Foreign Legion, if you like. I hate the word since novelists have made it so fashionable.'

'But surely a priest—' I stammered.

'Priests? We've plenty of priests out there. My colonel's orderly—he'd been a priest at Poitou, at one time. We only knew afterwards.'

'After what?'

'After he was dead, of course.'

'And how did he—?'

'How did he die? Strapped to a pack-mule like a sausage. He got a bullet in his belly.'

'That wasn't my question.'

'Well, I won't lie to you. At those times our boys like to swank. And their way of doing it consists of two or three formulae which closely resemble blasphemy from your point of view, and that's the truth.'

'How very terrible.'

Something inexpressible was taking place in me. God knows I had never given much thought to those harsh men, to their terrible, mysterious vocation, because for all of my generation the word 'soldier' brings to mind the very usual sight of a civilian during military service. I remembered how those fellows on leave used to turn up weighed down with haversacks, and the same evening you came across them back in their corduroys—peasants, like all the rest.

But now the words of this stranger were awakening in me untold curiosity.

'There are blasphemies and blasphemies,' my companion went on, in his quiet rather callous voice. 'In the mind of those blokes it's a method of cutting off your retreat, a way they have. It's stupid, I consider, but not foul. They're outlaws in this world, and they make themselves outlaws in the next. If God isn't going to save soldiers, all soldiers, just *because* they're soldiers, what's the good of trying? One more blasphemy for the sake of good measure, running the same risk as the other lads, avoiding a "non-proven" verdict, that's the idea—and then—' He snapped his fingers. 'You see, always the same motto: All or nothing! Don't you agree? Why, I bet you yourself—'

'Me?'

'Well, there's a shade of difference, perhaps, but— If only you'd take a look at yourself.'

'Look at myself?'

He couldn't help laughing. We laughed together, as we had laughed earlier on the road, in the sun.

'I mean that if your face didn't express—' He stopped dead. But his pale eyes were no longer disconcerting. I could read his thought in them. 'The habit of prayer, I suppose,' he went on. 'Lord, that kind of talk isn't altogether in my line. . . .'

'Prayer! The habit of prayer. If you only knew—I pray so badly.'

He found a strange reply which has made me think ever since.

'The habit of prayer, as I see it, would mean a continual anxiety with regard to prayer, a fight, a struggle. It is the perpetual dread of fear, *the fear of fear*, that shapes the face of a brave man. Your face—you don't mind if I tell you?—looks *worn* by prayer; it reminds me of a very old missal, or even of one of those half-rubbed-away engravings on ancient tombstones. Anyway, I don't think it would take much to outlaw that face, after our fashion. Besides my uncle says you have no sense of social life. You'll admit our order isn't theirs?'

'I don't deny their order,' I said. 'I reproach it for being loveless.'

'Our boys don't know all you do. They simply identify God with a kind of justice they despise, because it's a justice without honour.'

'But honour itself—' I began.

'Oh, honour of their own dimension, I agree. Though it may seem pretty rough to your casuists, their law has at least the merit of standing at a high, a very high price. . . . It's like the sacrificial stone—a mere pebble, hardly bigger than another, but streaming with the blood of victims. Of course our case is hard to define, and theologians would have their work cut out, if such worthy gentlemen had time to consider us. But not one of them would dare say that, alive or dead, we belong to this world on which the only curse in the New Testament has been falling for the last twenty centuries. Because the world's law is to refuse, but we refuse nothing, not even our skin; pleasure, but for us an orgy is mere rest and forgetfulness, a form of sleep; gold-lust, but most of us do not even possess the dirty old bags we're buried in. You'll agree such poverty can stand comparison with that of certain fashionable monks, specialized in the lay-out of rare souls. . . .'

'Look here,' I said, 'there is such a thing as a Christian soldier. . . .'

My voice was shaking as it always does when I am aware, through some unknown sign, that whatever I do my words will bring solace or offence, according to the will of God.

'A Knight?' He smiled. 'Our good fathers at college used still to swear by helmets and bucklers, and we were given the *Chanson de Roland* to read as the French *Iliad*. Mind you, those famous gentlemen were not what old maids think 'em, but who cares? You must take 'em as they showed up to the enemy, shield to shield, elbow to

[243]

elbow. They were well worth the fine ideal they were trying to represent. And they didn't borrow that ideal from anyone. Our peoples had chivalry in their blood. The church merely had to bless it. Soldiers, just soldiers, that's all they were, the world has known none better. They were protectors of the City, not slaves to it, and they dealt on an equal footing. The highest military incarnation of the past, that of the soldier-labourer in ancient Rome—why they just blotted it out of history. No doubt they were neither just nor pure—all of them—but they did stand for a kind of justice, which for centuries of centuries has haunted the sadness of the poor, or sometimes filled their dreams. Because you see, justice in the hands of the powerful is merely a governing system like any other. Why call it justice? Let us rather call it injustice, but of a sly effective order, based entirely on cruel knowledge of the resistance of the weak, their capacity for pain, humiliation and misery. Injustice sustained at the exact degree of necessary tension to turn the cogs of the huge machine-for-the-making-of-rich-men, without bursting the boiler. And then one day it was rumoured all over the Christian world that there was going to arise a kind of police-force of the Lord Jesus. A rumour isn't much to rely on, I agree. But look: when you think of the huge uninterrupted success of a book like *Don Quixote*, you're bound to realize that if humankind have not yet finished being revenged, by sheer laughter, for being let down in their greatest hope, it is because that hope was cherished so long and lay so deep! Righters of wrong, hands of iron! You can't get away from it: those men dealt great blows, heavy blows, they forced open our consciences with heavy blows. Even to-day women'll pay a high price to bear their names, poor soldiers' names and the artless allegories once drawn on their shields by some clumsy scholar, set coal and steel magnates dreaming. Don't you think that's rather comic?'

'No,' I said.

'I do. It's so funny to think of the upper ten imagining they can see themselves in those proud images of the past, over a seven-hundred-years' gulf of domesticity, sloth and adultery. Let 'em try. These soldiers belonged to Christianity alone, and Christianity belongs to no one now. There is no Christianity. There never will be again.'

'But why?'

'Because there are no more soldiers. No soldiers, no Christianity. You'll say the Church has survived and that's the chief thing. Sure. But Christ's Kingdom on Earth will never be again. It's over and done with, and all hope of it died with us.'

'With you?' I cried. 'There's no lack of soldiers.'

'Soldiers? Call 'em "army-men." The last real soldier died on May 30, 1431, and you killed her, you people. Not only killed her: condemned her, cut her off, burned her.'

'We made of her a saint, too.'

'Why not say it was the will of God? And that soldier was raised so high, because she was the last. The last of such a race had to be a saint. God also wished it to be a woman. Out of respect for the ancient covenant of chivalry. The old sword rests for ever across knees that the proudest among us could not kiss without shedding tears. How I love that discreet reminder of the tournament: "*Honneur aux Dames!*" Enough to make your doctors of divinity squint with spite, they who are so afraid of women!'

[245]

The joke would have made me laugh, for it was like many I had heard in the seminary, but I saw his eyes were sorrowful, a sorrow I knew. And such sorrow gets my soul on the raw, as it were, fills me with stupid insuperable shyness.

'What is your grudge against the Church?' I said at last, foolishly.

'Mine? Oh, nothing much. You've secularized us. The first real secularization was that of the soldier. And it's some time ago now. When you go snivelling over the excesses of nationalism, you should remember it was you who first pandered to the law-makers of the Renaissance, whilst they made short work of Christian right, and patiently constructed, under your very noses, right in your very faces, the Pagan State: the state which knows no law but that of its own wellbeing—the merciless countries full of greed and pride.'

'Listen,' I said, 'I don't know much about history, but it seems to me that feudal anarchy had its own risks.'

'No doubt. . . . You wouldn't take them. You left Christianity high and dry, it took too long, it cost a lot and brought in very little. You gave us the "state" instead. The state to arm us and clothe us and feed us, and take charge of our conscience into the bargain. Mustn't judge, mustn't even try to understand! And your theologians approve it all, naturally. With a simper, they grant us permission to kill, kill anywhere, anyhow, to kill by order, like executioners. We are supposed to defend our land, but we can also be used to keep down revolution, and if the revolution should win we serve it instead. No loyalty required. That's how you put us "in the army," and now we're so thoroughly "in the army" that in a democracy inured to all servility, the lawyers

[246]

themselves are really astonished at the servile ways of Ministers of War. "The army" is so entirely debased that even a fine soldier like Lyautey hated the very name of his profession. And besides, soon there won't be any army. We shall all be in it, from the age of seven to sixty—in *what*, come to think of it? The word "army" means nothing when entire nations are hurling themselves against each other like African tribes—tribes of a hundred thousand men! And your theologians, more and more disgusted, will still "approve" of it, still print "dispensations," or so I imagine, drawn up by the Secretary of the Board of National Conscience. But between you and me, when do your theologians intend to stop? The cleverest killers of to-morrow will kill without any risk. Thirty thousand feet above the earth, any dirty little engineer, sitting cosily in his slippers with a special bodyguard of technicians, will merely have to press a button to wipe out a town, and scurry home in fear—his only fear—of being late for dinner Nobody could call an employee of that description a soldier. Can he even deserve to be called "an army man"? And you people, who refused Christian burial to poor mummers in the seventeenth century, how do you mean to bury a guy like that? Has our trade become so debased that we are no longer responsible for any one of our actions, that we share in the horrible innocence of our steel machines? Don't tell me! A poor lad who puts his girl in the family way one spring night, is considered by you to be in mortal sin, but the killer of a whole town, whilst the kids he's just poisoned'll be vomiting up their lungs on their mothers' lap, need only go off and change pants to "distribute holy bread"! Frauds you all are! What's the use of pretending to "render unto Caesar"? The ancient world is dead, as dead as its gods. And the titulary gods of the modern world—we *know* 'em; they dine out, they're called bankers. Draw up as many agreements as you like. Outside Christianity there is no place in the West for soldiers or fatherland, and your shifty compromises will soon have permitted the final shame of both.'

He had risen and was still enfolding me in his strange gaze, always the same pale blue, but which looked golden in the shadow. He threw his cigarette furiously into the cinders.

'I don't give a damn,' he said. 'I'll be killed before then.'

Each of his words stirred the very depths of my heart. Alas, God has entrusted Himself in our hands—His Body and Soul—the Body, the Soul, the honour of God in our consecrated hands—and all that those men lavish over the highways of the world. . . . Should we even know how to die as they do? I asked myself. For one moment I hid my face, appalled to feel the tears slip between my fingers. To weep in his presence, like a child, like a woman! But our Lord restored some of my courage. I stood up, let my arms drop, and with a great effort—the thought of it hurts me still—I let him see my sorrowful face, my shameful tears. He looked at me for a long time. Oh, pride is still very much alive in me! I was watching for a smile of scorn, or at least of pity on those wilful lips— I feared his pity more than his scorn.

'You're a good lad,' he said at last. 'I wouldn't like any priest but you around when I was dying.'

And he kissed me, as children do, on both cheeks.

I have decided to go to Lille. My substitute came this morning. He said I was looking well. Certainly I am better than I was, much better. I am continually making plans, rather mad plans. I'm convinced I have never had enough self-confidence. To doubt oneself is not to be humble, I even think that sometimes it is the most hysterical form of pride, a pride almost delirious, a kind of jealous ferocity which makes an unhappy man turn and rend himself. That must be the real truth of hell.

I feel that in me there must be the germ of great pride. For a long time now I have felt such indifference for all that is usually called earthly vanity—but this gives me more mistrust than satisfaction. There must be something clouded in the kind of insuperable disgust which I feel for my absurd self. The way in which I neglect my appearance, my natural clumsiness against which I no longer struggle, even the morbid pleasure which I feel at the thought of certain small injustices—those which smart worse than many greater ones—does not all this cloak an illusion whose origin in God's eyes is impure? Doubtless for what it is worth, this state of mind is conducive to charity towards my neighbour, since instinctively I put myself in the wrong; I *can* see other people's point of view. But surely this tends to rob me gradually of confidence, of life, and the hope of doing better? My youth—at least what there is of it—is not my own; have I the right to hide it under a bushel? I was pleased with what M. Olivier said to me, but by no means carried away. It only made me realize that people of his kind are in instant sympathy with me, people so much better than I am in so many ways. What does that mean?

I also remember how one day M. le Curé de Torcy said to me: 'You're not made for wars of attrition.' And this *is* a war of attrition.

God, supposing I get well! Supposing this illness were

only to be the first symptom of that physical change which sometimes occurs at thirty. . . . For two days I have had in my mind a sentence read in some book: 'My heart is with those in the front line, with those who throw away their lives.' Soldiers, missionaries—

The weather is only too greatly in keeping with my— I was going to write 'my delight,' but that word would not express it. Expectation is more what I mean. Yes, a great, miraculous expectation which continues even during sleep, for truly it woke me up last night. I found myself in the dark with my eyes open. It was almost painful to be so happy, as I knew no reason for it. I got up, drank a glass of water, and prayed till daylight. It was like a great murmuring of the spirit. It made me think of all the rustling leaves which herald the dawn. What morning can be breaking in me? Will God's grace shine on me?

Two letters in the box this morning; one from M. Olivier at Lille, where he tells me he will be spending the last of his leave with a friend, 30 rue Verte. I don't remember having told him I should soon be visiting that town. What a queer coincidence!

M. Bigre will send his car for me at five o'clock tomorrow morning.

Last night I went to bed good and early. But no sleep would come to me. For a long time I resisted temptation to get up and go on scribbling in this diary. How fond I am of it! The very thought of having to leave it here, even for such a short time, is literally more than I can bear. I don't think I shall be able to resist—at the last moment I shall pack it. And in any case drawers never shut properly, there is always a chance of somebody reading it.

We imagine we have freed ourselves from everything, but, alas, one day we have to realize that we are trapped in our own self-deception, that the poorest man has his hidden treasure. Those which appear the least valuable are by no means the least insidious, on the contrary. Certainly there must be something unhealthy in the way I cling to these pages. Still, they were a great help to me at my worst moments, and to-day they still bear precious witness, precise enough to remind me of what I was, but too humiliating to dwell on pleasantly. They broke my dream. That is a great deal.

It's likely enough that in future they'll cease to be of any use to me. God has been so good, so unexpectedly, strangely good. My heart is full of trust and peace.

I have thrown a log on to the fire. And now I sit and watch it flame, before starting to write. If my forebears had too much to drink and never enough to eat, they must also have known what it was to be chilly, for whenever I get in front of a big fire, a vague sleepy surprise steals over me, the surprise of a savage or a child. How still the night is! I feel that I shall get no sleep.

This afternoon I was finishing off my packing, when I heard the creak of the front door. I was expecting my substitute, I thought I recognized his step. If the truth must be told, I was moreover engrossed in a ridiculous job. My shoes are still quite sound, but the damp has given them a rusty look, and I was blackening them with ink before polishing. Hearing nothing more, I went into the kitchen where I found Mlle Chantal sitting on a low chair in the chimney corner. She didn't look up, but stared into the embers.

I admit I was not particularly surprised. Since I know in advance that every mistake I make, intentional or otherwise, must be paid for, I always feel as though I were being allowed a respite, a delay of execution; so why look ahead, what is the use? My 'good afternoon' seemed to trouble her somewhat.

'So you're going away to-morrow, are you?'

'Yes, mademoiselle.'

'Are you coming back?'

'That'll depend.'

'It only depends on you.'

'No, it depends on the doctor. I'm going to Lille, to see him.'

'You're lucky to be ill. I should think illness gives one a chance to daydream. I never daydream. All my thoughts are so horribly precise, like the account-books of a lawyer or a bailiff. The women of our family are so frightfully downright, you know.'

I was still carefully polishing my shoes. She came towards me. I took my time over this polishing, and I certainly wouldn't have minded if our talk had ended in a burst of laughter. She may have guessed what I was thinking. Through her clenched teeth she suddenly asked:

'Has my cousin been talking about me?'

'Yes,' I said. 'But I couldn't tell you anything he said. I can't remember.'

'What do I care? What does his opinion matter to me? Or yours either?'

'Listen,' I said to her, 'you're only too anxious to hear mine.'

She hesitated, and then simply answered: 'Yes,' for she doesn't like lying.

'Priests have no right to any opinion. I wish you could manage to realize that. You people judge one another according to the harm or good you can do each other, but you can neither harm me nor do me any good.'

'Well at least you ought to judge me by—well—I don't know—some moral precept, I suppose.'

'I can only judge you according to the graces which God has given you, and those I don't know and never shall.'

'Rot! You've got eyes and ears. I suppose you can use them like anyone else.'

'They wouldn't tell me much about you.' I think I smiled.

'Go on. Say what you want to say.'

'I am afraid of hurting you. I remember seeing a Punch and Judy show when I was a child. Punch had hidden his money in an earthenware pot and he was waving his arms about at the other side of the stage so the policeman might not notice it. I think you are always waving your arms to prevent other people from seeing the reality of you, or perhaps to hide it from yourself.'

She listened carefully, her elbows planted on the table, her chin in her hands, biting the little finger of the left hand.

'I'm not afraid of truth, monsieur, and if you dare me, I don't mind confessing to you at once—I won't hide anything, I swear.'

'I'm not daring you. And you'd have to be in danger of death before I agreed to hear *your* confession. Absolution will come in its own time, I hope, and I know I shan't be the one to give it you.'

'Oh, it isn't hard to prophesy. Daddy swears he's going to have you shifted, and now everyone here says you drink, because—'

I turned on her roughly.

'That's enough,' I said. 'I don't want to be rude, but don't start that nonsense over again, you'll end by making me ashamed of you. Since you *are* here—against your father's wishes, too—help me to tidy up the house. I'll never get it done by myself.'

On thinking it over I still can't understand why she obeyed me. At the time it seemed to me quite natural. In a few minutes the presbytery looked a different place. She worked in silence and each time I happened to glance at her face, it looked paler and paler. Suddenly she flung away the duster with which she had been polishing the furniture, and came towards me again, her face contorted with fury. I was almost afraid of her.

'Is that enough? Are you satisfied? Oh! You play an underhand game! People think you so harmless, they're almost sorry for you. But you're hard as nails.'

'It is not I who am hard. It is the inflexible part of you, which belongs to God.'

'What rubbish! I know perfectly well God only loves soft meek little people. And if only you knew what *I* think of life!'

'At your age one doesn't think of it much. One wants this or that, and that's all there is to it.'

'Well, I want everything, good and bad. I intend to know everything.'

I began to laugh. 'You'll soon manage that,' I said.

'Not at all. I may be only a girl, but I know quite well that lots of people die before they manage to find out anything.'

'Because they were not really looking. They were only dreaming. You'll never dream. The people you mean go round in circles. When you go straight ahead, the world is small.'

'What do I care if life lets me down. I'll get my own back. I'll just do evil out of spite!'

'And when you do,' I said, 'you'll discover God. Oh, no doubt I'm putting it very clumsily. And besides, you're no more than a child. But at least I can tell you this: you are setting off with your back turned on the world, for the world does not stand for revolt, but for submission, submission to lies, first and foremost. Go ahead for all you're worth, the walls are bound to fall in the end, and every breach shows a patch of sky.'

'Are you saying all this for the sake of talking—or are you—'

'It is true the meek shall inherit the earth. And your sort won't try and get it from them, because they wouldn't know what to do with it. Snatchers can only snatch at heaven.'

She was blushing deeply, and shrugged her shoulders.

'You make me feel I could say anything. . . . I'd like to insult you. I won't be disposed of against my will. I'll get to hell all right, if I want to.'

'I'll answer for your soul with mine,' I said impulsively.

She washed her hands under the kitchen tap, without so much as looking round. Then she quietly put on her hat, which she had taken off when she started working. She came slowly back to me. If I did not know her face so well, I might have said it looked tranquil, but the corners of her mouth trembled a little.

'I'll make a bargain with you,' she said, 'if you're what I think you are.'

'The point is I am not what you think me. You see yourself in me, as you might in a mirror, and your fate as well.'

'When you talked to mother I was hiding under the window. And suddenly her face became so—so gentle. I hated you then. I don't believe much in miracles, not any more than I do in ghosts, but I did think I knew my mother. She cared no more about pretty speeches than a fish for an apple. Have you a secret, yes or no?'

'It's a lost secret,' I replied. 'You'll rediscover it, and lose it again, and others after you will pass it on, since your kind will last as long as the world.'

'My kind? Whatever do you mean?'

'Those whom God sends on and on for ever, who will never rest while the world remains.'

8

I AM ASHAMED, for I can hardly hold my pen. My hands
are shaking. Not all the time, but in sudden spasms: it
only lasts a few moments. I force myself to record this.
If I had enough money left I would take a train to
Amiens. But I had that absurd impulse just now, when I
left the doctor's. How stupid! I have only my return
ticket and thirty-seven sous.

Supposing everything had been all right: I should
probably be sitting just here, writing as now. I remember catching sight of this quiet little pub, with its deserted back room, so convenient, and its big clumsy deal
tables. (There was a good smell of new bread from the
baker's next door.) I was even hungry. . . .
Yes, I would surely have been here. . . . I would have
got this exercise-book out of my bag, I would have asked
for pen and ink, and the same girl would have brought
them with the same smile. And I would have smiled too,
for the street is flooded with sunshine.

When I re-read these pages to-morrow, or in six weeks
—six months perhaps?—I know I shall be hoping to find—
What, O Lord? . . . Well, just the proof that to-day I was
going and coming as usual. How childish!

At first I walked straight ahead towards the station. I went into an old church—I don't know its name. It was too crowded for me. That is childish too, but I would like to have been able to kneel freely on the stone floor, or lie down rather, lie with my face to the ground. Never have I known such sheer physical revolt against prayer—and it was so real that I felt no remorse. My will was powerless. I would never have believed that prayer, which is commonly called a mere recreation, could have assumed this tearing, crumbling quality. For I was not struggling against fear, but against a number of fears which seemed infinite: a fear for each fibre of my being, myriad fears. And when I shut my eyes to concentrate, I seemed to hear the rustling voices of this huge invisible crowd lurking in the depths of my anguish, as in the deepest night.

Perspiration was on my forehead and my hands. In the end I went out. The cold outside caught me in the face. I began to walk quickly. Had I been aware of any suffering, I think I might have taken pity on myself, cried over myself, over my loss. But I felt only an incredible lightness. My stupor, as I was caught up by the noisy crowd, was like the shock of joy. It gave me wings.

I have found five francs in the pocket of my cassock. I had been keeping it for M. Bigre's chauffeur, but I forgot to give it him. So I ordered black coffee and one of those fresh rolls which I had smelt earlier.

The manageress of this pub is called Mme Duplouy; she is the widow of a bricklayer who at one time used to work in Torcy. For the last few minutes from behind the bar and over the partition into the back room she had been keeping an eye on me. Then she came and sat beside me and watched me eat. 'You should be really hungry at your age,' she said. She made me sample some of her butter, that Flanders butter, smelling of nuts. Mme Duplouy's only son died of consumption, and her grandchild of meningitis at two years old. She suffers from diabetes herself, her legs are all swollen; but she can't find a buyer for this pub, which is so badly patronized. I did my best to cheer her up. The resignation in all these people puts me to shame. It seems in no way supernatural because they express it in their own language, and that language is no longer Christian. Or rather they don't express it, they don't express themselves any longer. They make do with a few well-worn sayings, and phrases out of the newspapers.

When she heard that I was waiting until the evening train, Mme Duplouy very kindly let me have the backroom to myself. 'That way,' she said, 'you can go on writing your sermon and not be disturbed.' I had a job to prevent her lighting the stove (I am still rather shivery). 'In my young days,' she said, 'priests ate a lot too much, they'd too much blood in 'em. Now it's the other way round—you're as lean as stray cats.' I think she mistook the face I made at her, for she hastily added: 'It's always hard in the beginning. Never mind! At your age you've all your life before you.'

I opened my mouth to answer and— At first I didn't understand. Yes, without having decided anything, thought of anything, I knew I would keep silent. Keep silent, what a strange expression! Silence keeps us.

(You wished me to be silent. I knew Your hand as it closed my lips.)

Mme Duplouy left me and returned to the bar. Some people had just come in, workmen, for lunch. One of them caught sight of me over the partition, and his pals burst out laughing. The row they make does not trouble me, on the contrary. My inner quiet—blessed by God—has never really isolated me. I feel all human-kind can enter, and I receive them thus only at the threshold of my home. I feel they do come to me, in spite of themselves. Alas, mine is but a very precarious shelter. But I imagine the quiet of some souls is like a vast refuge. Sinners at the end of their tether can creep in and rest, and leave comforted, forgetting the great invisible temple where they lay down their burden for a while.

I realize it is rather foolish to evoke one of the most mysterious aspects of the Communion of Saints regarding this resolve of mine, which mere common sense might as easily have advised. But I am not to blame if I always depend on the urge of the moment, or rather on some sign of the gentle mercy of Our Lord, to which I confide myself. The fact is I suddenly realized that ever since leaving the doctor's I had been burning to tell my secret, to share its bitterness with somebody. And I realized, too, that to recover my peace, I only required to be silent.

My sorrow is not unusual. This very day hundreds, thousands of us perhaps, all over the world, will be dazed by a similar sentence. I am probably among the least able to control a first impulse—I know my weakness so well. But experience has also taught me that I have inherited from my mother, and no doubt from other poor women of our kind, a sort of endurance, which in the long run is almost unlimited, because it doesn't attempt to vie with pain, but slips within, makes of it a habit in some way: that is our strength. Otherwise how can one explain the obstinate will to live in so many poor creatures, whose amazing patience finally wears down the callousness and cruelty of husband, children, relations. . . . Mothers—Mothers of the Poor!

Only you mustn't talk about it. I mustn't talk for as long as silence is mine. And that may last for weeks, months. When I think how one word then, one look of sympathy, a mere question, possibly—might have sufficed to draw out my secret. It was there on my lips— He held it back. I know the compassion of others is a relief at first. I don't despise it. But it can't quench pain, it slips through your soul as through a sieve. And when our suffering has been dragged from one pity to another, as from one mouth to another, we can no longer respect or love it, I feel—

I am back at this table. I wanted to see the church again, the one I deserted this morning, so ashamed of myself. But it is a cold, black place. What I had hoped for did not come to me.

When I got back, Mme Duplouy made me share her lunch. I didn't like to refuse. We talked about M. le Curé de Torcy, whom she knew when he was Vicar of Presles. She was very frightened of him. I had some soup and vegetables. While I was out she had lit the stove, and she left me alone after lunch, very cosy, with a cup of black coffee. I felt warm and comfortable, I even dozed off for a while. When I awoke—

(Dear God, I shall have to write it. I think of those mornings, those last mornings of mine this week, the welcome of those mornings—the cocks crowing. That high window, so peaceful, full of night as yet, but one pane, always the same one, the right one, would begin to light up. . . . How fresh it all was, how pure. . . .)

Well, I got to Dr. Lavigne's very early. They showed me in almost at once. The waiting-room was upside down, a servant was rolling up the carpet. I had to wait a few minutes in the dining-room, which did not appear to have been touched since the night before; shutters were down, curtains drawn, the cloth still on the table and crumbs crackled under my shoes; there was a stale smell of cigar smoke. Then the door behind me opened and the doctor beckoned to me to come in.

'I must apologize for receiving you here,' he said. 'It's my little girl's nursery. The flat's in an awful mess this morning; once a month the landlord is determined to have it vacuum-cleaned in this way—a silly fad of his. On that day I don't see anybody till ten. But it seems you're in a hurry. We've a divan you can lie on in here, which is the chief thing.'

He drew the curtains and I saw him full in the light. I had not expected him to be so young. His face is as lean as mine, and of such a strange colouring that at first I thought it was a trick of the light. It seemed to be shaded with bronze. And his black eyes were watching me with a kind of detached impatience; yet there was no hardness, quite the opposite. He turned his back as I struggled out of my much-darned woollen vest. I sat down on the divan, foolishly, too uneasy to lie down. Besides, there were odd, broken toys scattered all over it, including an ink-stained rag doll. The doctor lifted it onto a chair, then after a few questions he prodded me carefully, at times closing his eyes. His face was exactly over mine, and his forelock of black hair just touched my own brow. I saw his scraggy neck, cramped into an old stiff collar that was turning yellow, and the blood which was slowly creeping into his cheeks now gave them a copper hue. I felt nervous of him, and slightly repelled.

His examination lasted a long time. I was surprised he paid such little attention to my poorly chest, he merely placed his hand several times on my left shoulder, under the collar-bone, whistling softly. The window opened out on a tiny courtyard, and through the panes I saw a soot-blackened wall pierced by such narrow slits they made me think of loopholes in a fort. I had certainly had a very different notion of this specialist, Professeur Lavigne, and his surroundings. The little room seemed to me really dirty and—I can't think why—those broken toys, the rag doll, troubled me profoundly.

'Get dressed,' he said.

A week earlier I should have expected the worst. But for the last few days I had been feeling so much better. All the same, the minutes seemed to drag. I tried to think of M. Olivier, of our ride together last Monday, that bright, sunny road. So badly were my hands shaking that as I was putting on my shoes the lace broke twice.

The doctor was walking up and down the room. At last he came towards me, smiling. His smile only half reassured me.

'Well, now I think I'd just as soon have an X-ray. I'll give you a note to take to Dr. Grousset at the hospital. Unfortunately you'll have to stay till Monday.'

'Is it really essential?'

For one second he seemed to hesitate. Heavens, I believe I could have taken any news just then without flinching. But I know from experience that when there arises in me that voiceless, that profound appeal which precedes prayer, my face assumes an expression akin to that of terror. I think the doctor must have mistaken it for such. His smile became more stressed, an open, very affectionate smile.

'No,' he said, 'it would only be a formality, really. What's the use of keeping you here any longer? You go quietly home.'

'Can I go on with my work.'

'Surely.' (I felt the blood rush to my face.) 'Oh, I don't mean to say your troubles are at an end, those attacks may recur. We have to come to terms with our aches and pains—we're all in the same boat, more or less. I shan't even bother you with a diet-sheet; feel your own way, don't swallow anything you can't keep down. And when what you *used* to keep down won't stay down any longer, don't force yourself. Get quietly back on to milk and water with a little sugar in it. . . . I'm speaking to you as a friend. If the pains get very bad you can take a tablespoonful of the prescription I'm going to make out for you now; a dose every two hours, never more than five a day, do you understand?'

'Yes, M. le Professeur.'

He moved a little table next to the armchair opposite me and found himself face to face with the rag doll, who seemed to be gazing up at him with her shapeless head from which the paint was peeling off in patches, like scales. He flung her wrathfully to the other side of the room, and she made a funny noise against the wall before flopping to the ground. And there she lay on her back with her arms and legs sticking up in the air. I did not dare to look at either of them.

'Look here,' he said suddenly, 'I really do think you should be X-rayed. But there's no hurry. Come back in a week.'

'But if it isn't absolutely essential?'

'I'm bound to advise it. After all, we are none of us infallible. But don't let Grousset put ideas into your head. A photographer's a photographer, we're not asking him for a lecture. We'll talk it over together, afterwards, just you and I. . . . At all events if you follow my advice you won't change your habits in any way; our habits are our friends in the long run. Even bad habits. The worst thing that could happen to you would be to give up your work for any reason.'

I was hardly listening, I was so eager to be out in the street, free. 'Thank you, M. le Professeur. . . .'

I got up. He was fiddling nervously with his cuffs.

'Who the hell sent you here?'

'Dr. Delbende.'

'Delbende? Never heard of him!'

'Dr. Delbende is dead.'

'Dead, is he? Ah, well, can't be helped. Come back in a week. On second thoughts I'll take you round to Grousset myself. Tuesday week, then, that's settled.'

He almost pushed me out of the room. For the last few minutes his grave face had taken on a strange expression: he looked gay, in a wild, jerky sort of way, like a man who has great difficulty in hiding his impatience. I left hurriedly without daring to shake hands, and as soon as I was in the hall I realized I had come away without the prescription. The door had just closed; I thought I heard steps in the drawing-room and that therefore the room would be empty and I could just take the prescription off the table without disturbing anyone. He was standing there by the narrow window, with one trouser-leg rolled up; a tiny metal syringe shone between his fingers as he moved it towards his thigh. . . . I cannot forget his terrible smile, which surprise did not immediately efface: it hovered round the parted lips whilst his eyes glared with rage.

'What's come over you?'

'I came back for the prescription,' I stammered. I took one step towards the table, but it was no longer there.

'I must have put it back in my pocket,' he said. 'Wait a second.' He jerked out the needle and stood before me, motionless; his eyes did not leave me, the syringe was still in his hand. He seemed to be defying me.

'With *this*, my dear fellow—you can do without God.' I think my confusion must have disarmed him. 'Sorry. Only a student's joke. I respect all beliefs—even religious ones. I haven't any myself. There are no beliefs left for a doctor. Only suppositions . . .'

'M. le Professeur—'

'Why do you keep calling me "M. le Professeur"? *Professeur* of what?' I decided he was mad. 'Answer me, can't you? You're introduced by a colleague whose name I've never even heard of, and now you call me *Professeur*—'

'Dr. Delbende sent me to the Professeur Lavigne.'

'Lavigne? Are you trying to pull my leg? Your Dr. Delbende must have been a bloody fool! Lavigne died last January at the age of seventy-eight. Who gave you my address?'

'I found it in the Directory.'

'But look here, my name isn't Lavigne, it's Laville. Can't you read?'

'I'm very absent-minded,' I said. 'I beg your pardon.'
He now stood between me and the door, and I began
to wonder if I would ever get out. I felt trapped. Sweat
was running down my face, almost blinding me.

'It is I who must beg *your* pardon,' he said. 'If you
wish I can give you an introduction to another specialist:
Professeur Dupetitpré, for instance. But between you and
me, I consider it waste of time. I know my job as well
as these provincial men, I've been house-surgeon in the
Paris hospitals, and I even got a third place when I took
my final. Excuse me for blowing my own trumpet. Anyway, your case isn't at all puzzling, anyone could have
diagnosed it as I have.'

I made another move towards the door. His words in-
spired no mistrust in me, but his eyes alone made me feel
terribly uncomfortable. They were very bright and
steady.

'I don't want to be in your way,' I said.

'You're not.' He pulled out his watch. 'My appoint-
ments don't start till ten. I must confess,' he added, 'that
this is the first time I have had one of you as a patient—
I mean a priest, a young priest. Does that surprise you?
I suppose it *is* rather strange.'

'My one regret is to be giving you a very poor opinion
of us all,' I said. 'I'm a very ordinary priest.'

'What nonsense! On the contrary, you interest me im-
mensely. You have a very—very remarkable face. Have
you ever been told so?'

'Certainly not,' I exclaimed. 'I think you must be making fun of me.'

He turned his back, shrugging his shoulders: 'Are
there many other priests in your family?'

'None, doctor. But I don't know much about my people. Families like mine have no history.'

'That's where you're wrong. Your family-history is engraved in each line of your face, and you've got plenty.'

'I've no wish to read it. What good could it do? Let the dead bury their dead.'

'They can very easily bury the living. Do you consider yourself free of them?'

'I don't know what is my share of freedom, whether it be great or small. I only know God has given me all that is needed so I may return it, some day, to Him.'

'Forgive me if I appear very rude,' he said, after a moment's silence. 'But I belong to a family—a family rather like yours, I should think. When I saw you just now I had the unpleasant feeling of meeting—almost myself. Do you think I'm mad?' I couldn't help glancing at the syringe. He began to laugh. 'Don't worry, morphia doesn't make one drunk. It clears the brain, mostly. It helps me in the same way that prayer no doubt helps you: to forget.'

'You're wrong,' I said. 'I don't look for forgetfulness in prayer, but strength.'

'Strength would be of no use to me now.' He picked up the rag doll and placed her carefully on the chimney-piece. 'Prayer'—he went on in a dreamy voice, 'I wish you *could* pray as easily as I can push this needle into me. But restless folk like you don't really pray, or pray very badly. Confess that all you truly enjoy in prayer is the effort, the coercion. You're in conflict with yourself without knowing it. The real neurotic is always his own tormentor.' When I think it over, it is hard to explain the strange shame I felt at what he said. I could no longer look up. 'Don't take me for an old-fashioned materialist. The instinct of prayer is deep in all of us, and it is no easier to explain than all the others. It may be a form of the mysterious struggle of the individual against the race. But the race absorbs everything, silently. And then the species eats up the race, that the yoke of the dead may the better crush the living. For centuries I don't suppose any one of my ancestors has ever felt the slightest wish to know any more than his fathers. In our own village of Lower Maine, where we have always lived, there's a saying: stubborn as Triquet. Triquet is our nickname, always has been. And stubborn, in our part of the world, means a dolt. Yet I was born with that thirst for knowledge which you call *libido sciendi*. I worked with a ravenous fury. When I think over the years of my youth, of my narrow room in the rue Jacob, of those nights, I am filled with a kind of terror, religious terror, almost. And what was it all for? What, I ask you? That curiosity, which my own people never experienced, I am now gradually jabbing it out—jabbing it out with morphia. And if it takes too long— Have you ever been tempted to commit suicide? It's not rare, it's even pretty usual in neurotics of your kind. . . .' I could not answer. I watched him, fascinated. 'Of course the urge to commit suicide is a gift, a sixth sense or something: you're born with it. Mind you, I should be very discreet. I still go out shooting now and again. Anyone might climb through a hedge, dragging his gun behind him—bang! And the next dawn will find you with your face in the grass, all covered with dew, fresh, peaceful, early mists rising over the trees, a cock beginning to crow and the birds singing. . . . Well? Doesn't it appeal to you?' God! For one moment I thought he knew of Dr. Delbende's suicide and was playing a horrible game with me. But I was wrong. His eyes were sincere. And though I was very disturbed myself, I felt that my presence—for some unknown reason—was terribly disturbing to *him*, that each second it was becoming more intolerable, yet he felt unable to let me go. We were prisoners of each other. 'People like us should stick to the fields, at a cow's tail,' he went on in a muffled tone. 'We don't spare ourselves, we don't spare anything. I bet you went on the same at the seminary as I did at the Provins *lycée*. Religion or Science, we hurled ourselves upon it, we'd a fire in our bellies. And now! Here we are facing the same—'

He broke off suddenly. I should have understood then, but I was still itching to get away.

'A man of your kind,' I said, 'doesn't turn his back on the goal.'

'The goal's turning its back on me,' he answered. 'I'll be dead in six months.' I believed he was still referring to suicide, and no doubt he read the thought in my face. 'I don't know why I play-act to you,' he said. 'You've eyes that make me want to show off and romance. Me, commit suicide? Not in my line. That's a game for your lords and poets, a luxury quite beyond me. I don't want you to think me a coward, either.'

'I don't think you a coward,' I said. 'I was only wondering if the—that drug—'

'Don't go talking at random about morphia. . . . Some day *you* might—' He was looking gently into my eyes. 'Have you ever heard of malignant lymphogranulomatosis? You haven't? Besides it's not an illness the public know anything about. But I wrote my thesis on it, so there's no chance of my being mistaken; I don't need to wait for a laboratory test. I give myself three months, six at the most. You see, I'm not turning my back on the goal. I'm looking it in the face. When the itching is too great I scratch myself, but you see a doctor's practice makes certain demands; a doctor has to be optimistic. I dope myself a bit on consulting-days. Lying to the patients is a necessary part of our calling.'

'Perhaps you lie too much. . . .'

'Do you think so?' he said, and his voice had the same gentleness. 'Your lot isn't so difficult as mine! You only deal with them when they're dying, I suppose. Most deaths sound worse than they are. It's quite another matter to kill a man's hope with one blow, one word. I've done it once or twice. I know what you'll answer: your theologians have made a virtue of trust in the future, your trust has folded hands. All very well for "trust"— nobody's ever seen that angel very closely. But hope is a wild beast, I tell you: a beast within a man, powerful and fierce. Better let it die very slowly. Or if you must kill it, don't miss. If you miss, it'll scratch and bite. And the sick are so malicious! However well you know them, you get caught in the end. There was an old colonel I knew, a tough colonial, who asked for the truth, as one man to another. . . . Brrr!'

'One should die little by little,' I stammered. 'Get used to the idea.'

'You don't say! Is that what *you* do?'

'At least I have tried. But I'm not comparing myself to others who have their work, their families. The life of a priest like myself matters to no one.'

'Perhaps. But if you only preach resignation to fate, there's nothing new in that.'

'Joyous resignation,' I said.

'Pooh! Man sees himself in his joy, as in a mirror, and can't recognize himself, the fool! Joy must have its price, the price of your own substance. Joy and pain are the same thing.'

'What you call joy, no doubt. But the mission of the Church is to rediscover the source of lost joy.' His eyes were as gentle as his voice. I was utterly weary. I seemed to have been there hours. I cried out: 'Let me go now!'

He took the prescription out of his pocket, but without giving it to me. And suddenly he put one hand on my shoulder, with his arm outstretched; his head was on one side, his eyes half shut. His face recalled visions of my childhood.

'After all,' he said, 'perhaps we do owe the truth to people of your sort.'

He hesitated before going on. Absurd though it may seem, his words reached my ears without awakening any response. Twenty minutes earlier I had entered that house with my mind prepared, ready for anything. The previous week at Ambricourt had left me with an inexplicable sense of safety and peace, almost a promise of happiness, but the reassuring things Dr. Laville first said to me came nevertheless as a great joy. And I realize this joy must have been much greater than I thought, much deeper. It was that same feeling of gay release which I had known on the road to Mezargues, only now there was mingled with it the exaltation of a strange impatience. First to get away from this house, these walls. And at the very moment when my eyes seemed to be answering the doctor's silent question, I was hardly attending, my mind was on vague noises in the street. Escape now. Get out! Get back to that clear winter sky, where this very morning, through the carriage-window, I had seen dawn break! Dr. Laville must have mistaken my expression. But now the truth came in a flash, lighting up my mind. Before he had finished his sentence I was no more than a dead man among the living.

Cancer. . . . *Cancer*—of the stomach! The very word struck me. I had been expecting another: tuberculosis. It required a great effort of concentration to realize that I was to die of an illness actually so rare in persons of my age. I must have been merely frowning as though at some difficult sum. I was so puzzled that I don't think I turned pale. The doctor's eyes hadn't left mine, I read in them trust, sympathy, and more—I knew it was the look of a friend. His hand pressed my shoulder again.

'We'll go and see Grousset, but honestly, with a mess like that, I don't think an operation would be any good. I'm even surprised you've gone on as long as you have. The abdominal spreading is very extensive, the distention considerable, and unfortunately I've just discovered an unmistakable symptom under the left side of the collar-bone, which we call Troizier's gland. Of course the development can be more or less slow, though I'm bound to say that at your age—'

'How long do you give me?'

Again he must have been mistaken, for my voice was steady. But my steadiness was sheer stupor. I distinctly heard the trams rumbling by, their bells clanging, and in thought I was already out of the deathly house, lost in scurrying crowds. . . . May God forgive me! I never thought of Him.

'Hard to say. It depends on the haemorrhage very largely. It's not often fatal, but in the long run— Bah! Who knows? When I told you just now to go quietly on with your work, I wasn't joking. With a bit of luck you might die standing up, like that famous emperor—or nearly. A matter of guts, really. Unless—'

'Unless what?'

'You're persistent,' he said. 'You'd have made a good doctor. I'd as soon tell you all there is, now, rather than you should go ferreting it out of books. Well, if one of these days you should ever feel a pain on the inside of the left thigh, with a slight rise of temperature, go to bed. Phlebitis is pretty usual in your case, and there's a danger of embolism. And now, my dear fellow, you know as much as I do.'

At last he gave me the prescription, which I placed in my note-book mechanically. Why didn't I leave then? I don't know. Perhaps I couldn't repress a rising of anger, of rebellion against this stranger who had just disposed of me as though I were his property. Perhaps I was too absorbed in an absurd endeavour to reconcile in a few miserable seconds, my thoughts, my plans, my memories even, my whole life, with this new certainty which made of me another man. But I think it was merely my shyness paralysing me as usual—I didn't know how to take my leave. I think Dr. Laville was surprised by my silence. The uncertainty of his voice made me realize this.

'Mind you, there are many thousands all over the world, condemned to death by their doctors at odd times, and now quietly progressing towards their hundredth birthday. Malignant tumours occasionally get reabsorbed into the system. At all events a man like you wouldn't have been taken in for long by Grousset's patter, nobody but a fool would believe him. There's nothing more humiliating than to get the truth bit by bit out of those prophets; they don't give a damn for the yarns they spin, anyway. Hopes that are alternately raised and dashed cause one to lose all self-respect in the end, and finally the bravest toe the line like the rest and go blindly to their fate with the crowd. Come back tomorrow week, I'll go with you to the hospital. Till then go on saying your mass, confessing your penitents, make no change in your life. I know your parish well. I've a friend who lives at Mezargues.'

He held out his hand. My mind was still outside it all, wandering. However hard I try now, I know I shall never understand by what terrible mischance I was able at such a time even to forget the very name of God. I was alone, utterly alone, facing my death—and that death was a wiping out, and nothing more. With fearful speed the visible world seemed to slip away from me in a maze of pictures; they were not sad, but rather so full of light and dazzling beauty. How is this? Can I have loved it all so much? Mornings, evenings, roads. Mysterious changing roads, full of the steps of men. Have I loved roads so much, our roads, the roads of the world? Is there any poor boy, brought up in their dust, who has not scattered there his dreams? And the slow, stately roads shall bear them on, to what unknown seas—? Great rivers of light and shadow bearing the dreams of the poor. I think it was the word Mezargues that broke my heart. My mind seemed very far from M. Olivier and our ride—and yet it wasn't. I was still watching the doctor's face, but suddenly it disappeared. I didn't realize for the moment that I was crying.

Yes, I was crying. I was crying without a sob, I believe even without a sigh. I was crying with my eyes wide open; as I have seen the dying cry, it was life, again, passing out of me. I wiped my face on the sleeve of my cassock, and once more I saw the doctor. He was watching me with an odd mixture of surprise and pity. If one could, I would have died of self-loathing. I should have gone but I couldn't. I waited for God to inspire me. I waited for the gift of one word, one word that a priest might utter, for that one word I would have given my life, what was left of my life. But I could barely stammer the beginnings of the apology on my tongue, tears in my throat were choking me; they had a taste of blood. How I wish they *had* been blood! I don't know where they came from. I was not weeping over myself, I swear. I was never so near to hating myself. I was not weeping over my death. When I was a child I often used to wake up in such tears. From what dream had I awakened now? Alas, I had thought I was crossing the world almost without seeing, as one walks with downcast eyes in a glittering crowd, and sometimes I believed I despised it. But that was because I was ashamed of myself—not of life. I was like an unfortunate lover who loves without daring to say so, without even admitting it to himself. I know my tears may have been cowardly. But I think, too, they were tears of love. . . .

At last I turned and left, and found myself outside in the street again.

Midnight at M. Dufréty's.

I don't know why it never occurred to me to borrow twenty francs from Mme Duplouy, so I could have stayed the night at the hotel. The fact is I really didn't know what I was doing yesterday evening, and I was in despair at having missed my train. Anyhow my poor friend received me very kindly. I think all is well.

No doubt I shall be blamed for having accepted even one night's hospitality with a priest whose status is no longer accepted (it's even worse than that!). M. Le Curé de Torcy will call me a muddler. He won't be far wrong.

I thought so yesterday as I climbed the dark stinking stairs. I hesitated a moment or two at the door of the lodging. A yellowing visiting-card was fixed up by four drawing-pins: *Louis Dufréty, commercial traveller.* Horrible!

A few hours earlier I doubt I would have ventured in. But I am not alone, now. There is this in me, this thing. . . . So I rang the bell vaguely hoping to find no one at home. He opened the door himself. He was in shirt-sleeves and a pair of white cotton pants which we wear under our cassock, his feet were bare in slippers. He said almost crossly:

'You might have let me know! I've an office, rue d'Onfroy. I merely camp here. It's a foul place.' I embraced him, and he began to cough. I think he was rather more affected than he wished to show. The remains of a meal were still on the table. 'I just *have* to eat,' he said gravely, poignantly. 'But unfortunately I have no appetite. Remember those beans at the seminary? The worst of it is we have to do our cooking in the one room, in the recess. And I simply can't bear the smell of frying—just nerves. Anywhere else I'd be ravenous.' We sat down together; I could hardly recognize him. His neck seemed to have grown much longer, and his head looked very small—like a rat's—at the top.

'It's nice of you to come. To tell the truth I was surprised you answered my letters. Between ourselves, you used not to be so very broadminded in the old days.' I muttered some reply. 'Excuse me while I tidy up a bit,' he said, 'I've been slacking to-day, it doesn't often happen. Active life has its points, you know. But don't go on thinking I've turned into a dull business man. I read a great deal, I have never read so much. Maybe even some

[277]

day— I've made some very interesting notes—all my own experience. We'll talk it over. I seem to remember you were quite a poet at one time. Your advice will be very helpful.'

A few minutes later, through the door which he had left ajar, I saw him go downstairs with a milk-can in his hand: again I was alone with—God, how I would have preferred a different death! Lungs slowly dissolving like a lump of sugar in water, a heart played out and must be for ever stimulated, or even that queer illness of Dr. Laville's, of which I have forgotten the name: I should think the menace of all those things must remain somewhat vague and abstract. But when I merely place my hand over my cassock where the doctor's fingers explored me so thoroughly, I seem to feel— Imagination, perhaps? But though I tell myself again and again that nothing has changed in me for weeks—or hardly anything—the thought of returning home—with this *thing*, shames me, sickens me. Already I was only too inclined to be disgusted with my own body, and I know the danger of such a state of mind, which would eventually rob me of all courage. Faced with the ordeals which await me, my first task is surely to become reconciled to myself.

I have given much thought to the humiliation of this morning. I think it was due to error of judgement rather than cowardice. I have no common sense. Obviously, when facing death, my attitude cannot be the same as that of men so greatly superior to me, M. Olivier, for instance, or M. le Curé de Torcy. (I compare these two purposely.) At such a time they would both have retained a kind of crowning distinction, which is merely the natural expression, the freedom of great souls. Mme la Comtesse, herself. . . . Oh, I know these are qualities rather than virtues, it would be impossible to acquire them. Yet there must be traces in me, as I respond to them so in others. Like a language which I can understand very well, without being able to speak it. Repeated tests have not hardened me. For then, just when I need most strength, the knowledge of my weakness so entirely overcomes me, that I lose the thread of my paltry courage, as a clumsy speaker loses the thread of his speech. This discovery is not new to me. I used to comfort myself with the hope of some marvellous unforeseen possibility—martyrdom, perhaps? At my age, death seems so far away that the daily experience of our own mediocrity does not as yet convince us. We do not wish to believe that such a happening will be in no way unusual, that it will probably be neither more nor less ordinary than ourselves, made in our image, the image of our destiny. It doesn't appear to belong to our familiar world, we dream of it as of fabulous countries whose names we have discovered in books. It has just occurred to me how my agony was that of a cruel, sudden disappointment. What I had believed was so far away, beyond imaginary seas, stood out before me. My death is here. A death like any other, and I shall enter into it with the feelings of a very commonplace, very ordinary man. It is even certain that I shall be no better at dying than I am at controlling my life. I shall be just as clumsy and awkward. So often have I been told to be 'simple.' I do my best. It is so hard to be simple. Worldly men talk of 'simple people' as they do of 'humble people,' with the same indulgent smile. But they should speak of them as of kings.

Dear God, I give You all, willingly. But I don't know how to give, I just let them take. The best is to remain quiet. Because though I may not know how to give, You know how to take. . . . Yet I would have wished to be, once, just once, magnificently generous to You!

I was very tempted to go round and see M. Olivier, rue Verte. I was even on my way there, but turned back. I think I should have been unable to hide my secret from him. As he is going to Morocco in two or three days it would not have greatly mattered, but I feel that in spite of myself, in his presence I would have played a part, and spoken in a way that doesn't belong to me. I don't want to be daring and defiant. My courage shall be to know that I have none, and as I am lacking in strength, I would now wish for my death to be a small one, as small as possible, no different from the other events of my life. After all, my innate awkwardness has won for me the kindness and friendship of a man like M. le Curé de Torcy—an awkwardness worthy, perhaps, of such affection. Maybe it is that of childhood? Though I have judged myself severely at times, I have always known that I possessed the spirit of poverty. The spirit of childhood is much akin. No doubt they are really one and the same thing.

I am glad not to have seen M. Olivier again. I am glad to have started on the first day of my ordeal, here in this room.

It isn't really a room at all. They put up a camp-bed for me in this narrow passage where my friend keeps his drug-samples: they all smell horrible. There is no greater loneliness than a certain type of ugliness, the devastation of ugliness. A gas jet—of the kind referred to, I believe, as a fish-tail burner—is hissing and spluttering over my head. I seem to lose myself in this foulness and misery. At one time I would have been filled with disgust. But to-night I am glad of such a shelter to my misfortune. Not that I sought it, or even recognized it at first. When last night, after a second period of unconsciousness, I found myself on this bed, my impulse was to get away, get away at all costs. I remembered how I had fainted in the sun, outside M. Dumouchel's field. This was worse. I not only remembered that hollow pathway, I saw my presbytery too, my small garden, I seemed to hear the rustle of the great poplar that wakes up long before dawn on the stillest of nights. Stupidly I thought my heart had stopped—'I won't die here,' I cried out. 'Carry me down, drag me where you like, I don't care!'

I had certainly lost my head, but nevertheless I recognized the voice of my unfortunate friend. He sounded excited and very angry. (He was talking to someone else on the landing.)

'What d'you want me to do? I can't carry him myself, and you *know* we can't ask the concierge to help us any more!'

Then I was ashamed, and I knew I was a coward.

I must really explain things once and for all. I will go back to the point where I left off a few pages earlier. After my friend had gone out, I was alone for quite a while. Then I heard a whispering in the passage, and in he came at last, still carrying his milk-can, very red in the face and out of breath.

'You'll have some supper, won't you?' he said. 'We can have a talk while we're waiting. I might read you some of my—it's a kind of diary, the title is: *My Stages*. My case would be of interest to many people. It is typical!'

A first giddiness came over me whilst he was talking.

He made me drink a big glassful of wine, and I felt much better except for a violent pain around the navel, which wore off slowly.

'The fact is,' he went on, 'we've only bad blood in our veins. These little seminaries have no notion of hygienic progress, it's dreadful. A doctor said to me once: "You're under-nourished intellectuals from childhood." That explains many things, don't you agree?' I couldn't help smiling. 'Don't think I'm trying to justify myself. I believe in one thing only: complete honesty towards oneself and towards others. *Right You Are if You Think You Are:* that's the title of a remarkable play by a very well-known dramatist.' These are his exact words. They would have seemed absurd to me, if at the same time I had not seen in his face some deep distress which I had given up hope of ever being told. 'If it hadn't been for this illness,' he continued after a moment's silence, 'I think I might still have been where you are now. But I read so much. And when I came out of the san., I had to find a job. I was up against it. It's a matter of determination and guts. Especially guts. Of course you must think there's nothing easier in the world than to get orders. You're wrong, entirely wrong! Whether you sell drugs or gold mines, whether you're Ford himself, or a mere commercial traveller, you've got to know how to deal with men. Dealing with men is the best way to develop your own strength of mind, I know something about it now. Fortunately the worst is over. Within the next six weeks my business will be on its feet, and I shall enjoy the relief of independence. Mind you, I'm not encouraging anyone to follow my example. There are difficult times to go through, and if I hadn't had to sustain me then, my sense of responsibility towards—towards a lady

[282]

who gave up for my sake a most promising career, and to whom— But forgive me for alluding to this matter, which—'

'I know about that,' I said.

'Yes—I suppose you do. Anyhow, we can speak of it quite objectively. Of course, you know, I have taken every precaution this evening to spare you a meeting that—' My eyes were obviously worrying him, he certainly couldn't find what he had hoped to read in them. Faced with this poor and tortured vanity, I got the same unhappy impression which I had experienced a few days earlier with Mlle Louise. The same inability to sympathize or share, the same closing-up of the spirit. 'She generally gets in about this time. I asked her to spend the evening with a friend, a neighbour of ours.' Timidly he stretched out his arm across the table to me, a lean, white arm in a sleeve too wide; he put his hand over mine, it was wet with perspiration and very cold. I think his feeling was real, yet his eyes continued to lie. 'She has nothing to do with my intellectual evolution, though at first our relationship was merely an exchange of views, opinions on men and life. She was chief sister at the san. A most refined, cultured girl—her education was much above the average: one of her uncles has a government post at Rang-du-Fliers. So you see I felt bound to keep the promise I had made when I was over there. Above all don't go thinking I was carried away, infatuated. . . . Does all this surprise you?'

'No,' I said. 'But I think you are wrong to vindicate yourself for loving the woman you have chosen.'

'I never thought *you* were sentimental.'

'Listen,' I went on. 'If ever I had the misfortune to go back on the vows of my ordination, I would rather it

[283]

were for the love of a woman than as a result of what you call "intellectual evolution." '

He shrugged his shoulders. 'I don't agree with you,' he answered dryly. 'Allow me in the first place to say that you don't know what you're talking about. My intellectual evolution—'

He must have talked on for some time, as I seem to remember a long monologue to which I listened without understanding. Then my mouth suddenly filled with a kind of insipid mud, and his face appeared before me with remarkable clarity and precision, before sinking into the darkness. When I opened my eyes again, I was getting rid of a sticky substance that stuck to my gums (it was a clot of blood) and the next minute I became aware of a woman's voice. She was saying in a Lens country accent: 'Now don't ye move, Father, ye'll soon be all right.'

Consciousness returned all of a sudden, the vomiting had greatly relieved me. I sat on the bed. The poor woman wanted to go. I had to hold her back by the arm.

'Beggin' yer pardon,' she said, 'I was over with a friend, t'other side o' the passage. M. Louis lost his head, like. He was wantin' to run all the way to the chemist's —Rovelle's place. Rovelle's his pal. But the shop don't stay open at night-time, worst luck, an' M. Louis can't go hurryin' along, he's soon out o' breath. It's his health, ye see, he don't have much strength to spare.'

To reassure her I walked up and down the room a few times, and finally she agreed to sit down. She is so tiny she reminds me of the little girls you find in miners' cottages, whose age it is so hard to guess. Her face is not unattractive, quite the contrary, yet if you but turned your head, you would forget it at once, I feel. Her faded blue

[284]

eyes have in them a gentleness so resigned and humble that they resemble those of an old woman—a very old woman at her weaving.

'When ye feel better, I'll be goin',' she said. 'M. Louis wouldn't like to find me here. He don't want us to get talkin' together, as he went out he specially told me to say I came from next door.' She sat down on a low chair. 'I don't know what ye'll be thinkin' o' me, the room not done, everythin' so dirty! It's because I go out to work very early, five o'clock. And I'm none too strong either, as ye can see—'

'Are you a nurse?'

'Nurse? Ye must be crazy! I was a ward-skivvy at the san., when I met monsieur—but ye'll be thinkin' me funny callin' him "Monsieur Louis," seein' as we live together.' She bent her head, pretending to straighten the folds of her worn skirt. 'He never sees anythin' of his old—of his—well, of his old pals, as ye might say. You're the first. In a way I quite see I'm not the right one for him. But ye see, at the san., he began thinkin' he was cured and got ideas in his head. It was the religion really, for I don't see no harm in livin' as husband and wife, but he'd *promised*, ye see, hadn't he? And a promise is a promise. Anyway, just then I couldn't go talkin' to him of a thing like that, especially as—savin' yer presence— I was in love with him.'

The last words were spoken so sadly that I didn't know what to say. We both blushed.

'An' there was another thing. An educated man like him isn't easy to nurse, he knows as much as the doctor, he knows all the stuff to take, and though he's in the racket now and gets his fifty-five per cent off, still medicine's expensive.'

[285]

'What is it *you* do?'

She hesitated for a moment. 'I go out charin'. The most tirin' part of our job is harein' from one spot to another.'

'But what about *his* business?'

'Seems it's *goin'* to pay a lot. But he had to borrow for the office-furniture and typewriter, and then, ye see, he don't go out much. Talkin' wears him out. I can manage all right, mind, only he's got it into his head to go educatin' me, as he calls it, like goin' back to school!'

'When does this happen?'

'Well, in the evenin's, at night, he don't sleep much. But folk like me, workin' people, we got to get our sleep. 'Course he don't do it on purpose, he don't think, that's all. "Midnight already!" he says. He's got it in his head I ought to be a lady. A man of his standin', it's only natural, come to think of it. . . . Ye may be sure I'd never have been the girl for him if—' She was watching me with amazing intentness, as though her very life hung on the words she was about to utter, the secret she was to tell. Not that I believe she didn't trust me, but her courage failed at having to speak that fatal word before a stranger. In a way she was ashamed. I have often noticed among the women of the poor, the same reluctance to speak of illness, a reticence. Her face became very red. 'He's dyin',' she said. 'But he don't know.' Her colour deepened. 'Oh, I know what you're thinkin'. We've had the parish vicar round already, such a polite man he was; M. Louis don't know him anyway. Accordin' to him I was stoppin' M. Louis from returnin' to his duty, he says. Duty, I'm thinkin', ain't so easy to understand. I know those gents 'ud look after him better'n me, seein' how bad the air is here, an' the food ques-

[286]

tion, which ain't all it should be, I know. (It's nourishin' food, I manage that, but there's not much change, and M. Louis soon gets tired o' one thing—) But I'm thinkin' he ought to make up his own mind, if he's goin', it 'ud be better, don't ye think? If *I* went he'd think I'd let him down. 'Cause between you an' me, an' savin' yer presence, he knows I ain't got much religion. . . . So ye see—'

'Are you married?' I asked. 'No, father.' I saw a cloud pass over her face. Suddenly she made up her mind. 'I'm not lyin' to ye, it's *me* that wouldn't.'

'Why not?'

'Because— Well, because o' what he is. When he left the san., I thought he'd go on all right, get better. An' then in case some time he was wantin' to—ye never know? I didn't want to be standin' in his way, I was thinkin'.'

'And what did *he* think of that?'

'He didn't mind. He thought I didn't want to 'cause of my uncle, he's a retired postman at Rang-du-Fliers, he don't like priests, an' he's got a bit put by. I said he'd be cuttin' me off with a shillin'. An' the joke is the old man *has* cut me off, just because I ain't got married, gone on bein' a "concubine" as he calls it. He's a very respectable man in his way, he's mayor of his village. "So ye can't even get yer priest to marry ye," he wrote, "it's pretty low ye've sunk!" '

'But when—' I couldn't finish my question. She finished it for me in a voice which many would not have understood, but I know it well, and it awakens in me so many memories: the ageless voice, the voice both brave and resigned, which soothes drunkards, scolds naughty brats, lulls naked babes, argues with relentless tradesmen, beseeches bailiffs, comforts the dying—the voice of the working-woman which goes on through time probably never changing, the voice which holds out against all the miseries of the world. . . .

'When he's dead, I'll still have me charin'. Before workin' in the san. I was kitchen-maid at a children's hospital, near Hyères, in the south. Nothin' better in this world than kiddies, I'm thinkin'—they're my notion o' heaven.'

'You may be able to find another job like that,' I said. She blushed again. 'No more, I'm thinkin'. Because—I don't want this gettin' round—but, just between you an' me, I was none too strong an' I've caught it from him.' I didn't speak and my silence seemed to trouble her greatly. 'P'raps I had it already'—she seemed to be excusing herself—'Mother wasn't strong either.'

'I wish I could help you,' I said.

She must have thought I was about to offer her money, but after looking at me carefully she seemed reassured and even smiled.

'Look,' she said, 'I'd be very grateful if you'd drop him a hint, sometime, about his notion o' teachin' me. When ye think that— Well, seein' as we've not much time left together, it's a bit hard. He's never been any too patient—after all, ye can't expect an invalid— But he says I do it on purpose, that I could be learnin' if I'd a mind to. Sure, I think it's somethin' to do with me bein' ill, 'cause I'm not stupid really. Only what can I say? D'you know, he's been startin' me on Latin—think of it! And me not so much as got me school certificate! Anyway, when I've done me work me head's swimmin', I'm just longin' to get to sleep. Couldn't we just talk quietly, like?'

She bent her head, playing with a ring she wore. When

she saw I was looking at it, she hastily hid her hands under her apron. I was longing to ask one question, but I didn't dare.

'You've a hard life,' I said. 'Don't you ever despair?' She must have thought I was laying some trap, her face clouded and became very intent. 'Aren't you ever tempted to rebel?'

'No,' she said. 'But sometimes I don't understand no more.'

'And then?'

'Ye get thinkin' that way when ye've a chance to rest. Sunday notions I calls 'em. An' sometimes when I'm tired, very tired— But why are ye askin' me that?'

'As a friend,' I said. 'Because there are times when I too—'

She was watching me steadily. 'Yer not lookin' any too grand yerself, father, I must say! . . . Well then, as I was sayin', when I can't go on no more, and me legs are givin' way with that pain in me side, I creep into a corner by meself an' I—ye'll be laughin' at me—instead o' tellin' meself cheerin' things to buck me up, I think of all the people that I don't know of like me—an' there's plenty of 'em, a wide world it is—beggars ploddin' through the rain, kiddies with no home, all the ailin' and the mad folk in the asylums cryin' to the moon, an' plenty, plenty more! I slip into the crowd of 'em, makin' meself small, and it's not only the livin' but the dead as well who was sufferin' once, and those that are comin', an'll be sufferin' too. . . . "What's it for? Why suffer?" they all keep sayin'. . . . I feel I'm sayin' it too, with 'em, I can hear it like a great murmurin', sendin' me to sleep. I wouldn't be changin' places then with a millionaire, it's so happy I'm feelin'. . . . 'Deed, I don't know why I get that way, an' I don't go arguin' it out with meself. I'm like mother. "Sure, if it's the best o' luck to have no luck, then I'm lucky," she was always tellin' me. I never heard her complainin'. Yet twice she was married, an' both drunkards; a time of it *she* had! Father was the worst, a widower with five lads and regular devils they were! She got so fat, ye'd never be believin' it, all her blood was turnin' to fat. Still— "There be nothin' so endurin' as a woman," she'd say, "she don't go to bed till she be dyin'." There was a pain catchin' her over the chest an' shoulder an' one arm, she couldn't breathe no more. Father came rollin' home drunk as ever on the last night. She was wantin' to put the coffee-pot on the fire an' it slipped out o' her fingers. "A big fool, I am," she says, "run over the road an' borrow another, an' don't be long comin' back or father'll be wakin'." When I got in she was about dyin', one side o' her face was all black, her tongue was hangin' out, an' that was black too. "I got to lie down," she says, "I'm not feelin' well." But father was snorin' on the bed an' she didn't dare wake him, so she went an' sat down by the fire. "Ye can pop the bacon in the broth, now," she says to me again, "it's boilin'." An' she died.'

I didn't want to interrupt her, for I felt sure she had never told so much to anyone before, and she really seemed to be waking suddenly from a dream; she was confused.

'I go talkin' and talkin' an' there's M. Louis comin' back, it's his step I can hear in the street. I'd better be goin'. He'll be callin' me back I'm thinking,' she added blushing. 'But don't say nothin', he'd be that angry!'

He was quite pathetically pleased to find me up: 'The chemist was right after all, he just laughed at me. Any little faint scares me so, you must have had indigestion, that's all.'

Then we decided I should spend the night here, on the camp-bed.

I have been trying once more to get some sleep. It seems hopeless. I was afraid the light, and especially the hissing of the gas-jet might be disturbing my friend. I half opened the door and looked into the room. No one there.

No, I am not sorry I stayed here, quite the opposite. I even think M. le Curé de Torcy would approve. And anyhow if it is foolish, it should not count against me now. My follies don't count any more: the game is up.

There were obviously many things in me to worry my superiors. But we viewed it all from the wrong angle. The Dean of Blangermont, for instance, was quite right to be uneasy about my future capabilities. Only I had no future, and we neither of us knew it.

And I know now that youth is a gift of God, and like all His gifts, carries no regret. They alone shall be young, really young, whom He has chosen never to survive their youth. I belong to such a race of men. I used to wonder: what shall I be doing at fifty, at sixty? And of course I couldn't find an answer, I couldn't even make one up. There was no old man in me.

This awareness is sweet. For the first time in years—perhaps for the first time ever—I seem to stand before my youth and look upon it without mistrust; I have rediscovered a forgotten face. And my youth looks back at me, forgives me. Disheartened by the sheer clumsiness in me which always kept me back, I demanded of my youth what youth alone can't give, and I said it was a stupid thing and was ashamed of being young. But now, both weary with our silly quarrels, we can rest awhile, silent by the road, and breathe in the deep peace of evening where we shall enter together.

It greatly comforts me also, to think that nobody has been guilty of real harshness towards me—not to say the great word: injustice. I certainly respect those victims of iniquity who are able to find in that knowledge some basis of strength and hope. Somehow I should always hate to think myself—though unwittingly—the cause, or merely the pretext of another's sin.

Even from the Cross, when Our Lord in His agony found the perfection of His saintly Humanity—even then He did not own Himself a victim of injustice: *They know not what they do.* Words that have meaning for the youngest child, words some would like to call childish, but the spirits of evil must have been muttering them ever since without understanding, and with ever-growing terror. Instead of the thunderbolts they awaited, it is as though a Hand of innocence closed over the chasm of their dwelling.

And so I find great joy in thinking that much of the blame, which sometimes hurt me, arose from a common ignorance of my true destiny. A sensible man like the Dean of Blangermont was obviously over inclined to anticipate what I should be later, and he was unconsciously reproaching me now for mistakes that were to come.

I have loved without guile (I think that is the only way I can love). Such guilelessness was a danger in the end, both for myself and for others. I know it. I always struggled against this natural impulse, and so ineffectually that I may believe it was invincible. The thought that this conflict is over—there is no more reason for it—had already occurred to me this morning, but I was still dazed by Dr. Laville's revelation. It seeped into me only very slowly, like tiny drops from a stream at first. But now there are rising waters freshening to my spirit, overflowing. Quiet and peace.

Of course, during the last weeks or months that God may spare to me, while I can still look after a parish, I shall do my best, as always, to be careful. But I shall give less thought to the future, I shall work in the present. I feel such work is within my power. For I only succeed in small things, and when I am tried by anxiety, I am bound to say it is the small joys that release me.

This day of realization will have been like others: with nightfall fear had gone, but the coming dawn brings no glory. I do not turn my back on death, neither do I confront it bravely as M. Olivier surely would. I have tried to open my eyes to death in all the simplicity of surrender, yet with no secret wish to soften or disarm it. Were the comparison less foolish, I would say that I look upon death as I did on Sulpice Mitonnet or Mlle Chantal. . . . Alas, one would need also to become as a little child. . . . Before I realized my fate, I often feared I should not know how to die when the time came, as there is no doubt I am too impressionable. I remember a saying of dear old Dr. Delbende, which I believe was recorded in this diary, about monks and priests not always being the best at dying. . . . But I have no more qualms about that now. I can understand how a man, sure of himself and his courage, might wish to make of his death a perfect end. As that isn't in my line, my death shall be what it can be, and nothing more. Were it not a very daring thing to say, I would like to add that to a true lover, the halting confession of his beloved is more dear than the most beautiful poem. And when you come to think of it, such a comparison should offend no one, for human agony is beyond all an act of love.

God might possibly wish my death as some form of example to others. But I would rather have their pity. Why shouldn't I? I have loved men greatly, and I feel this world of living creatures has been so pleasant. I cannot go without tears. Nothing is farther removed from me than stoic indifference, so how can I hope for the death of a stoic? Plutarch's heroes both terrify and bore me. If I were to go to heaven wearing such a mask, I think even my guardian angel would laugh at me.

Why worry, why look ahead? If I feel afraid I shall say: I am afraid, and not be ashamed of it. As soon as Our Lord appears before me, may His eyes set me at rest. . . .

I fell asleep for a few moments with my arms on the table. Dawn cannot be far off, I seem to hear the milk-vans.

I would like to go without seeing them again. But I hardly know how I can, even were I to leave a note on the table promising to return soon. My friend wouldn't understand.

What can I do for him? I fear he would never agree to meet M. le Curé de Torcy. I fear especially that M. le Curé de Torcy might hurt his vanity cruelly, and so provoke him to some absurd desperate act of which, in his obstinacy, he is so capable. My old master would certainly win in the long run. But if that poor woman is right, there is so little time.

So little time for her, too! Last night I avoided looking at her; I think she would have read in my eyes that I was none too sure of myself. No, I wasn't sure enough! Though I tell myself that another would have forced the issue which I feared, instead of waiting for it, I am still not convinced. I suppose he would have said to her: Go, leave him, let him die reconciled, far from you! And she would have gone. Gone without understanding, following the instinct of her kind, a gentle kind which for centuries past has always awaited the knife. She would have lost herself in the crowd of men with her humble sorrow, her innocent rebellion that she can only express in words of acceptance. I don't think she is capable of hate, for the amazing ignorance, the supernatural ignorance in her heart is such that angels guard it. Will no one ever teach her to lift brave eyes to the Eyes of all Resignations? Perhaps God would have received from me the priceless gift of a hand that knew not what it gave? But I dared not. M. le Curé de Torcy can do what he likes.

I have said my rosary at the window, opened wide over a courtyard like a dark well. But above me, the east corner of the building seems to be showing lighter.

I have rolled myself up in the blanket, and even drawn it a little over my head. I am not cold. My usual pain isn't troubling me, but I feel sick.

If only I could I'd get out of this house! I would love to walk again through empty streets the way I went this morning. My visit to Dr. Laville, and the time I spent in Mme Duplouy's café are now but a confused memory, and when I try to concentrate and recall precise details of those hours, I become aware of a strange insurmountable weariness. What was hurt in me then is no longer, must have died. Some part of me cannot feel any more and will not feel—until the end.

I certainly regret my show of weakness in the presence of Dr. Laville. But I should be ashamed of feeling no real remorse, considering the impression of us priests I must have given to that determined, resolute gentleman! Well, it's all over now. The strange mistrust I had of myself, of my own being, has flown, I believe for ever. That conflict is done. I cannot understand it any more. I am reconciled to myself, to the poor, poor shell of me.

How easy it is to hate oneself! True grace is to forget. Yet if pride could die in us, the supreme grace would be to love oneself in all simplicity—as one would love any one of those who themselves have suffered and loved in Christ.

Letter from Monsieur Louis Dufréty to Monsieur le Curé de Torcy:

Lille, February 19—.

MONSIEUR LE CURÉ,

I am sending you at once the information you were so kind as to request. I am writing a really detailed account of what occurred for the Lille Youth Herald, *a very modest periodical of ours to which I contribute at odd times. But owing to my present state of health I have been unable as yet to complete the article. I shall take pleasure in sending you a copy as soon as it comes out.*

My friend's visit was a great satisfaction to me. Our affection for each other sprang from the best years of our youth, and was such that time does not efface. His first intention, I believe, was just to spend the evening here with me, chatting over old times. At about seven o'clock he was not feeling too well. I decided he had better stay the night. My home, simple though it is, seemed to attract him, and I had no difficulty in persuading him to stay. But at the same time I felt it would be tactful myself to put up with a friend, whose flat was on the same landing.

Towards four o'clock in the morning, being restless and unable to sleep, I went quietly to his room and discovered my poor friend lying unconscious on the floor.

We carried him to bed. And though we used all possible care, I fear this moving him was fatal. He vomited blood in great quantities. The lady who shares my life had made a thorough study of medicine, and was able to inform me regarding his condition and do all that was required. Her diagnosis was a very grave one. But the haemorrhage had subsided. While I was awaiting the doctor, our friend regained consciousness. Yet he did not speak. Great beads of perspiration were rolling over his brow and cheeks. His eyes, which I could scarcely see under his heavy half-closed lids, told of great anguish. I felt his pulse and it was rapidly growing weak. We sent a boy to go and fetch our parish priest. The dying man motioned to me to give him his rosary. I found it in one of his pockets; and from that moment he held it pressed to his breast. Then some strength returned to him, and in a voice one could hardly hear he asked me for absolution. His face became more at peace, he smiled even. Although I realized I had no right to accede over hastily to this request, it was quite impossible in the name of humanity and friendship, to refuse him. May I add that I was able to discharge this duty in a spirit which need leave you with no possible misgivings.

The priest was still on his way, and finally I was bound to voice my deep regret that such delay threatened to deprive my comrade of the final consolations of Our Church. He did not seem to hear me. But a few moments later he put his hand over mine, and his eyes entreated me to draw closer to him. He then uttered these words almost in my ear. And I am quite sure that I have recorded them accurately, for his voice, though halting, was strangely distinct.

'Does it matter? Grace is everywhere. . . .'

I think he died just then.

[298]